ICARUS AND THE DEVIL

A SOUL TO FIND NOVEL

LAYLA REYNE

ABOUT THIS BOOK

My name is Icarus for a reason.
If there's a way to screw up a plan, I'm your man.

Case in point:
Falling for the man I'm supposed to seduce and ferry to his death.
Adam Devlin, aka the Devil.
A vigilante ex-cop and a thorn in the side of the mobster blackmailing me.
Should be easy.
Except Adam's longing for intimacy—for submission—is irresistible.
Seduce him, yes. Lead him to his death, world of no.

There's only one solution to save us both: kidnap the Devil.
I mentioned my name is Icarus, right?
Three guesses how this plan will go.
Bet you only need one.

Icarus and the Devil is a steamy M/M urban fantasy romance novel. It features two danger-magnet men trying to stay alive and failing to stay away from each other. Chaos ensues on their way to happily ever after.

For Hailey,
who gave me the courage to go for it,
vampires, shifters, and all

PART ONE

ICARUS

ONE

THIS WAS the definition of fucked. And not in the good way. Not in the way Icarus liked to be fucked, and not in the well-fucked way he made sure his clients left his bed. Nope, this was just plain old five-minutes-from-being-dusted fucked.

A far cry from the good kind of fucked of five minutes ago when he'd been putting on a show for the online client who'd paid for a virtual solo session. Icarus had nestled his favorite plug in his ass, clamped the rose gold cage around his cock, and tightened the leather cuffs around his ankles and wrists, naked and spread for his client on the other end of the private live stream. With a remote in each hand, he'd been slowly ramping up the vibrating plug and tightening the cock cage, his and his client's moans escalating together. And then his remotes had stopped working. The vibrating plug had died, and the cage had gone mad, clamping down and strangling his dick.

Not mad.

Hacked.

By the client—the warlock—formerly onscreen who had

materialized in his room, yanked open the curtains, and replaced Icarus's soft leather cuffs with silver-laced ones that kept Icarus bound and pliant. The warlock stood beside the bed, finger hovering over a different remote that he'd promised would ruin Icarus's dick or destroy his ass for good if pressed. In either event—or both—it would cut off Icarus's primary source of income.

Assuming he survived the next five minutes. There was a reason he was called Icarus, and it had nothing to do with his currently magenta hair.

Ignoring the shaft of sunlight that crept across the foot of his bed, ever closer to his foot, ever closer to dust, Icarus tried sexy pouting at the warlock who held his dick and ass at his mercy. "Is this any way to treat the guy who was putting on a bang-up show for you?" He eyed the tent at the front of his captor's kilt. "Now that you're here, I could put on an even better show. Suck that for you. Make you come so—"

"He's not the one calling the shots."

Icarus's attention snapped toward the voice, toward the movement at the far end of the room. A tall, broad-shouldered white man dressed in a high-dollar suit stood in the bedroom doorway. Icarus sniffed. Human. He didn't carry the rotting wood stench of dark magic like the warlock beside the bed, but that didn't make the new visitor any less frightening. The bulging impressions of pistols under each arm, likely packing lead and silver bullets, wasn't the scariest thing about him either. No, it was the cold, hard malevolence that swirled in his big brown eyes. Such a beautiful color, one only humans possessed, one Icarus loved seeing bright with cheer or dark with desire. This man's eyes were dark, but the only desire swirling in them was for power—no matter how deadly and violent the path—and that frightened Icarus to his chilly core.

He deflected the only way he knew how. "I can suck your cock too. Let you call the shots. Or you can watch while I suck his."

The stranger nodded, and hope flared, but only for a second before the warlock's open palm smacked Icarus's cheek with unchecked force.

"Ow!" Icarus howled as stinging, magic-laced pain seared across his face. He'd cradle his cheek if he could but had to settle for gritting his teeth, waiting for the worst of it to pass. Once he could see straight again, he whipped his gaze back to the human standing at the foot of his bed. "That was fucking shitty! Your warlock has my cock in a cage and could tear my ass apart with the vibrator still in there, and I'm this fucking close to being dust." He wriggled his toes enough to put the little one in the sunlight, a spark catching and a tendril of smoke pluming in the air. He yanked it back into the narrowing shadow before it fully caught fire. "You didn't have to fucking hit me."

"And you don't have to keep running your mouth. I'll have him hit you again if you persist." He eyed the encroaching sun. "You don't have time to waste."

Meaning he intended to let Icarus live.

Meaning Icarus needed to shut the fuck up.

He pressed his lips together.

"Good," the human said. "Now, at last count, you were fifteen grand in debt to me."

"To you?"

"By way of Paris Cirillo."

Icarus hung his head back and groaned. Again, not in the good way. "Of course this is about that fool."

"That fool is my son."

Icarus gasped and righted his head. Seeing the truth of the statement on the big man's face, he slammed shut his mouth again.

"You're learning." Paris's father smiled, a wicked, cruel thing, as he circled the end of the bed and came to stand beside the warlock. "I don't dispute your assessment, but the fact remains that you owe us, and I'm here to collect."

"I don't have anything. Not worth that."

"On the contrary . . ." He trailed a hand up the inside of Icarus's thigh, hitching the leg higher and wider, as much as the ankle cuff would allow. Demonstrating his power, given the circumstances. He dipped his hand into the crease of Icarus's groin, fingers skirting the edge of the cage. "You have exactly what we need."

Icarus gnashed his teeth, fighting a moan and his fangs, the natural reactions of his body as the cage clamped painfully around his cock. "I thought—"

"Not for me." He removed his hand from Icarus's groin and palmed the warlock's straining cock. The magician moaned deep in his throat, and the sharp, salty scent of precome tinged the air. "My needs are well taken care of."

"You wanna fuck and make me watch?" It would hurt like hell. Just the thought was making him harder, making the cage tighter, despite his fear, despite the pain. But right then, he feared the creeping sun more, the pain the warmth on the side of his foot was already causing. "Fine, I'll watch, but you gotta let me out of the sun first."

Paris's father shook his head. "As soon as we're done here,

Mr. Magic is gonna snap us back to my car parked in the alley behind this shithole building, and I'm gonna bend over his lap, flip up that skirt, and take his uncut cock in my mouth and suck him dry." He pumped the warlock's erection, and the scent of precome intensified. "Then he'll crawl onto his hands and knees in the back seat, and I'll shove my cock into his ass, over and over, until I fill him so full he'll be sore and dripping for days. So no, we don't need your help in that department."

Icarus stared, turned on and confused all at the same time. "I don't . . ."

If he thought the man's grin was wicked and cruel before, the one he flashed then was downright deadly, so full of rank hunger—for power—that Icarus's erection waned, even as the magician's continued to strain.

"We'll let you out of the sun," the terrible man said. "Then tonight, you're gonna put on the show of your life. For the Devil." He released the trembling warlock, circled to the foot of the bed, and snapped the laptop closed. "If you fail, it'll be the last show you ever perform."

Icarus gulped. If this man wasn't the Devil, who the fuck was?

TWO

ADAM DEVLIN, aka the Devil.

That was who Vincent—Paris's power-hungry father who'd eventually introduced himself—had commanded Icarus to seduce. To what end, Icarus hadn't asked. Not like he had a choice. Once they'd given him his "mission" and made clear what would happen to Icarus if he failed, Vincent and his warlock, Atlas, had fizzled into thin air. Five minutes later, so had the cuffs. Five seconds after that, Icarus had freed his cock from the cage, removed the plug, and chucked both toys out the open window. Shame, as they'd been personal favorites, but he could never trust them again.

Hours later, lurking in the shadows of a crowded club, Icarus thought the same about the human sitting by himself at the end of the bar. He could never trust someone that good-looking, who sat that eerily still, and who went by the moniker the Devil. Six feet, broad shoulders, fit build. Not as fit as Icarus, but not everyone was frozen in time at twenty-five. Not everyone was in peak physical condition in their twenties either. Something about Adam Devlin made Icarus think he was far more dangerous in what looked like his forties than he would've been in his younger years. Maybe it was the dark hair and beard flecked with silver, or the peaks and valleys of his long, sharp face, or his pale weathered skin, or the blue-gray eyes that never stopped surveying his surroundings, even as he lifted a glass of amber liquid to his lips.

Barrel-aged whiskey.

Icarus had tasted it once on the lips of a ridiculously wealthy, seriously buttoned-up pack leader who occasionally liked to take a walk on the wild side. Warm and spicy with hints of oak and vanilla. Flavors derived from natural resources that didn't exist in abundance anymore—precious, expensive commodities. Only the rich and powerful were able to afford vintage bottles or the sky-high price tag of a single shot in a place like Club Sutro.

Icarus bet on both about the Devil—rich and powerful. A rival of Vincent, who Icarus was beginning to understand was rich and powerful too, especially to have a warlock in his thrall. Of course the internet was scrubbed clean of their identities—Adam, Vincent, Atlas, and Paris, all of them erased persons—rich-and-powerful clue number whatever count Icarus was up to. He probably should have known better, probably should have kept an ear closer to the ground of Yerba Buena, especially where his dealers and clients were concerned, but staying oblivious was generally better in his line of work. The performance was easier when his sole focus was seducing his mark and keeping his own secrets.

Tonight's performance was going to be the opposite of easy. "The show of your life," Vincent had said. And the curtain continued to rise higher with each sip of whiskey Adam took, until the drink was all but gone and the stage lights were shining bright.

Showtime.

Icarus cinched his corset around his bare torso, tugged up his sheer black gauntlets, checked his garters were secure, and finger combed his hair, making sure his magenta strands were spiked to maximum height. He might have been a fuckup in every other aspect of his life, but in this one area, he was in control. He was the best. As if this was what he'd been born for—turned for. He relished the rare slice of confidence.

Emerging from the shadows, he sauntered across the club at human speed, his stilettos clicking on the cement floor, his lace garters and nylon stockings brushing with each step. Every paranormal in the club could hear his approach and how, after two steps, Icarus adjusted his gait so his steps were in time with the Devil's heartbeat. On the hunt, no other paranormal in the club would interrupt him. Not unless they wanted their heart torn from their chest or their jugular ripped from their throat.

Adam, however, shouldn't have been able to hear him, not over the thumping club music. Shouldn't have been able to sense him at all, Icarus approaching from his blind spot, but the human's frame stiffened with awareness. Maybe not completely human. Adam whipped his face around, glaring over his shoulder. Storm clouds gathered in his steely gaze, a back-off warning aimed squarely in Icarus's direction.

Icarus didn't falter; he didn't scare that easily. He swayed his hips as he closed the distance between them, sidling up to the bar beside Adam. "I'd offer to buy you another"—he ran a black-painted fingernail along the rim of the glass—"but even

I don't have whiskey-kind-of-money, and I'm the best courtesan here."

The Devil shifted on his stool as if to leave. "Not interested."

"Yes, you are." Icarus propped a foot on the bottom rung of Adam's stool, planted a hand on his bent knee, and boxed Adam in. "If you weren't, you would have ignored my approach."

"You're new here."

"Nine months or so, up from Portola." A practiced line. Never mind the decades between when he'd left Portola the first time and arrived in Yerba Buena.

"Which is why you don't know." Adam's gaze darted past Icarus, sweeping the club again—along the wall of windows, the actual stage, the crowd, the exits—before landing back on him, impatient and unamused. "I used to be a cop. Not my instinct to ignore danger at my back."

Icarus didn't think that was Adam's only instinct at work. He went to work on another, widening his stance and giving Adam a bird's-eye view of everything being offered. The skimpy boy shorts beneath his garters did little to hide his package. Intentionally. "The only danger you're in is missing out on the best night of your life if you leave here without me."

Adam didn't take the bait. He lifted a hip, withdrew his wallet, and pulled out two bills. "I already had the best night of my life. Ten years ago." He slipped the bills under the glass, then tucked his wallet away. "Just here to commemorate it and move on. Same as every October first."

A hole opened in Icarus's chest, dark and fathomless, the sadness and loss in Adam's voice a wrecking ball like Icarus had only experienced one other time in his life: the day he'd been turned, which was why he'd never turned anyone himself. He couldn't bear to be the cause of that feeling. Couldn't bear it now for Adam either. He lifted a hand, ignoring Adam's flinch and the gun he'd glimpsed on the Devil's hip, and cupped his cheek. It was warm despite the gray clouds that hung around the man. "I can make you forget it. For a night." His own instincts—beyond mere self-preservation—demanded it.

Gray gave way to blue, a deep sad shade that reminded Icarus of Picasso's Blue Period. "I don't want to forget it," Adam said. "I can't."

"Relive it, then?"

Adam's bitter laugh made ragged the edges of the hole his earlier words had torn open in Icarus's chest. "You'd end up dead."

He already was, but Adam's instincts hadn't caught on to that detail. Hadn't caught on to the fact that the opposite of his words was doubly true. If Icarus didn't succeed in seducing him, Icarus would be dead. For good this time. He teased the corner of Adam's mouth with his thumb. "Risk I'd be willing to take."

Faster than he should have been able, Adam clasped his wrist. To yank it down and push him away, Icarus expected— but Adam did the unexpected. He pulled Icarus closer and swiped his tongue over his own bottom lip, the tip brushing the pad of Icarus's thumb. "Could I even afford you?"

Icarus bit back his gasp—surprise, victory, and lust all warring for a voice. Any of which, if spoken, would crater the mission.

The mission.

"If you can afford that whiskey"—he flicked his gaze to the glass—"you can afford me."

A shaky breath coasted over Icarus's palm, and Adam's gaze finally drifted down, taking in all of Icarus. His pulse sped, a blush streaked across his high cheekbones, and when he lifted his eyes back to Icarus's, a lake of fire stared back at him. The same fire that roared through Icarus, unlike anything he'd ever experienced. "Where—"

A phone rang, shattering the moment. A single blink and Adam disappeared, retreating into his shell, banking the heat as the storm clouds returned. The Devil tiptoed back under his skin, and he released Icarus's wrist, shifted away, and pulled out his phone. "Devlin."

The call lasted less than a minute, and when it was over, the Devil slid off his stool without another word. Without another look. Without the slightest clue that he'd just sentenced Icarus to death.

THREE

ICARUS ORDERED a cheap shot of vodka, sulked the length of it, then got over himself. Yes, he was good at his job, but not every job was easy, and he hadn't expected this one to be. In fact, he'd been doing better than expected before that phone call had interrupted them. Success—*Adam*—had been at his fingertips. It—*he*—could be again if Icarus was in the right place at the right time when Adam finished doing whatever that call had summoned him away to do. The night wasn't over, and neither was the mission.

He paid the bartender and grabbed his trench and combat boots from the coat check. Swapping his heels for the boots, he shoved the former into his coat pockets and wrapped up tight before heading outside into the cold night. Neither the temperature nor the dark affected him, but his work attire might draw the kind of attention he didn't need at the moment. He already had a mark; he wasn't looking for another.

He sniffed the air and caught the lingering aroma of whiskey, and on its heels, the oily odor of gasoline, another thing only the rich and powerful could afford for their gas-powered automobiles. He followed the scents, keeping to the shadows as he moved at his preternatural pace, heels never touching the ground, leaping from toe to toe, block to block. The path took him down Sutro Hill and east across town toward the Canyon Lands.

Humans rarely ventured into this part of Yerba Buena, their reaction times too slow for the frequently shifting land and their eyesight too poor for an area that was shrouded in fog day and night. Magically so. It was a demented sort of fun house for paranormals—a place to hide, to trade in illicit goods, to do bad things, a playground for one's darkest fantasies—but for humans, it was a sightless, dangerous nightmare. A deadly maze that could change shape in the blink of an eye.

Icarus wasn't surprised to find a vintage Camaro parked at the end of a road in front of the barbed wire fence that ran the length of the Canyon Lands border. He was surprised, however, that Adam's scent didn't diverge left or right into one of the alleys, garages, or abandoned buildings where all sorts of shit went down. Instead, it continued straight ahead, beyond the fence and out toward the canyons of deep dark water that cut into the crumbling ruins of structures that used to stand tall and magnificent, glass and metal that had once shone in the sunlight.

Before the Rift.

Before that day thirty years ago when Nature and her allies had gone to war with Chaos and the darker forces of magic, with Yerba Buena as ground zero. When what had started as a balmy October day had turned into a dark and stormy nightmare, when the contours of the land had been irrevocably altered by earthquakes, landslides, and tsunamis, and when battle lines had been etched in stone. Skirmishes were constant in the three decades since, the push and pull between Nature and Chaos waxing and waning with the seasons and the power grabs of beings—human and paranormal—in between. But where the Canyon Lands were concerned, Nature had conceded the territory, and she hadn't left it a hospitable place.

Icarus ducked through the wire fence, cursing low when a barb snagged the lace band of his stocking. He could try to save it, but the wafting whiskey scent was growing fainter, dissipating in the heavy fog as Adam moved farther into the canyons. Cutting his losses, Icarus unclipped the garter—*that* he wasn't losing—and clawed through the thinner nylon beneath the lace top of the stocking.

Freed, he climbed the rest of the way through the fence and hustled to catch up to Adam, worrying more with each step. The ground beneath his boots was a debris-filled mess of buckled roads and sidewalks, sand and silt, and all around, in buildings and makeshift hovels, in the swirling fog that filled alleys and crevices, bright eyes glowed, their owners snarling a warning.

What the fuck was Adam doing out here? Meeting someone—or doing something—he shouldn't? In either case, was it worth risking his life?

Icarus got his answer twenty or so yards later when an explosion overhead sent him scrambling behind a rusted-out dumpster. Smoke and flames billowed from the shattered windows of a corner building, the metal fire escape rattling as another explosion wracked what was left of the crumbling structure.

"Go, go, go!" someone shouted from inside the building, and in the wake of another plume of smoke and shattering glass, a slim figure in jeans and a dark hoodie emerged from the broken window onto the fire escape. They turned back toward the building, arms outstretched, and Adam appeared at the window, leaning his torso out, a blanket-wrapped something in his arms. As Adam handed off the bundle, an arm slipped loose of the blanket, and a head fell back onto the rescuer's shoulder, exposed. Human, maybe? Dark hair, skin that was too pale and too thin, translucent almost, stretched across jutting bones. Emaciated, barely hanging on to life, a fluttering heartbeat compared to the stronger two—no, four— in its vicinity. And glowing too, a red-orange sheen the likes of which Icarus had never seen, rippling over the being's skin. A shifter, then, of some sort? Icarus sniffed, but the smoke drowned out any other scents.

"Go!" Adam shouted. "Get him to Jenn and the coven before he flames out."

Flames out?

The hooded figure wrapped their arm tight around the young man, turned, and jumped off the metal platform. Icarus muffled his shout in the crook of his arm. The jumper landed on their feet, dark hair escaping the hood, delicate features visible in profile. A woman. Definitely a shifter for how gracefully she'd landed and how fast she took off, disappearing into the fog.

The building gave another terrible shake and a groan as wood and metal scraped together, as smoke and flames gushed out of every hole, as hunks of concrete crashed to the already-splintered asphalt. Icarus whipped his gaze back to the fire escape. No sign of Adam. But three heartbeats still inside. Adam plus two other friends . . . or two other foes? *Fuck.* A tinny voice of self-preservation rang in Icarus's head.

Let the building come down; let it end Adam; let Vincent blackmail Icarus to do something—anything—else. The louder voice inside Icarus's chest rebelled at the notion of leaving Adam to such a fiery fate, especially after he'd just saved a paranormal of some sort from the same.

Icarus moved to step out from behind the dumpster, to zip into the building and rescue the man he was supposed to deliver to Vincent, only to freeze midstep when a coughing Adam staggered out of a glassless window on the ground floor. The two other heartbeats emerged and rushed to Adam's side, helping to hold him up as he gulped in breaths of air. Icarus silently sank behind the dumpster and waited for Adam to recover, which happened far too quickly for Adam to be only human. Icarus didn't have long to ponder what he was, though, because the trio moved again, Adam leading them away from the burning building and deeper into the fog, stopping only when they reached the outer edge where the ground had fallen away in massive chunks, only ruins and unstable jetties left between the deep dark crevices of rushing water.

Icarus ducked inside the nearest hollowed-out ruin, inching closer to where Adam and his associates gathered on the buckled road outside. He hopped from one rusty steel pile to the next, ignoring the murder of crows perched on the broken beams overhead, the gaping holes in the slab floor around him, and the muted crash of waves somewhere far below.

"What did you find out?" Adam asked.

A growl belied the voice that answered. "He pulled the trigger on the contract. Even before that stunt tonight."

He? As in Vincent? It had to be.

"How much?" a third voice asked, solemn and dutiful, all business.

"Five million," the growly one replied.

Someone whistled. Mr. Solemn, if Icarus had to guess.

"Probably more now," Mr. Growly added. "You cost him another one." Icarus couldn't get a read on his accent. It was practiced and unnatural, like it had been pieced together from a million different dialects. Icarus crept closer, wanting to get eyes on them. Were they mostly human, like Adam? He didn't think so, at least not the growly one.

"You didn't pick the contract up?" Adam asked.

Mr. Growly laughed, and when he spoke again, some of the put-on accent was stripped away, his growl softened to an affectionate rumble. "She'd never forgive me."

She who? Someone they worked for? The Devil didn't seem the sort to work for anyone.

"She might haunt you for passing it up," Adam replied.

A dead someone. A dead and gone someone. Icarus's kind didn't "haunt." That was a term strictly reserved for ghosts. But the three men in the street didn't seem to have the same dark connotations with the word as Icarus did. They laughed, quiet and low, tender almost. Whoever *she* was, they all remembered her fondly.

Mr. Solemn's voice was gentle, beseeching when he spoke again. "Come up to the mountain."

Sneaking closer, Icarus inched into a crumbling cement corner, only rebar left on his side but still solid enough on the street-facing side to hide behind.

"I'm not running," Adam said. "I haven't run for ten years. And she—they—deserve vengeance."

They, not only *she*. And there was that ten years again.

Icarus peeked around the corner just as Mr. Growly got in Adam's face. Golden eyes glowed beneath a headful of rusty-blond hair. Definitely not human. "What good is vengeance if you're dead?" His words were full of anger and something deeper, something like brotherhood.

Icarus's own chest clenched. He batted down memories before they rose higher and instead focused on the here and now.

The present in which Adam shifted his focus, calmly rotating his face to the other man standing in the street with them. His words and expression were resigned. "Then you'll come get me and take me to them."

"Fuck." The man flinched and rotated, the tails of his long dark trench flying, and before he dipped his chin, before he raked a hand through his jet-black hair, Icarus caught the flash of violet eyes. Also not human. He spun back around the next instant, solemn long gone, anger and anxiety straining his voice. "I swear, you've had a ten-year death wish. You just ran into a burning building, for fuck's sake. Do you have any idea how hard it's been keeping you alive?"

"Can you blame me?" Adam swung his attention back to the golden-eyed man. Icarus risked a sniff, far enough away from the smoke to smell again—a canine of some sort. "If Vincent's coming after me this hard, he knows I'm close, and he can't afford that with whatever he's banking power for."

"The Rift anniversary," the dog said. "Or Samhain."

"Whatever he's planning, we have to stop him. We have to finish their work."

There was that *their* again. Mr. Solemn started to argue something, maybe about them, but his words were dampened by a wave crashing into the canyons below so thunderous the silt beneath Icarus's feet shifted, the earth giving way. Icarus bit out a low curse. "Fuck."

"Who's there?" the dog barked, and the crows above screeched an awful chorus.

Icarus debated bounding away, but he couldn't without being seen, without exposing what he was. He scooted farther into the corner instead, fingers scrabbling at rusty rebar and crumbling cement.

Voices and footsteps drew closer. "Show yourself!" Adam shouted.

Gunshots were not the answer any of them expected.

FOUR

THE GUNFIRE CAME from behind Icarus, from the direction of the burning building they'd fled. From the only path out of the Canyon Lands. Cliffs and dark water—all that existed the other way.

"I'll cut a path," the dark-haired man said, and in the blink of an eye, he was in the air, transformed into a crow bigger than any of the ones overhead.

No, not a crow. A raven.

The crows, though, followed his lead, taking flight and barreling through the hole in the ceiling, out past Icarus and into the street, falling into formation behind the shifter and slicing through the fog.

A hand clasped Icarus's wrist and yanked him out from his hiding place. Adam shoved him against the other side of the disintegrating wall and rammed the muzzle of a gun into the underside of his chin. "What the fuck are you doing here? Did you shoot—"

More gunfire rent the air, and birds scattered as cones of bobbing light shone through the fog. Flashlights, held by the gunmen. At least two of them. Icarus pointed their direction. "Clearly, the shots came from them."

"You heard the bird," the dog said. "Get the fuck behind me, and let's get the hell out of here." And by behind him, he meant the giant back end of a rusty-blond coyote that appeared after several bone-cracking seconds.

Icarus pretended to be shocked; it wasn't much of a stretch. While he wasn't surprised by the actual shifts—he'd known they were shifters, had witnessed shifts before—he was still struggling to grasp why Adam was working with shifters in the Canyon Lands to rescue a kid and foil Vincent's evil plans. Shifters he seemed to know well and share some history with.

"We have to get out of here!" Adam tugged him by the wrist and sprinted behind the coyote, barely stumbling over the uneven ground. "Stay behind me."

Icarus pretended to struggle, enough to be believable but not enough to slow them down. He didn't know if the bullets flying were lead or silver or both; it didn't matter. He wanted the fuck out of there too. Dark magic was closing in around them, making the hairs on his arms stand on end and the fog so heavy there was no trace of the earlier fire. "How can you see in this muck?" he asked Adam, who at no time had used a flashlight or his phone.

"Long story," he replied.

A snipe about giving the shortest answer possible was on the tip of Icarus's tongue, but then gunfire popped close enough to steal his words. The sharp, rich scent of blood spiked the air, and Adam grunted before hauling Icarus close. He slammed Icarus against the nearest wall and pressed against him, shielding him with his body, hot and thrumming with adrenaline.

Driving Icarus wild.

Instincts on hyperdrive, they threatened to tear Icarus apart, ripping him in conflicting directions. Take Adam's mouth with his; it was right there, lips parted and panting, open for the plundering, so goddamn tempting. Sink his fangs into Adam's shoulder where a bullet had sliced through fabric and skin, blood welling in the open cut. Wrench free and rip out the throat of whatever monster—human or otherwise— had harmed Adam and was trying to kill him. Icarus couldn't say where that last instinct had come from—the absolute need to protect a virtual stranger, a target he was supposed to deliver to his death—but it was there, stronger than all the rest.

He didn't get the chance to act on any of his urges. Didn't even get the chance to try and blink his senses off. Adam fired into the darkness, a curse echoed out of the fog, and the coyote launched toward the sound. A bloodcurdling wail pierced the misty air, followed by a piteous gurgling. The coyote had taken care of the threat to Adam, same as Icarus would have.

The giant raven screeched overhead again, croaking an urgent warning, and Adam peeled Icarus off the wall. "Let's go! This way."

They sprinted through the dark, the wire fence coming into sight, but then a flashlight flickered on from the other side of the border, momentarily blinding them and making Adam's steps falter.

Making a shot impossible.

Adam's pulse spiked, and his hand around Icarus's wrist tightened. Fear flooded the air, more pungent than the blood dripping down Adam's arm. Whatever the raven thought about Adam's death wish, Adam still feared it.

Which ramped Icarus's instincts higher. His vision sharpened despite the blinding beam. He saw a gun, rising next to the flashlight, aimed at them. The shooter clicked the safety off.

No time left, and no coyote or raven to save them.

No one to see him.

Moving at his preternatural speed, Icarus shoved his free hand in his coat pocket, yanked out a high heel, and chucked it at the shooter with all the might the darkness could hide.

A squelch echoed back—direct hit—and the flashlight fell to the ground, rolling away as the gunman wailed.

With the bright light gone, Adam didn't waste a second. He tugged Icarus toward and through the fence. On the other side, he paused long enough to fire two bullets into the downed shooter—one in the chest, one in the head—before dragging Icarus the rest of the way to the Camaro.

He shoved Icarus against the passenger door, one arm braced on the car's roof, the other hand pressing the muzzle of the gun under Icarus's chin. Again. "Did you lead them to me?"

Two of the three earlier urges returned, stronger now that the danger had passed. Icarus blinked, the world going gray and odorless, and his fangs receded. One instinct suppressed. But there was no help for the other, his cock stiffening against Adam's thigh.

"Lead who?" Icarus ignored the sinking feeling in his gut that told him he knew exactly who had used him as fucking bait, assuming Vincent's thugs hadn't already been drawn by whatever diabolical plan Adam had foiled. "*If* I did," Icarus said. "If it was me and not the burning building you ran out of, I didn't mean to."

"You saw that?"

Icarus slammed shut his lips before more things escaped.

"I should leave you here."

"Fine." Icarus lifted his chin off the gun. "You killed the bad guys. We're back on this side of the border fence. I'm safe now."

Adam scoffed. "That's the furthest thing from what you are." He yanked Icarus off the side of the car and opened the passenger door. "Get in."

"Where are we going?"

"Somewhere that's actually safe." He lowered the gun and stepped back, giving Icarus the choice.

Icarus slid into the car, closing his eyes and palming the soft leather seats as Adam circled to the driver's side door. A brief reprieve before Icarus steeled himself and brought his other senses back online, focusing on the scents of leather and whiskey to distract from the blood, opening his eyes to color and sharpening his gaze instead of his fangs. He glanced out each window, checking all directions and making sure they weren't being followed.

Making sure they were safe. That was what he'd been turned for, after all. To protect. Now it seemed the Devil was his charge too.

FIVE

AT THE BEGINNING of the night, if asked where he thought Adam lived, Icarus would have guessed one of the grand mansions in the Heights, or maybe a unit in one of the glitzy high-rises that rose on Sunset Hill above the Pacific cliffs. Those were the areas of Yerba Buena where most people who could afford whiskey and gas cars lived, if they lived in the city at all. He'd bet the single designer heel still in his pocket that that was where Vincent Cirillo and company lived. They probably had a whole floor or two in one of those high-rises.

After the events of the past hour, Icarus had reconsidered his guess about the Devil's habitat and had changed it to the Lost Valley, a patch of relatively stable land bound on all sides by this or that area where illegal activities of this or that variety were the norm. Property was cheap in the Valley, the weather a mix of sun and fog. Not bad if one had the means of protecting themselves from the occasional spillover violence. Icarus had thought that was where they'd been headed as

Adam had sped away from the Canyon Lands toward the interior of Yerba Buena.

But then Adam had driven right past the Valley and continued across the city—to the Terrace. In no event would Icarus have guessed that Adam lived a neighborhood over from him in the foggy corridor known as the Gap. Between the max-capacity, run-down apartment buildings of Icarus's Lakeside neighborhood and the jammed-together, equally run-down rentals of the Manor, the Terrace was several blocks of single-family homes on decent-sized lots. Once affluent, the houses were now considered too modest for the wealthy and too expensive for everyone else. It was an upper-middle-class enclave for an upper-middle-class that no longer existed in YB, their numbers dwindling since the Rift, then falling precipitously since the turn of the century two decades ago. Nice middle-class folks like the ones who'd inhabited the Terrace had either been financially squeezed out or fled the epicenter of the centuries-old war between Nature and Chaos. Add to that the less stable ground—exacerbated by the Rift—and more fog than anywhere outside the Canyon Lands—naturally occurring, in this case—and the Terrace was a sort of residential graveyard where only a house every few lots was occupied.

"You live here?" Icarus asked as he stepped outside the garage where Adam had parked. From the driveway, he stared up at the two-story house, the exterior painted the same blue-gray shade as Adam's eyes. It was in better shape than any of the surrounding homes—the pitched roof whole, the chimney in one piece, the white molding peeling only a little, the yard neatly kept—and the only one occupied on the street, as far as

Icarus could tell by the lack of other cars, lights, or heartbeats. "Does anyone else live here?"

Adam didn't answer either question, just slapped a button on the wall with the arm that wasn't bleeding. The garage door began to lower, and Icarus skirted back under in the nick of time and followed Adam across the garage to an interior door. Using a key, Adam opened a control panel, entered a code on a keypad, and waited for a lock to disengage before pushing open the door and flipping on the lights inside.

No biting back the gasp this time. The armory Adam ushered him into shouldn't have been a surprise. Especially not after the location of the house, the trip into the Canyon Lands, or the shifters Adam had met with, but it was still a shock. Guns, crossbows, throwing stars, and knives hung on three walls; beneath them on workbenches were tools and explosives in progress; in the drawers under the benches were ropes, cuffs, tape, and more; and in wooden crates all about the room were rocket launchers, grenades, tranq darts, and stakes.

"You're at war," Icarus said.

"I'm trying to stop a bigger war." Adam withdrew the gun from the holster on his hip and emptied the bullets into a lined case. Silver, then, deadly to most magical creatures, including Icarus, versus lead bullets, which would have no effect on him but were deadly when fired at those on the more human end of the scale. Adam placed the weapon back in the open spot on the wall.

"And that kid you rescued tonight?"

"A weapon we couldn't let the other side have." Sadness in Adam's eyes belied the simple statement. That wasn't all the kid was, at least not to him. Before Icarus could read deeper,

Adam turned to the one wall in the room that was the antithesis of violence. A utility sink stood beside a washer and dryer, fluffy gray towels piled atop the latter, and above the sink and appliances was a built-in cabinet from which Adam withdrew a green box with a white cross on it. "I need to clean up, then I could use your help with the cut."

Icarus slammed shut his olfactory senses and blinked the color from his vision. The entire drive across the city he'd been able to ignore the blood—mostly. But now, what Adam was asking . . . damn near impossible. Not without shutting off his triggered senses and dampening his instincts, activating the defense mechanism he'd been "gifted."

Maybe it was all for naught. Vincent clearly intended to kill Adam. Icarus could kill him tonight—probably, especially, once they left the armory—but that wasn't his mission. And Icarus was too damn curious for his own good. Med kit in hand, he followed Adam up the stairs to the main level of the house. "I don't think a gunshot wound is exactly a cut."

Adam went through the keypad routine again at the top of the stairs. "Relatively, this is a minor cut."

Icarus believed it, given the weapons stockpiled downstairs. The Devil was ready to do battle. For someone armed like that, tonight was merely a skirmish.

Adam pushed open the door and held it for Icarus to enter first. He closed the door behind them, rearmed it, and flicked on the lights. The same empty feeling that had first socked Icarus in the club returned, not as sharp but more encompassing. The air in the house was heavy with it. Just as the former mudroom downstairs had been turned into an armory, the main level of what had once been a cute family home—Icarus could sense the lingering warmth of it—had been transformed into a sort of basecamp. A kitchen that looked like it hadn't been used in a decade other than as a storage area for water bottles and a receptacle for take-out containers. A dining table covered in photos and files. A living room with card tables and desk chairs for furniture, the former laden with computers and monitoring equipment, wires crisscrossing the dull wood floors.

Icarus's tiny apartment wasn't much, but it was lived in and cozy, a home. This was not. It was a lonely, tactical, sterile place.

Except for the mantel above the fireplace.

Icarus set the med kit on the kitchen island, then drifted into the living room toward the mantel. Adam drifted in the opposite direction down the hallway, turning on lights as he went. Icarus blinked color back into his vision, just for a moment, and regretted it immediately. The framed pictures on the mantel made his chest ache worse than it had in the club. A younger Adam in police blues. A dark-haired man and blond woman in military camo, holding up a sign that read We Miss You. The same man and woman in numerous other pictures with Adam. One with the man dressed in a tux, the woman in a white gown, and Adam in his dress uniform between them, the two strangers kissing either side of Adam's face. Adam's smile was sublime, bright enough to power a solar grid. Another picture of the grinning three, holding up their hands with matching wedding bands. Obviously happy, obviously in love. The family of three in front of this house, arms over each other's shoulders, standing next to a SOLD sign in the yard. Then, on either end of the mantel, triangular cases of polished wood and gleaming glass, each holding a flag and medals. Deborah Levin, a shined brass plaque read at the bottom of one. David Levin, read the plaque on the other.

Something about their names . . . Icarus squinted, concentrating, then a moment later, it clicked—anagrams were a favorite family game—and his eyes widened with another surprise. The D from their first names, plus an anagram of their last names—Devlin.

And beneath the name on each plaque was a date exactly ten years ago.

Icarus lifted a hand to touch, drawn to the contradiction of joy and misery radiating from this one spot in the otherwise emotionless environment, as if it were a giant black hole, melancholy's gravitational pull sucking him in. He caught himself at the last second, clutching the beveled edge of the mantel, then removing his hand as the wood cracked under his tense grip. He stepped back, blinked away the pain-laced color, and folded his arms over his chest.

"Who were they?" he asked when he heard Adam return from the bathroom.

"I belonged to them, and they belonged to me."

SIX

ICARUS DUG his fingers into his biceps, trying and failing to displace the agony from the gaping hole in his chest torn open again by Adam's words.

"What's your name?" Adam asked from behind him.

"Icarus."

Adam's sharp bark of laughter was enough to break the mantel's hold over him. He turned and focused all his attention on the bare-chested Devil moving around the kitchen, a towel around his neck, another around his injured arm. Icarus was tempted to see color again but resisted the urge, already too shaken by the emotional tides of this place.

"Okay, not really." He stood on the other side of the island from Adam. "But let's just say I have a way of fucking up and getting myself into shit. Family nicknamed me Icarus."

"King of crash and burn?"

"All my life, until I became a courtesan, but by then, the name had stuck."

Adam pulled a bottle of vodka out of the freezer and two shot glasses from a cabinet. "Your family back in Portola?"

Icarus diverted his gaze. Talk about a fuckup. "Your name?" he asked, diverting attention from himself to a question he wasn't supposed to know the answer to.

"Adam." He nudged the med kit toward Icarus. "Could use that help now." Not waiting for a reply, he carried the vodka and glasses with him down the hallway.

Med kit in hand, Icarus followed the man supposedly called "Adam" to the bathroom at the end of the hall. He peeked into the bedroom on his way there—a lonely bare room with a cot, several books on the floor, and a single chest of drawers. There was another room to the right of the bathroom, but its door was closed. Judging by the lack of scuffs and the layer of dust on the floor beneath the door, it had been that way for a while, no traffic over its threshold.

"In here," Adam called.

Icarus shook off the melancholy he'd gotten mired in again and squeezed into the bathroom. The room was too small for two men their size, but Adam didn't give him a choice, sitting on the closed toilet and sliding the med kit from his hands. He opened it and unpacked items onto the ledge of the tub—a tube of antiseptic skin glue, a strip of butterfly bandages, and a large square of gauze. "Why did you follow me tonight?"

Icarus rolled off his gauntlets, shoved them into his coat pocket, and washed his hands in the sink. "To finish what we started."

"We didn't start anything."

"You wanted to."

Adam bobbled the vodka bottle he'd picked up, spilling a little over the side of the shot glass he'd filled for Icarus.

Icarus didn't call him on it, just accepted the shot, clinked the glass against Adam's, and tossed the alcohol back, confirming his senses were as dulled as he could make them. He set the glass aside next to Adam's empty one, then stepped between his spread knees and unknotted the makeshift tourniquet around his outer shoulder. His skin was warm, as if it burned from the inside, and the muscles under the skin were lithe and strong. Icarus removed the hastily slapped-on bandage, and dark liquid welled in the open cut, a metallic tang teasing the edges of his senses.

His fangs threatened.

Until Adam loosened the knot of his trench, pushed aside the coat's lapels, and ran a callused hand up the back of Icarus's thigh, under the lace strap of his dangling garter.

Instincts rushed in a different direction, arousal overriding the urge to bite, giving Icarus just enough headspace to treat the wound on Adam's arm quickly and efficiently.

"You're good at that," Adam said, voice low and rough.

"I was going to be a nurse."

"You still could be."

Icarus didn't answer, didn't breathe for what would be a minute too long for a human. If he did, it would be the last minute the not-quite-a-human in front of him lived. And that was the last thing Icarus wanted right then.

He finished patching the cut, tossed the capped tube back on the ledge, and snagged the matches from the windowsill above the toilet. He struck one and dropped it into the sink, the used bandage and towel catching fire. Standard operating procedure for erased persons.

Smoke filled the air, and Icarus could breathe again. He blinked and saw the world in color once more, just in time as Adam tipped forward, resting against him and exhaling a heavy breath. He inched his hand higher, rough fingertips brushing the curve of Icarus's ass.

Icarus gasped, in pleasure and desire, in chest-aching hope that he could give the same to the man nuzzling the bottom edge of his corset. He threaded his fingers through the strands of Adam's dark hair—coarse, uneven, self-cut. Icarus could happily run his hands through it all night. "What do you want?" His own voice was raspy, naturally so, not a performance.

Palming his ass, Adam nudged him closer, and his lips skirted the edge of the garter, his hot breath skating through the dips and valleys of Icarus's groin like the fog through the Gap.

Making Icarus hard, the evidence right in Adam's face.

Similar evidence making itself known behind the fly of Adam's jeans.

"What do you need?" Icarus urged.

Adam pressed his nose, then his lips against Icarus's erection. "Just this." He lowered his hand back to Icarus's thigh, holding him close. "Just for a minute. It's been so long."

Ten years, if Icarus had to guess. A guess he was sure was right this time. Ten lonely, melancholy-filled years without a caring, intimate touch from anyone. The Adam-sized hole in his chest ruptured into a canyon like the one they'd run through tonight. Ever-changing, life-threatening, terrifying and beautiful all at the same time.

A minute lasted five, and Icarus relished all three hundred seconds of them. When Adam stood, Icarus relished more the glide of Adam's hard body along the front of his. He brushed his lips over Icarus's cheek. "Thank you."

Icarus barely resisted grinding his stiff cock against the erect one nudging his hip. "You're welcome."

Adam shifted them, making enough room so he could step back and close Icarus's coat, cinching it tight and knotting the belt. "Take the cot."

Icarus shook his head. "Unnecessary." Adam needed the rest, he didn't, and the hours until dawn were dwindling. "It feels like you're running a fever already."

"Wasn't a request." Adam ducked out of the bathroom first, claimed a spot on the bedroom wall opposite the cot, and slid down to the floor. Icarus shot him a glare as he entered the room, and Adam glared a path for him to the cot. "We'll talk in the morning." He waited until Icarus was curled on his side under a blanket on the cot before shutting his eyes.

"You did good tonight, rescuing that kid," Icarus whispered, sensing Adam needed that too. A kind word, an acknowledgement of the victories in this war he was fighting.

A divot formed between Adam's brows, pain streaking across his features. It was gone the next second, a flinch to anyone not watching as closely as Icarus. Eyes still closed, the Devil's face smoothed, his breaths evened out, and he was fast asleep in less than two minutes.

Icarus wondered if he'd picked up that skill from David and Deborah. He recalled how the soldiers in the veterans' hospital where he'd started his training could fall asleep anywhere, anytime, on a dime—in those awful plastic hallway chairs, on the too-short waiting room sofas, on the cold hard floor of a platoon mate's room. It was a talent Icarus did not possess. He stretched out his legs and his senses, keeping watch over Adam, the house, and the surrounding area.

Hours passed without incident, and when the night sky began to lighten from black to early morning blue, when Icarus's head hurt from the math he couldn't square—those happy family pictures on the mantel had to have been from before the Rift, over thirty years ago, yet Adam didn't look thirty years older now, and he'd also lost Deborah and David during that time—Icarus climbed off the cot. He left his orphaned designer heel on the folded blanket and moved with the speed and silence he hadn't dared display last night. Crouching in front of Adam, he studied the lonely man and tried to find the smiling one from those pictures under the rough yet not old enough exterior.

Icarus barely resisted the urge to run his fingers through Adam's hair again, to skate his fingertips over his cheek and drown in his warmth. Temptation, a long-forgotten drug, was riding him hard. "What are you?" he mumbled to the sleeping man, to the dawn, and to whatever twist of fate had put the Devil in his path.

SEVEN

THE TRIP back to his apartment took Icarus less than five minutes, the morning fog heavy, the sun still shy of the horizon. Good cover for him to move through the shadows at a quickened, inhuman pace. His mind likewise operated on high speed, replaying images from last night. To say the performance—the mission—had not gone where expected was an understatement. He couldn't say he understood where it had gone at all. And that was fucking dangerous. On so many levels. He needed to excavate—Adam, David, and Deborah—and needed to sort a strategy for dealing with Vincent. Sort a way out of Yerba Buena if he had to.

At his apartment door, Icarus inserted the key in the lock, then recoiled as magic blasted through the metal, prickling his skin and lifting the hairs on his arms. Same as it had yesterday when Atlas had first appeared in his bedroom. He backed away from the door, clear across the hall, and contemplated running. To Adam and his armory? To Portola? To some place else altogether? But as sure as he'd felt the current of magic, so had its wielder felt him. He could try to run, but would he even make it out of the building?

Debatable.

Better to buy time and work on his survive-until-tomorrow to-do list. He crossed the hall and gritted his teeth, prepared for the shock this time. He grasped the key, turned it quick, and shoved open the door. His unit was dim, the blinds drawn and the lights off, but Icarus had no trouble seeing—and smelling—Atlas on the sofa in his living room. The warlock sat in the far corner, one ankle resting on the opposite knee, an arm stretched across the top of the couch, the other along the armrest, hand dangling off the end in the muted light that crept around the blinds of the sliding glass door.

How long had he been waiting there?

Icarus shut the door, undid his trench, and hung it on the metal wall hooks. He continued with his routine as if the warlock wasn't there, venturing into the tiny kitchen, laying his phone on the charger, and grabbing an express meal out of the fridge. He tipped back the vial and forced himself not to cringe. Fresh and warm was better, but convenient and safe was more valuable—and his default, absent a willing food source or an agitator who found the pointy end of his fangs.

Atlas tutted, tongue clicking behind his teeth. "Where are your manners, Icarus?"

He lowered the empty vial and licked his lips. "Oh, did you want one? I didn't think these were on your diet."

"They're not. I was thinking along the lines of vodka. You know, basic hospitality."

"I reserve hospitality, basic and otherwise, for invited guests." Icarus tossed the vial into the waste bin. "Which you are not." He crossed his arms and leaned a hip against the end of the kitchen counter. "What are you doing here?"

Atlas dropped his leg and reached between them, stroking his half chub through his slacks. "Came to finish what we started yesterday."

Icarus rolled his eyes, not the least bit tempted by the warlock's cock anymore. "World of fuck no, and aren't you supposed to be sore and dripping?"

Atlas smirked. "Who says I'm not?"

It was a shame he was a liar and an ass. He'd been filthy as fuck during their private online sessions and hands down one of the most gorgeous beings Icarus had ever seen. A toned, compact body under flawless fair skin, blond hair with an enviable wave, sinfully long lashes, and green eyes the color the forests used to be. Through computer screens, Icarus had pegged him as a white-collar professional sort. The fake profile Atlas had given him—Pierce Wilkes—confirmed as much. Perfectly groomed, expensive business casual attire that "Pierce" liked to trade for buckles and kilts, a kink or twenty that needed regular working out. He'd been Icarus's best client the past two months between solo sessions and live stream hits. The "businessman" with money and upbringing and access to resources.

Which he had, only magically.

Magic that was tied up by another.

"Where's your master?" Icarus asked.

"He sent me alone this time."

Icarus pushed off the end of the counter and peeked inside the bedroom. Sniffed. No one else that he could detect, assuming the warlock—the *lying* warlock—hadn't disguised their presence. Icarus made a swift lap around the room, checking the other side of the bed, under the bed, in the closet, and in the bathroom. All clear.

Icarus returned to the living area and rested back against the wall opposite Atlas. "You can understand how I don't trust you."

"You can understand how I can snap my fingers"—he rotated the hand hanging off the armrest, fingers at the ready—"and he'd be here."

"Hmm." Icarus caught the corner of his mouth with a fang. "I don't think so."

Their stare down lasted a good half minute before Atlas shifted forward, elbows braced on his knees. "He's overseeing a healing. There was an altercation with a coyote last night."

Icarus jolted. "That *was* you who followed me."

"Wasn't that your intent?"

The opposite was on the tip of Icarus's tongue. He bit his lip, silencing his too-truthful reply.

"That's what I thought." Grinning, Atlas pushed to his feet, brushed down his slacks, and made no effort to disguise that he was still half hard. "We'll give you another chance."

Icarus lifted his chin, defiant. "I led you to him. Not my fault he got away."

Atlas stalked the edge of the plush white rug that lay between the couch and where Icarus stood. "Maybe we found him because of that burning building and not by following you, in which case, your debts are not repaid."

"What if I could get you the money?"

"From the Devil?"

"Does it matter?"

Atlas stopped directly in front of him. "You know as well as I do that this isn't about the money."

"What does Vincent want with him?"

"He's the last thing standing in Vincent's way. Time's short. Vincent's done fucking with him."

That explained the five-million-dollar bounty on Adam's head. But if Vincent had the means to hire assassins . . . "Why do you need me?"

"Covering all our bases."

"Why would the Devil be interested in me?"

Atlas's gaze skipped over Icarus's shoulder, out of this space and time it seemed, but only for a second before returning to the present. "Everyone has a weakness."

"He doesn't know me. I can't be a weakness."

The warlock chuckled darkly, a curious mixture of condescension, amusement, and beleaguered resignation. "You've got three days, Icarus. Deliver the Devil back to the Canyon Lands by Friday night, and we'll take care of him. For good."

Atlas turned toward the door, and Icarus shot out a hand, grabbing his biceps. The warlock's green gaze snapped back to his—anger, surprise, and something more hiding in the forest. "What does Vincent have over you? You were in his thrall last night, but he's a human. Their kind can't—"

"Not everything is about magic."

"Are you in love with him?"

If the warlock's earlier laugh had been dark, this one was well past midnight. And so cold, like the frozen tundra way up north with its thinned-out trees and utter desolation. "Do your job, Icarus." He wrenched his arm free. "Leave me to mine."

EIGHT

ONCE HE GOT THE STINKY, horny warlock out of his apartment, Icarus helped himself to the vodka Atlas had suggested. He poured himself a generous shot and sipped it slowly, savoring the freezer-chilled liquor, letting it cool and calm him after a long, strange night and morning. He needed to be steady—focused—for the hours of work ahead of him.

He finished his drink, then changed out of his corset and garters and into his most prized possession—a pair of worn, comfy as sin blue jeans he'd rescued from a dumpster and patched a dozen times over. He yanked on a tank over his head, and over that, an equally comfy sweater he'd knitted last winter. He'd probably end up ditching the sweater, as he'd been unusually warm since last night, but until it became unbearable, his favorite soft garments would also help him focus. Grabbing his laptop out of the closet safe, he carried it into the living room, claimed the opposite end of the couch from where Atlas had stunk it up, and commenced excavation.

Hours passed with the daylight outside, the sun only

coming close to his toes once, when it burned off the midafternoon fog for an hour or so and snuck in around the sides of the balcony blinds. By dusk, he'd ditched the sweater and was two seconds from ditching his laptop as well. He had little to show for his daylong efforts. Nothing about Adam Devlin—or Adam Levin, he'd checked—and only one article about Deborah and David Levin. It was in an obscure local newsletter, something the hired scrubber must have missed. They'd died in a fire in Talahalusi, the area north of Yerba Buena and the Bay. That was all Icarus could find about them or the incident. No survivors were listed, and no mention was made about whether the fire was natural, man-made, or magical. Talahalusi was a popular destination for Yerba Buena refugees. There was vegetation and agriculture, jobs and homes, and a thriving cultural scene. A different proposition than YB's dreary fog, unstable ground, and magical mayhem or the twenty-four-seven, hyper-business scene of Portola, a grimy rat race powered by drugs and money with a highly polished, highly fake veneer. And don't even get him started on the religious zealots farther south who would tie him and any other paranormal to the stake and roast them.

Talahalusi could be roasting too, though, with its increasingly long, increasingly hot summers. While much had been done in Talahalusi under the leadership of the local Indigenous communities to fight the effects of climate change, the lack of similar foresight and concern by those in the areas around them meant climate change was encroaching nonetheless, driving up Talahalusi's average daily temperature, decreasing the rainfall, and sparking wildfires.

Maybe Deborah and David had died in one of those. Or

maybe they'd died because their husband was a cop? Retaliatory arson? Something to do with Vincent? Adam spoke of vengeance to the raven and coyote. Against Vincent? Were their deaths in the past connected to whatever it was Vincent was planning in the present and what he needed the Devil out of the way for? Had Adam always been the Devil—had he always been Adam—or only since his need for vengeance pushed out whatever else remained? Or because he'd survived the fire? Like he'd survived that burning building last night? He was unscathed in either instance. Icarus hadn't noticed any fresh burns or scars from old burns on him, but he'd only seen his torso; his lower half had remained covered the entire time.

He looked again at the picture accompanying the article. The Levins were slightly older in it than in the pictures on Adam's mantel, and something about Deborah looked familiar. Long blond hair, honey-colored eyes, freckles. Recalling the pictures on the mantel, something about her had looked familiar in them too, but Icarus had been too caught up in surprises to process it then. Now, he was too caught up in frustration to make a connection.

Sighing, he set his laptop on the floor, stood from the couch, and snagged his phone off the charger. Drawing back the door blinds, he found a crow on the balcony rail outside. They were frequent visitors, having overrun the old golf courses in the area, but tonight he gave his visitor a closer look. Checked its beak—narrow, its tail—fan-shaped, the scruff of its neck—smooth, the color of its eyes—black.

Just a crow, then. Not a raven.

Not *the* raven.

He slid the door open, and his visitor flew off with a

parting caw. The bird didn't go far, just to one of the lonely cypress trees beside an overgrown putting green, wobbling for several seconds until it found the point of equilibrium on the branch.

Caw.

"All right, then, bravo," Icarus said, giving the bird its due.

Caw.

His chuckle eased the tightness in his chest and made it easier to punch in the numbers on his phone. He hung up after two rings, counted off thirty seconds, then dialed again.

"I was expecting your call," a woman greeted.

The smirk in her voice made Icarus smile. "I need an excavation."

"I taught you how to excavate."

"Enough to check out my clients, though apparently, I'm not even good at that."

The smirk vanished, concern coloring her words. "What happened?"

"Long story involving a stinky warlock and a hacked cock cage."

"What?"

"Blackmail ensued."

"What the ever-loving fuck, Icarus?"

He rolled his eyes and held the phone away from his ear as she continued her chiding. Once she'd blown out the well-placed, endearing concern, he brought the phone back to his ear. "Point is, what I need to know is beyond my capabilities."

"About the warlock?"

"No, about someone who's been erased."

A ping sounded, a request for visual. He accepted, and her face filled the screen. She looked as worried as she sounded, eyes wide and brows halfway to her dyed-green hairline. She'd been wearing it that color since they were teens. A fucking beacon, unintentionally, and then intentionally because she liked giving the world the middle finger. And she chided *him* about being reckless. He rolled his eyes.

She huffed. "Icarus . . ."

"I don't have a choice."

"You always have a choice."

He glanced away from the screen, back out at the weed-covered green and the crow still perched on the cypress branch, watching him as the evening grew darker. Reminding Icarus of the choices he'd made and the choices he'd closed off for good. Reminding him of last night. Making him wonder what choices Adam had made, what choices he had left, and how Icarus played into those. He returned his gaze to the woman onscreen. "I don't." She opened her mouth to protest, but Icarus continued before she got the chance. "But it's more with this one. I want to know. I need to. Can you help me, please?"

Expression softening, she lowered her brows and smiled, but worry still swirled in her hazel eyes, all the colors of the earth mixed in them. "Of course, babe."

"Thank you. I'll wire payment when I can."

She shook her head, her long green curls bouncing with the motion, still none of the silver strands one would expect to see at her age. Magic had slowed her aging too—not stopped it like with him, but slowed it to as near as possible for a living being. "You'll do no such thing. You're my family."

He gulped down the lump in his throat. "You don't need—"

"Zip it, Icarus." Her voice was scratchy, like she had a lump in her throat too, but the tone brooked no argument.

He'd learned decades ago not to argue with her when she'd made up her mind. "All right," he said. "Thank you."

"Now, who is it?"

"He goes by the name Adam Devlin, aka the Devil."

NINE

ICARUS FELT it the second Adam entered the club, their connection a live wire electrifying the air around them. Adam's gaze seared a path across his bare back, and Icarus could hear his heartbeat over the thumping music, over the heartbeat of the client in front of him. Mike, one of his regulars, was a sweet, handsome commodities trader from out of town who always called when he was in Yerba Buena. Polite, generous, and decent in bed, he was a good, calm, and safe night's work. And as good an excuse as any to stall while excavation continued.

According to Atlas, Icarus had three days to deliver Adam back to the Canyon Lands. Three days to figure out what he was actually going to do. He could take this first one to gather his info, gather his wits, and gather extra money in case he needed to bolt. And no matter how loudly Icarus's instincts screamed at him to run Adam's direction, a night off from Mister Stranger Danger across the room was a smart decision. He needed to make more of those and less of the run-toward-danger sort.

Beside him, Mike slid some bills into the folio the bartender had left for them. "You mind if we grab a quick dinner on the way to the hotel?" He dipped his chin, and a blush reddened his dark cheeks. "I dropped off my bags and came straight here."

Icarus lifted his chin with a crooked finger. "Of course not, babe. Need you—" The rest of his words died as a hand spread across his bare back, snuck beneath the drape of his open-back halter, and inched around to clasp his side. Icarus didn't need to look to know who the hand belonged to. The heat and strength of the body that pressed against his back, the scent of whiskey that flooded his senses, and the muscled arm that draped over his shoulder, a single designer heel dangling from his fingertips, confirmed what he already knew.

As did Mike's wide eyes.

"I need a word with you," Adam said, voice deliciously rough.

Icarus shivered, and he was sure that Adam, snug as he was against Icarus's back, felt it. Adam spread his fingers over Icarus's hip, teasing the side laces of his leather shorts. Icarus would be lying if he said his dick didn't perk right up. Rude of his dick, and of Adam, seeing as Icarus was standing at the bar next to a client. "I'm busy," he said to Adam as he attempted to step forward, hand on Mike's forearm.

He failed, Adam's fingers digging into his side. "I'll outpay him."

Snatching his shoe from Adam, Icarus whipped his head to the side and glared at the too-presumptuous, too-fucking-handsome man. "That's not how it works."

One corner of the Devil's mouth hitched up. "Fine." He turned his smirk to Mike. "How much did you pay him?"

"Five hundred."

Adam removed his hand from beneath Icarus's blouse, and Icarus didn't want to admit how much he missed the touch. Adam stepped more fully beside them and withdrew a wad of bills from his wallet. He held out the cash to a slack-jawed Mike. "That's a grand. Enough for you to go away?"

Mike's gaze bounced between the cash, the two of them, and down to Icarus's erection straining the front of his shorts. "But he's the best."

Icarus chuckled. Leave it to the thirsty trader to try and negotiate.

Adam, though, had an answer for Mike's thirst: quench it with a different one. He lifted a hand, catching the attention of the bartender, who, catching sight of Adam, bobbled his shaker. He finished pouring the drink, slid it in front of the customer, then hustled in their direction. "Didn't expect to see you back so soon."

"Unfinished business," Adam replied, gaze flicking to Icarus, then to Mike. "Get . . ."

"Mike," Icarus's client supplied.

"Get Mike a barrel-aged whiskey."

"Coming right up."

"That settle us?" Adam said to Mike while the bartender accessed a secure cabinet beneath the back bar.

Mike shot Icarus a chagrined smile. "Sorry, Icarus, but I've never had the real stuff before. Rain check?"

"Of course, and I can't blame you." He leaned forward, ready to flex a bit of extra strength if Adam tried to stop him. He didn't, and Icarus gave Mike a long, lingering kiss. It was the least he could do for the money and the fleeting hope of a normal evening. He drew back, leaving the trader more than a little dazed and more than a little hard, his erection tenting his slacks and nudging Icarus's fishnet-covered thigh. Not a total waste of a night, then. A firm reminder to Mike to call again next time he was in town. "Enjoy your whiskey."

Icarus slipped out from between Mike and Adam while the latter settled the tab with the bartender. Adam caught up with him halfway across the club, slinging an arm over his shoulder again. "What happened to 'We'll talk in the morning'?"

"Somewhere else I had to be." Icarus made it one more step before his forward momentum was halted.

Adam dragged him backward instead, toward the panoramic windows that overlooked the city. "Where do you think you're going?"

"To find another client."

The speed at which they reversed accelerated, and Adam shifted their course toward a dark corner off to the side of the windows. Arm still over his shoulder, Adam slunk around to his front and planted a hand against the wall behind Icarus, caging him in. "You don't need another client tonight."

"Are you jealous?"

Adam bent his elbow, crowding closer, and Icarus backed the rest of the way up, hissing at the cold cement wall against his back. It was no match, however, for the heat that blanketed his front. "I woke up hard as a rock this morning," Adam growled in his ear. "First time in I can't remember how long."

Icarus shifted, wedging a thigh between Adam's spread legs. "Are you still hard?"

Adam took the hint, dragging his erection along Icarus's thigh, denim catching on fishnet.

Icarus pushed up against the dick and balls he'd love to get his lips around. So much for running away from danger, but when it was this goddamn tempting . . . "I can do something about that."

"You can tell me why you followed me last night."

Icarus dropped the shoe to the floor, freeing both hands to glide up Adam's chest, over the soft, worn fabric of his sweater, relishing the heat that seeped through the material to his palms, warming him to his core. "We've been over that already." He pressed his own erect cock against Adam's hip. Evidence aplenty on both their parts. "Still seems we have some—what was it you said?—unfinished business."

Adam coasted a hand over Icarus's hip, making space between the wall and his back, and snuck his fingers under the dip of the draped top, under the waistband of his shorts, inches away from where Icarus would kill to have them, spreading him open, breaching his—

"You're lying."

Icarus bit back the groan on the tip of his tongue, the fantasy interrupted, but not for long. Not if he could help it. And this right here—seduction—was what he did best. Smirking, he lifted the leg not between Adam's and hooked it over the Devil's hip, encouraging him to dip his hand lower, to grind his cock along the hard one pressed snug to his. "Am I?"

A push too far, fucking finally. Adam's hand dropped off the wall, fingers threading through the fishnet, clutching Icarus's raised leg almost painfully. But it was nothing compared to the force of the kiss he laid on Icarus—scorching in its heat and hunger, in its sheer need. Adam's lips moved over Icarus's, rough and greedy, a tongue demanding entrance, which Icarus granted without hesitation, his own desire surging to meet Adam's.

Icarus opened for him, mouth and body, hooking his leg

around Adam tighter and curling his fingers in the front of his shirt, hauling him closer, rutting cock to cock. He growled down his throat as Adam shoved a hand farther down his shorts, diving into his crack, clasping a cheek and spreading him. So close to where Icarus wanted him.

Danger had never felt so fucking good. And Icarus wanted more. "Please."

As if the plea had broken a spell, Adam pulled back—lips, body, hands, the latter adorably tangled in fishnet for a few seconds before he fully separated himself. Icarus could have kept him locked tight in his hold, but not without giving away his strength, and in any event, not without Adam's consent.

Eyes half-lidded, Icarus swooned against the wall and flicked the corner of his mouth with his tongue. "You want more?"

Adam paced in front of him and roughly ran a hand over his nape, seemingly at war with himself, his angry tone confirming as much. "Of course I want more."

Icarus lifted the hem of his blouse with one hand and slid the other inside the front of his shorts, adjusting his erection, making sure Adam got a good look at how hard he'd made him. How much he wanted more too.

As good as crooking any finger, Adam's gaze went right to the intended target. Icarus could see how hard it was for the Devil to tear his gaze away. Adam stepped closer, then caught himself. "Are you in trouble?"

Icarus yanked his hand out of his shorts. "Is that what this is about? Some rescue fantasy shit? Can't get enough of playing hero after last night?"

"I am no one's fucking hero." Adam closed the distance between them and palmed Icarus's dick through the leather.

"Even if I were, this isn't me trying to rescue you. This is me trying to find any excuse not to haul you into the bathroom and let you fuck me senseless with this piece."

Moaning, Icarus thrust into his hand, wishing for any other material so Adam could feel how hot and dripping he was for him already. "I fail to see the problem."

Adam curled his fingers around the ridge of Icarus's cock and slowly stroked the length of it, eliciting another moan. "You're trouble."

Icarus dropped his head back against the wall, eyelids fluttering closed. "You caught my name, right?"

Adam's lips brushed his neck, a tongue teasing in their wake. "But which of us will burn in the end?"

"Devlin."

Icarus righted his head and snarled at the intruder who'd spoken. The woman standing on the edge of the shadow they were hidden in snarled right back.

"Who's that?" Icarus spat.

Adam didn't step back or release his dick. "My second. Jennifer."

"Your second?" He aimed his next question in the intruder's direction. "Where were you last night?"

"On the receiving end of that rescue you witnessed," Adam answered for her as he licked along Icarus's collarbone, teasing the narrow halter strap.

"And after? She didn't have your back." None of them had. Not Jennifer, not the raven, not the enormous, growly coyote.

"I always spend that night alone."

Dragging his gaze away from their audience, Icarus dipped his chin and flicked the shell of Adam's ear with his tongue. "But you weren't."

Adam whimpered, and his erection dug harder into Icarus's hip. "Do you have any idea who you've decided to get into trouble with?"

"We're going to be late," Adam's second huffed.

Icarus nipped his earlobe. "Can you tell her to fuck off?"

"Unfortunately not. She's a coyote. She'll eat me." He glanced up through long dark lashes, and it was a good thing Icarus had the wall at his back. The smoldering look, the heat radiating off the man in his arms, was enough to make him swoon again. Almost enough to make him come in his shorts. "Not in the good way."

That thought didn't help Icarus's hard-on either. But as he glanced over Adam's shoulder, getting a glimpse of glowing golden eyes, Icarus came back to his cautious senses, a little. "Related to the one last night?"

"His cousin." Adam returned the earlier nip, teeth teasing Icarus's shoulder. "How do I reach you?"

Icarus dragged his leg along the outside of Adam's. "Seems you already know where to find me."

Adam kissed a path up his neck and along his jaw. "For a proper date."

Icarus laughed out loud. "Sweetheart, I am not the sort you date."

Adam drew back, smirk positively evil, positively addictive, and the fingers still around Icarus's dick tightened, bringing him back to fully erect with a single stroke. "Once I leave, I want you to go into a bathroom stall and jerk yourself off, and while you're doing that, pretend it's me on my knees in front of you, giving you the best blow job of your life." Icarus gasped, and Adam dipped his tongue inside his mouth, a parting sweep of heat and whiskey and everything Icarus wanted another taste of. "Or better yet, imagine your cock pounding my ass. It's been so long since anyone's breached me. Imagine how tight it must be, how good it'll feel." Adam dropped a final peck on his lips and stepped back. "Then decide if you want to be the sort who dates."

He turned on his heel and left without a backward glance. As soon as Adam and Jennifer cleared the exit, Icarus bolted to the bathroom, locked himself in a stall, ripped down his shorts, and yanked out his dick. He jerked himself off to the images Adam had seared onto his brain. Adam on his knees, mouth around his cock. Adam on his knees, ass in the air, taking every pounding thrust Icarus gave him. He sprayed the wall and floor in less than two minutes, coming with a shout, not the least bit ashamed if anyone heard him.

But after, forearm braced against the door, face resting in the crook of his elbow, reality set in. He hadn't been performing for anyone just now. Hell, not since he and Adam had left Mike at the bar. Icarus hadn't just fucked Adam in his imagination, he'd fucked himself in reality. A million different ways from Sunday. Living up to his name yet again.

TEN

ICARUS CURSED the phone vibrating on the bedside table. He wasn't ready to get up yet. Two rings, then it stopped. Didn't seem he had a choice. Thirty seconds, then, to wake the rest of the way up and activate the secure call channel. He peeled open one eye, then the other, wincing at the bright room. Midday already, judging by the ambient light that leaked in around the bedroom curtains. A longer than intended rest, but it had been a few days since he'd last slept. He snagged the phone off the charger, activated the secure channel, and was ready when she called back. He ignored the video request and lifted the phone to his ear. "I just woke up," he greeted. "You don't get to see this face."

"Eww!" she sputtered, and he could practically see her recoiling. Could imagine her curls whipping back and forth as she frantically shook her head. "As if I'd want to."

"I didn't mean it like that." Chuckling, he shifted onto his side in the bed and sank back under the cozy comforter he'd quilted. "It's my first rest in days, and I haven't eaten yet."

"So you look like death warmed over."

"Not even warm." He pulled the comforter higher, flipped the phone to speaker, and laid it on the pillow beside his head. "What'd you find out?"

"That you probably shouldn't be sharing any kind of morning face with the Devil."

He sighed and flopped onto his back.

"Wait," she squawked. "Did you already? Is he there?"

"No, but the word 'inevitable' comes to mind. I don't think I've ever wanted to fuck someone so badly in my life. It's bizarre. I hardly know the guy, I know he's dangerous, but the raging hard-on is real."

"Don't you have a whole assortment of cock cages? Have one on next time you see him. I'll hack it from here. Make sure you keep that dick locked down."

He half laughed, half groaned. "Yes, I have a whole collection. No, I don't think I'll ever use one again. They're ruined for me."

"Aww. Poor Icarus."

He pouted to no one over the loss of the toys and the inevitable bad news she was about to deliver. He retracted his jutted-out lip and ripped off the Band-Aid. "Tell me about Adam."

"Not much to tell."

"I thought—"

"The fact that he's so well-erased, his alias and his real name too, whatever that might be, and Deborah and David too, means he really doesn't want to be found. Someone who can pay for that good a scrub has something to hide. Something major."

"What *did* you find?"

She sighed, louder than his before.

"Come on," Icarus needled. "Surely you didn't think I was just going to give in?"

"A girl can dream."

"A zebra can't change its stripes."

She blew a raspberry over the line, and he covered the ache in his chest with laughter. He missed seeing and talking to her in person, missed sharing these moments together. Missed falling asleep to the sound of her rapid-fire keystrokes, the same sound that filled his room now, his phone screen lighting up with documents she pushed through.

"House is owned by a shell company, which is owned by a shell company, yada yada. Was purchased five years before the Rift." As Icarus had suspected. "The only person on the record is the attorney who set up the shell company—who set up all the shell companies—and he's dead. In the Rift."

YB had lost half its population in the Rift, most unfortunate victims in the wrong place at the wrong time, caught in the magical crossfire or pulled under the waves or into the earth that had cracked open. The number of fatalities in the Canyon Lands alone had been staggering. The half that had survived had continued to dwindle in the thirty years since.

Three decades. Icarus ran the math in his head, coming back to the same conclusion he'd reached at Adam's house the other night. The years weren't adding up. Adam wasn't adding up. And the Cirillos were mixed up in the equation too, somehow.

"Any connection to Vincent or Paris Cirillo?"

"They're just as scrubbed clean," she answered. "How'd you get mixed up with them, anyways?"

"Pretty face with a ready supply of Daylight."

"I told you that shit would get you in trouble."

"Yeah, yeah, yeah." He flapped a hand in the air, waving her off despite the fact she couldn't see him. "I don't even fucking want it. I'm fine being a hermit during the day, but it doesn't hurt to have an emergency supply."

"In case you have to rescue a certain someone during daylight hours."

"Worth it," he didn't hesitate to reply. It was the last time he'd seen her, for a few too-short hours. The time in the daylight with her was worth it, but even more worth it was keeping her safe. Worth every penny of the fifteen grand he owed to Paris—correction, Vincent—Cirillo.

"He's getting it from the warlock?" she asked.

"Probably," Icarus said. The serum that allowed Icarus's kind to withstand the sun was the sort of magic only a handful of warlocks could wield. And those that could generally wouldn't, which made Daylight exceedingly hard to come by and exceedingly expensive. Unless you had a warlock as powerful and morally bankrupt as Atlas on standby. "He's in their thrall."

"That's odd."

"No shit." Everything about the current predicament was odd.

"And you're sure the Cirillos are humans?"

"Brown eyes, and no, they're not contacts."

"Hmm." Keystrokes resumed, and a snapshot of computer gibberish appeared onscreen. "Also odd, this trace on the IP address you gave me for the warlock. It's bouncing all over the place. There's something else going on there, but I'm not sure what yet. I'm digging into it."

"Not a surprise. Atlas is all smoke and mirrors." He threw off the comforter and sat up, scrubbing a hand over his face.

"Speaking of smoke, anything on the Talahalusi fire?" Another bunch of documents came through. Police and hospital records. "Summary, please," he said. "Recall, I lack blood and a shower. Not awake enough yet."

She laughed. "When you get right, start with the Tal Gen Hospital records. There was a John Doe admitted to the ER there on the day of the fire. I think it's your guy. Third degree burns all over his body per the admitting report, but then he was discharged the next day, no treatment indicated."

"No burns on him that I could see." He stood, tiptoed around the sun dappling the floor, and grabbed his robe off the back of the bedroom door. "And the police reports?"

"As thin as the news article on details. The officer from the scene died. The case was assigned to Officer Cormac Kelley, who closed it after a respectable time of doing absolutely nothing."

"Is Officer Kelley still alive?"

"Detective Kelley now, and yes, he works the cold cases for the Talahalusi Sheriff's Office."

Had he been shuttled there because he was good at his job or bad at it? "Anything else on him?" Icarus asked as he snagged the phone off the pillow and went in search of food.

"He's local. Good cop by all accounts. No complaint charges filed against him. Asked for the cold case gig. Kind of a loner. Unmarried, no kids, lives on an outparcel of the family vineyard outside of Talahalusi proper."

"Which vineyard?"

"Monte Corvo."

Icarus almost dropped the vial in his hand. "No fucking way."

"That mean something to you?"

Crow Mountain? That couldn't be a coincidence.

"Maybe. You got a picture?"

He gulped down the meal and waited for the picture to load. Once opened, he spread his fingers across the screen, examining the man in uniform. Light tan skin, black eyes, black hair. Maybe it was the raven shifter from the other night. It had been dark, and Icarus had only seen him from behind, had only gotten a glimpse of a dark eye turning violet before he'd shifted. The man in the picture could be him or just as easily someone else with tan skin, black eyes, and black hair. But still . . . Crow Mountain, plus the case, plus a cop . . . Adam's partner, maybe?

"His what?"

Shit, he hadn't meant to muse that last part out loud.

"Former partner." He tossed the vial in the bin and left his phone on the far end of the counter, farther out of earshot as he prepared for the worst. "Adam used to be a cop," he confessed with a preemptory wince.

"*Icarus!*"

He winced more as the banshee was unleashed on the other end of the line. He pretended not to notice. "What was that?"

She saw right through the facade. "Don't play dumb with me. That was important info."

"Which would make you panic, hence—"

"Hence you should have fucking told me." She muttered a few curses, then the keystrokes started again, fast and furious. "What else didn't you tell me?"

Feeling like his eardrums were relatively safe from further damage, he retrieved his phone and ambled to the couch. "He drives a vintage Camaro and orders whiskey like it's tap water."

The typing stopped again, followed by a muttered, "Holy shit."

"Babe—"

"Don't fucking 'babe' me." She growled at him some more, and Icarus imagined she'd run her hands through her hair a dozen times by now, flattening the lovely curls. "I love you, you know that, but you are way out of your fucking league here."

"I'm starting to get that." He stretched out and clutched a pillow to his chest, ignoring the Adam-shaped hole that lingered there, that piqued his curiosity and hadn't dampened his desire for the man one bit, despite all the red flags.

Same as before, she saw right through his silence—saw right through him, period—and offered a tempting, impossible alternative. "Come home."

"You know I can't."

"Just meet me here, and then we'll go. I've got enough saved up. Enough for us to get settled somewhere else, then you can find work, and so can I."

He almost caved, but there was a reason he'd left Portola in the first place, a reason he only chanced seeing her when her life was in danger—at least, from someone other than him. He was powerful enough to protect her, but also dangerous enough to hurt her or those around her. "The last thing I want is to put you at risk."

"And the last thing I want is to lose you for good."

ELEVEN

ONCE NIGHT FELL, Icarus followed his intuition from Tuesday to the cluster of glitzy high-rises on Sunset Hill. He hunkered down on a park bench across the street, keeping to the shadows and keeping an eye on the multiple entry and exit doors of the buildings, waiting for his target to emerge or arrive. The night was relatively quiet, only the occasional passing car or departing guest interrupting the crash of waves against the nearby bluffs. His head wasn't nearly so peaceful. He couldn't help but contemplate the phone call from earlier. She would chide him for coming here, for making a direct approach, but he needed more information, needed a better sense of exactly what he'd gotten himself into. And what he might get her into if he took her up on the offer to run. Was there a way to slow the chase? Avoid it altogether? To protect them both? Because after last night, he couldn't be certain he could deliver Adam to the Canyon Lands tomorrow. Hell, he couldn't be certain he could deliver Adam anywhere but to his bed.

That was a whole other scenario his imagination wouldn't

stop spinning. Where would a kiss like the one from last night lead? What would it feel like to actually have Adam's mouth around his cock or to bury himself in Adam's ass? What would every inch of that hot skin taste like on his tongue, starting with the puckered rim of Adam's—

A yellow sports car screeched to a halt in front of the complex, shattering Icarus's fantasy. It didn't take a genius to guess who owned that flashy piece of trash. Paris Cirillo unfolded from the driver's side, and two women emerged from the passenger side, their doors opened by the valet. Paris rounded the front of the car and tossed the keys to the valet, then linked an arm through each of the women's. The one on Paris's right moved fluidly, like a cat of some sort. Vaguely familiar, but Icarus couldn't place her. The one on the left was like Icarus.

Paris had always insisted Icarus meet him elsewhere, at Club Sutro or at one of the other clubs or hotels where Icarus did business. So why had Paris brought these two paranormals here, to his home? Either Paris was a total fool, or the women worked for him. The latter, probably, which made Icarus's approach more precarious. Unless he wasn't the one who approached. He'd dressed for the possibility, knowing exactly what Paris liked, what would draw him in. He shrugged off his dark hoodie and slouched on the bench, legs spread, red lace panties peeking out from the top of the gray sweatpants stretched taut across his lap, nicely showing off the semi helped along by Adam-fueled fantasies. He laid one hand on his bare midriff below a cropped tee and shoved two fingers of his other hand into his mouth, amplifying his whistle.

The paranormals' heads swiveled his direction one second, their steps moved his way the next, and by the third second, they were across the street, into the park, and on him. The cat perched over him on the bench, claws around his wrists, holding his arms outstretched, while the other zipped behind him and circled his neck with her arm, putting Icarus in a chokehold.

"Wait!" Paris shouted. A car horn blew as he darted across the street, and once on the other side, he ran toward them at bumbling human speed, gravel crunching beneath his loafers. "I asked him to come here!"

Or maybe the women worked for Vincent, because that was a fucking lie.

The chokehold tightened. "You're not supposed to have visitors," Icarus's captor said to Paris. "Not here."

"I got hooked, okay?" An out-of-breath Paris arrived at their sides and made a sweeping gesture at Icarus. "I mean, look at him. Can you blame me?"

The cat cracked a sideways grin, dark eyes devilish in her tan face, as she glanced at his erection. "Not completely."

Icarus shifted to draw the fabric more taut. "I'm down to party."

The woman with her arm around his neck was not. "We already have a party to attend."

Paris grimaced, and Icarus suspected the party he was pretending to offer sounded way more fun than the party Paris was supposed to go to. "Fine," Paris huffed. "But can I have a minute with him first?"

Icarus tilted his head back as much as the chokehold allowed. "I promise not to bite."

Her blue eyes flashed, as did the white of her fangs. "You bite, it'll be the last bite you ever take." She cut her gaze to Paris. "And that would be a fucking waste of a last bite."

"Hey!" Paris protested.

She definitely worked for Vincent.

"Two minutes of his time," Icarus said. "Then I'm gone." He hoped they heard in his voice the finality he intended in the last word.

Whatever they heard, it was enough to back them off, and Paris slipped onto the bench beside him, his voice uselessly lowered. "What the fuck are you doing here?"

Icarus didn't waste time, cutting right to the chase. Or rather, how to end it. He hoped Paris had a different answer for him than Atlas had earlier. "How much will it take to get your father off my back for good?"

"There's not a number." Paris dipped his chin and laid a hand on Icarus's thigh, petting the soft fabric, petting him. His voice was rough when he spoke again. "It could have been a single dose of Daylight and it still wouldn't have mattered."

Icarus bumped off Paris's hand and crossed his legs. "You gave Atlas my number. I was the mark."

"Not you." He folded his hands and cast his gaze aside. "Not exactly."

"The Devil," Icarus reasoned, and Paris nodded. "Why me?"

"I don't know. I didn't want to know."

"So you sold me out instead?"

Paris clutched his hands in his lap, knuckles white. "They said you'd be safe."

Fool was right. But one who didn't mean to get in the trouble he did, at least not this time. Icarus knew something about being in predicaments like those. He laid a hand over Paris's fidgeting ones. "Why are you telling me this now?"

"Because you were always good to me." He lifted his eyes,

and sincerity and apology swirled in their beautiful brown depths. "I know I'm not the brightest. They know it, and so do you. I don't have the head for my father's business. I act before I think, but I don't know any other way to be, to survive this as me." He shrugged. "You never made me feel less for who I am."

Icarus forced out words around the lump in his throat. "You had something I needed."

Paris smiled, a soft, sad thing. "Don't sell yourself short." He gave Icarus's hand a squeeze, then withdrew his and stood. He leaned over, dropping a kiss on Icarus's cheek. "Goodbye, Icarus."

Icarus's face heated, shame at ever thinking or calling Paris a fool. He caught the young man's chin and gave him a proper goodbye kiss, sure it would be the last they ever shared. Maybe the last Paris ever received. Leaning back, Icarus held his chin and gaze. "Don't sell yourself short either."

"Thank you."

Paris made his way back across the street, shoulders drooping more with each step. The hideous yellow car was back at the curb, and Icarus overheard the cat mention a change in plans. She took the wheel, Paris the passenger seat, the other paranormal in the back. Icarus hoped like hell Paris got out of that car alive, but he couldn't be sure of any outcome. His stomach sank. He didn't like being set up, and he didn't like being the cause of someone else's setup either.

He didn't have long to beat himself up about it. Atlas and Vincent emerged from the building less than a minute later just as a hulking black SUV pulled out of the garage and around to the curb. It was hard to hear over the rumbling engine, but

Icarus flexed his powers, picking up words that made his stomach sink further.

"What's the backup plan," Vincent said, "if Icarus doesn't deliver?"

"I've got a line on the Devil's location," Atlas said. "But they want a human in return."

"Give them Paris," Vincent said without so much as a blink, not even a dollop of fatherly remorse.

Icarus had enough guilt for both of them. He'd never caused another human's death before. Tonight, it seemed he'd cursed Paris Cirillo to that fate twice over.

TWELVE

ICARUS CLOSED the computer window on his last live stream of the day, laid the remote beside it, and snagged the towel from his stash beside the bed. He wiped the come off his torso, then gently removed the massager from his ass and the cock ring from around the base of his dick. The toys were almost always a turn-on for his streaming clients, and the extra stimulation helped him too after a day packed with performances. He'd taken more appointments than usual, then an impromptu live stream, banking as much money as he could during the daylight hours so he could sneak away to Portola during the fast-approaching night.

Before Vincent or Atlas—or Adam—realized he was missing.

After what had happened with Paris last night, after hearing just how far Vincent and Atlas were willing to go to get to Adam, Icarus had decided running was his only option. He should probably also skip the stop in Portola—disappear altogether, from everyone—but this was her idea. If he left her behind, she'd keep digging, keep searching for him, and likely run afoul of the people he was trying to escape. Which would put her in danger, the very thing he was supposed to prevent, to protect her from. In Yerba Buena, he was close enough in case of emergencies but far enough away to avoid his past mistakes. Any farther, though . . . She'd be safer traveling with him than making herself a target without him.

He checked the time on his phone. Three hours until he was supposed to meet her in Portola. Enough time to finish packing, withdraw a stack of cash, and plant several false trails in case any of the aforementioned parties followed him.

Standing, he carried the toys into the shower with him, multitasking cleanup. Afterward, he snuggled in the terrycloth robe he'd treated himself to when he'd first moved to Yerba Buena, the fog-shrouded climate cooler than he was used to. He spent an indulgent few minutes sitting on the end of the bed, wrapped in the soft, cozy fabric, his last chance as the robe was too bulky to fit in his go bag.

He surveyed the room—the apartment—he'd be abandoning soon. Did he have everything? His drawers were half-open and rifled through, the bits he couldn't live without stuffed into the duffel by the door. He'd only been there nine months—not enough time to collect much more than what he'd arrived with—but enough time to get comfortable. He would miss this place and the promise Yerba Buena had held for him, including all the delicious dirty things Adam Devlin had promised him the other night. But if Icarus stayed, he couldn't be sure he or Adam would live to experience any of those delights. Misery and death were the more likely outcomes, and Adam, he sensed, had had enough of those nightmares already.

Shaking off the melancholy, he grabbed his jeans—no way

he was leaving those behind—and the black lace briefs he'd left on the dresser. He pulled them on and had just grabbed a fitted tee when the phone on the bedside table vibrated. He tossed the tee on the dresser and walked around to the side of the bed, expecting a text from her. Instead, the screen was lit by a message from Mike. **Last night in town. How about that rain check?**

Icarus checked the time again and ran train schedules in his head. Less sunlight hours in the fall meant the solar-powered trains didn't run as late into the night as they did in spring and summer, but if Mike was available now, Icarus could make it work. Pocket another five hundred, dash back here for his bag, then catch the last train to Portola. The extra money wouldn't hurt, nor would a final visit with one of his favorite clients. **When were you thinking?** he texted back.

Now? I'm on the red-eye out later tonight.

Icarus could make that work. **Hotel Ellis in 20.**

See you then.

The screen went dark, and Icarus shifted into high gear. Time was tight. He retrieved the toys from the bathroom and shoved them, the remote, and a tube of lube into a sparkly satchel he snatched out of his closet. One last hurrah for another favorite item that wouldn't fit in his go bag. Next, he hauled his duffel onto the bed and dug out a little black dress, stockings, a wine-colored jockstrap and garters, and his favorite black heels. Finally, he shut down his laptop, tucked it and the necessary peripherals into a pouch, and nestled it between clothes in the duffel. He carried the satchel and the duffel to the dusk-shadowed living room and set both bags on the couch. All that was left to do when he returned was retrieve the single dose of Daylight from his freezer and pack it with the rest of his express meals in an insulated pouch. Enough food to last him a few days and an emergency safety measure if needed.

Otherwise packed and ready, Icarus turned toward the bedroom to change but only got as far as the threshold when two hard knocks rapped against his door. Not a neighbor's knock that he recognized, nor the usual delivery person's. Keeping the lights off, he stepped back into the shadowed living area and extended his hearing.

And picked up a heartbeat he did recognize. "Fuck," he cursed low.

He glanced from his bag to the balcony door to his state of relative undress—barefoot, jeans undone, robe hanging open. It was dim enough outside, the fog rolled in by now, that he could make it to the cover of the cypress trees without a burn. But a certain human outside his door would hear the commotion inside—Icarus scurrying for the last most important item in the freezer, the hanging blinds on his balcony door rattling, the door opening. Given the speed at which he'd have to move and the height from which he'd have to jump, there'd be no disguising himself anymore. And all of that assumed a coyote wasn't waiting outside, ready to pounce.

Any exposure would be for naught, assuming Adam didn't know what he was already.

The knocks sounded again. "I know you're in there, Icarus." The gruff voice confirmed the owner of the heartbeat.

The Devil knew where he lived, and Icarus had no escape.

He looked down at himself again. He could dash back into the bedroom and quickly dress, but he'd wasted enough time already. Maybe the shock factor would work for getting rid of Adam faster.

He crossed to the door and swung it open. "How do you know where I live? And how did you know I was home?"

Adam's gaze raked over him like a brand, and when he spoke again, his voice was full of gravel. "Because you haven't left all day."

"Do you have someone following me?" Like a certain coyote?

Stormy eyes flicked to his, full of lightning, enough to startle Icarus back a step. Adam took advantage, slipping past him and inside. He was in work boots, jeans, and a Henley, and had a pistol in the holster at his waist. He ambled into the living room and stood next to the couch, staring down at the bags. "This is confusing."

Icarus closed the door and took up a spot on the wall between the bedroom and living room. "So stop trying to figure it out."

"This one will be useful." He picked up the satchel, and his eyes widened, surprised either at the weight of it or what he felt inside. The shape of the items, given what Icarus did for a living, was a dead giveaway. One Adam apparently caught on to and liked given his deepening smirk. "Very useful."

Icarus darted forward, barely containing his speed, and snatched the bag away. "It wasn't for you. I'm meeting a client."

"Not anymore. You promised me a date."

"I didn't—"

"You didn't go into that bathroom and jerk off after I left you Wednesday night?" He narrowed the distance between them, less than a foot apart. "Because when I got home, I sure did. Can't remember the last time I came that hard."

Icarus flattened himself against the wall, creating as much

room as he could between himself and the too-tempting man he wanted to plaster himself against instead. "I can't cancel on him again," he protested, voice breathy, not the least bit convincing.

The other corner of Adam's mouth hitched upward, a full-on devil's smile. He reached out a hand, and Icarus sucked in a breath, on the knife's edge anticipating where his warm, callused fingers might go. They slipped into Icarus's pocket, oh so close to where Icarus wanted them, but didn't venture far enough, withdrawing his phone instead.

Icarus glimpsed a message alert from Mike onscreen. As did Adam. "Mr. Whiskey from the bar?" He didn't wait for an answer. He clicked the call back option and put it on speaker.

"Icarus, hey," Mike answered, sounding winded. "I'm a little late, but on my—"

"Icarus isn't on his way," Adam replied. "But there'll be another whiskey waiting for you at . . ." Adam cut Icarus a questioning glance.

"Hotel Ellis," Icarus answered.

"Um . . . Icarus, you okay?"

"I'm fine, Mike." Icarus sighed and leaned his head against the wall, eyes closed. "But I can't be there tonight with you. I'm sorry. Enjoy your whiskey." He swallowed around the lump in his throat. "I'll see you next time."

The line went dead on whatever Mike started to say, and the phone thumped against his bags, Adam tossing it aside. Warm rough hands gently clasped Icarus's waist, inside the robe, just above the band of his jeans. "But you won't, will you?"

"Not if you keep fucking with my job."

"You know that's not what I meant." Adam ran the tip of

his nose along the column of Icarus's throat. "And besides, I'm your job."

Icarus froze midshiver. Did Adam know Vincent had sent him? That his job was to act as bait? To lead Adam to his death?

"I'm trying to refocus all your attention on me."

Or maybe Adam meant "job" in Icarus's usual sense of the word, in the way that involved an intimacy Adam missed, his gestures now so like the ones Tuesday night in his bathroom. He nuzzled the crook of Icarus's neck as his warm breaths and rapid heartbeat slowed. Every second like this made whatever it was Icarus was doing with Adam feel less and less like a job and more and more like something he also wanted. And somewhere between the jumble of conflicting emotions and priorities was the one thing that mattered most: not leading Adam to his death. Maybe if he took this "job" tonight, if he gave Adam the intimacy he so clearly needed, he could find a way to warn him away from Vincent Cirillo.

Or fuck, kidnap him if he had to. Make sure he didn't run to his death.

He lifted a hand and tangled his fingers in the coarse dark strands at the back of Adam's head. "Where are we going?"

Adam smiled against his skin. "Benton's."

Finding Adam's hair too short to tug, Icarus was forced to curl his fingers around his skull instead and gently tilt his face back so Icarus could see it. "How?"

The Devil grinned. "I'm me."

Icarus didn't know whether to slap him, kiss him, or knee him in the balls for being so damn arrogant. And he sure as fuck didn't know what to wear to a joint like Benton's. Yes, he worked YB's top clubs, but courtesans didn't frequent establishments like Benton's. Only the sort of people who drank whiskey and drove gas-powered cars dined there. People like Adam Devlin. "I don't have anything to wear to a place like that."

Adam tilted his head toward the bedroom. "There's that dress in there." When the fuck had he noticed that? In the half-second glance he'd cast that direction when he'd entered? *Cop,* Icarus's brain reminded him. Then his brain short-circuited completely as Adam coasted a hand over his hip and grabbed his ass. "But I'd rather you leave these jeans on and throw on that shiny top from the other night."

Despite his full day of work, Icarus was halfway to hard already. Zero need for toys. Not when Adam's erection was shoved up against his. It was a struggle even to hold the thread of conversation. All he wanted to do was wrap his legs around Adam's hips and get fucked against the wall. Or better yet, on the bed.

Bed.

Dress.

Benton's.

The thread.

"I can't go to Benton's in patchwork jeans."

Adam used the hand not clutching Icarus's ass to gesture at his own self, dressed in jeans and a sweater.

"Yeah, but you're . . ." Icarus shoved his shoulder. "You."

"And you'll be with me." Adam grabbed his retreating wrist and pinned it to the wall, spreading the robe open more fully, exposing more of Icarus's chest to lips and teeth that scorched a path across his collarbone on their way to a nipple. "I want to take you out for a nice dinner, some whiskey. A proper date."

He flattened his tongue for a long, rough lick, and Icarus scrabbled for purchase with his free hand. Scrabbled for the thread again. "I don't—"

Adam tightened his grip on his ass. "I want to stare at your ass in these threadbare jeans." He released the cheek and glided his hand up under the robe, spreading his hand over Icarus's bare back. "I want to splay my hand here and sneak my fingers beneath the drape of that sexy top." He licked a path across Icarus's chest to the other nipple, swiped and bit. Icarus hissed. Chuckling, Adam released the sensitive nub and nuzzled the thin patch of hair between his pecs. "I want everyone to see you on my arm, then I want to take you home." The hand on Icarus's back lazily drifted around front, then, with laser-sharp precision, dove into his open jeans and roughly palmed his cock over the lace, making Icarus achingly hard in an instant. "I want to peel these jeans down your incredible fucking legs, see you in nothing but lace, then lay you out on a bed and suck your thick shaft until you're about to blow."

Fucking hell, the swings from starved for intimacy to just plain starved were making Icarus dizzy and more turned on than he'd been in his whole damn life. "I'm about to blow now."

Adam kissed up his throat and around his mouth, tongue dipping and diving between his lips, teasing, never giving Icarus the kiss he wanted. "Not yet, baby."

Groaning, Icarus chased after his mouth and missed, lips scraping scruffy cheek. "When?"

Adam shoved the lace aside and grabbed his balls. Good thing, since his next words sent Icarus soaring. "When I'm on my hands and knees and you're fucking me senseless."

THIRTEEN

ICARUS TRIED NOT to focus on the heads that swiveled toward him and Adam as they crossed the restaurant to a corner booth. He wondered what was more of a shock to their audience—the fact he was wearing heels, jeans, and a slinky halter, or the fact he was walking arm in arm with Adam Devlin. Adam, who was arguably more dressed down than him in a sweater, nondescript—if well-fitting—jeans, and work boots. In one of the most exclusive restaurants in the city, where all the other patrons were dressed for a special occasion, where there were items on plates and liquids in glasses that Icarus never thought he'd see again. But the staff hadn't blinked when they'd entered. They'd greeted Adam like an old friend—definitely a frequent visitor—and led them to the table where two cut crystal glasses of whiskey were waiting.

The high-dollar liquor went a long way to helping Icarus ignore the stares they continued to catch over three courses of food the likes of which Icarus was sure he'd never taste again. He didn't need human food to survive, but he could eat and enjoy the fuck out of it. But in the moments when Icarus wasn't overwhelmed with the tastes and aromas of the food—or by the heat blanketing his side and the hand under the table nestled in his groin—he couldn't help wondering where this "date" might lead.

To Adam in his bed or to Adam dead?

That kidnap plan was sounding better and better if only Icarus had an ounce of faith he could execute it without fucking up.

He tossed back the rest of his whiskey, savoring the meld of smooth and spicy flavors and the internal warmth that rivaled the space heater beside him.

"You want another?" Adam asked.

"Lord, no, I can't—"

The rest of his words died on Adam's lips, stolen by the kiss Icarus had wanted so badly back at his apartment. Deep and slow, maddening in its intensity and its restraint. Maddening because they were in public, and Icarus couldn't crawl onto Adam's lap, grind down on him, and keep kissing like this until they came together, breathless and spent.

Adam drew back first, but only far enough to rest his forehead against Icarus's, sounding breathless already. "I've been dying to taste the whiskey on you."

Icarus ran the tip of his tongue along Adam's upper lip. "And?"

"Better than I imagined." He hummed contentedly and palmed Icarus's erection under the table. "Like I imagine this is going to be too."

"Oh, you have no idea." Icarus grinned. "How many more courses?"

"Just two." Adam kissed the hinge of Icarus's jaw while

slowly stroking his length. "Should I tell you all the ways I plan to worship this tonight?"

Icarus rolled his hips with the next stroke, eager for more friction. "I think you're enjoying this a little too much, Mr. Devlin."

Like a flipped switch, Adam withdrew into himself and away from Icarus, taking his teasing lips, warm breath, and claiming hand with him. Humor and desire fled his gaze, sadness and longing taking their place, the rain clouds moving in, the sight eerily similar to the one he'd worn that first night back at his house.

An awkward silence filled the space between them. Icarus had tripped a memory wire. Something Deborah or David used to say or do? What kind of explosion had he unintentionally set off? The Adam-shaped hole in his chest made itself known again. "Fuck, Adam, I'm sorry."

Adam wiped his mouth with the cloth napkin, then folded it on the table. "I'm sorry I interrupted your work tonight."

"I think I needed to be here instead."

"Why's that?"

Finger under his chin, Icarus refocused Adam's gaze on him. "Back at my apartment, and at the club the other night, you said you wanted me to"—he lowered his voice—"fuck you senseless." He shifted his hand to cup Adam's face and tapped a finger against his temple. "What are you running from in here?" Adam tried to look away, tried to knock Icarus's hand loose, but Icarus wasn't letting him or this point go that easily. "You want a good, hard fuck, I got that, and I'm more than happy to oblige, but there are other moments when you want something else, something you miss. Whatever those memories are, whatever you're missing, I don't want to make you forget that. Lust shouldn't blot them out." He firmed his grip on Adam's face, prepared for a reaction to his next words. "Neither should vengeance."

Adam's eyes narrowed, but he didn't jerk away—yet.

"I heard you," Icarus explained, giving part of the story, hoping it would be enough. "I heard you talking to the other two in the Canyon Lands the other night once you got away from the fire."

"Stay out of it, Icarus."

"You caught my name, right?"

Adam's hardened expression faltered on a chuckle. He lifted a hand, holding Icarus's to his face. He angled his face and kissed his palm. Another of those knee-stealing intimate moments. "I'm trying to keep you safe."

Icarus gave him more of the truth, more afraid not to, more afraid each second that Adam was headed the direction of dead instead of his bed. "Maybe I'm trying to do the same."

The grip around his hand would have crushed a human one. "What did you say?"

Icarus didn't flinch, didn't shy away from the cold, hard stare assessing his own. Adam apparently didn't like what he saw. He jerked away, yanked out his wallet, tossed a stack of bills on the table, and bolted out of the booth.

Icarus fisted his hand and thumped the seat of the leather booth. "Fuck!" He couldn't grab for Adam, couldn't block his path, and couldn't flex his speed or strength without making a scene and exposing himself. He was pretty sure Adam knew already given that grip, and he hadn't staked him for it, but Icarus couldn't be certain no other patron in this restaurant wasn't carrying. Namely the shifter two booths over who'd eyed him warily all through dinner. He just needed to get outside, into the dark, and follow the whiskey scent. He could catch up to Adam.

He slid out of the booth, calmly crossed the dining room, apologized to the waitstaff and host, then slipped outside. He sniffed the damp foggy air, caught Adam's familiar scent, and followed it around the corner into the alley where Adam had parked the Camaro.

And promptly met the business end of Adam's pistol. "What did you mean?"

Icarus held up his hands, palms out, and kept his voice as low and calm as the rising panic in his chest would allow. Not panic for his own life, but for Adam's. He argued with the only thing he thought might convince Adam to not race off. "Would Deborah and David want this for you?"

Adam shoved the gun's muzzle against Icarus's chest, backing him against the alley wall. "Stop with the fucking riddles."

"*You* stop chasing your own death." Icarus shared another truth, hoping it would convince Adam since appeals to sentiment had not. "Vincent is willing to sacrifice his own son to get to you. What do you think he'll do if he finally catches you?"

Adam's eyes flared, surprised perhaps that Icarus had given him the honest truth, but then they narrowed, and his mouth twisted into a sneer. "Nothing, if I catch him first. What exactly did Vincent say?"

"That they had a line on your location. That the source required a human in exchange for the information."

"Paris?"

Icarus closed his eyes and nodded.

"Is that source you? The location here?"

His eyes flew open. "No!" He made a slow show of moving

his hands toward Adam's face. Adam remained still, his grip on the gun firm. He could pull the trigger, lodge a silver bullet in Icarus's chest, and end him just as fast as Icarus could snap his neck. But he didn't, and Icarus lightly clasped his face. "I answered the door tonight because I knew the only hope for either of us was to convince you not to run into the fire again."

"But Vincent sent you to me?"

"Yes, but I'm trying to make sure they never catch either of us again." Icarus hoped to hell and back that he'd said enough to convince Adam to let this go. That maybe for once he hadn't made a complete fucking disaster of the situation.

But his name was Icarus for a reason.

Adam lowered the pistol, wrenched his face free, and turned away. He withdrew his phone with his other hand, tapped at the screen, and brought it to his ear. "Meet me at the pier in twenty," he told whoever answered on the other end of the line.

"Adam, don't!" Icarus grabbed him by the shoulder and spun him around. "Please don't! We can leave together. We can just go."

Heartbreaking sadness and aching loneliness stared back at him. Adam hung up the phone and tucked it in his pocket. "My name isn't Adam."

Icarus skated his hand down Adam's shoulder, gripping him by the biceps and pulling him closer. "It is to me."

As gently as Icarus had held his face earlier, Adam returned the gesture, using it to draw Icarus the rest of the way in, forehead to forehead. "Go back to your apartment and wait for that man."

"Like hell."

"I can't protect both of us."

"You don't—"

"I don't know how to turn it off, Icarus. It's who I am."

He remembered back to that first night in the bar, how Adam had sensed his approach, how the cop instincts just wouldn't turn off. Was that what had happened to Deborah and David? Could Icarus bear to put more of that guilt on Adam's shoulders? "How do I know you'll come back? That it won't be someone else knocking on my door?"

Adam shoved the butt end of the gun against Icarus's chest, forcing him to take it.

Icarus flailed. He didn't need it, and he sure as fuck shouldn't handle it if those were silver bullets in the chamber. "I don't—"

"They're real bullets, not silver," Adam said. "In case it's not me at the door."

The hole in Icarus's chest grew wider, and he closed his eyes, leaning more of his weight against Adam. "My name isn't Icarus."

"You've told me that before." Adam's lips brushed his. "But you're Icarus to me."

FOURTEEN

IT TOOK every ounce of willpower Icarus had to not flash his fangs and pin Adam to the ground, to not chase after the Camaro as it disappeared into the fog, to not follow the scent of whiskey and gasoline to wherever Adam was headed. Turning the opposite direction and making his way across town, back to his apartment, was one of the hardest things Icarus had ever done.

Once inside his four walls, staying there wasn't any easier. Conflicting instincts tore at him—run after Adam or run the fuck out of town. She had lobbied hard for the latter. Icarus had called her on his way home and explained he needed to stay. She hadn't bought his explanation. She might still win. His bag was packed and ready, or rather repacked for the third time, a fruitless exercise in passing the minutes.

He considered logging on and initiating a live stream or snagging a client for a solo performance, anything to whittle away the hours, but his focus was tenuous at best, and there was a damn good chance Adam's name would fall from his lips when he came. And Icarus only wanted that to happen once Adam was there and Icarus was buried to the hilt inside him.

An express meal and a long, hot shower finally began to settle him. He settled further as he pulled on his sheer black stockings and the delicate lace jockstrap and garters he'd laid out earlier. He slid his feet into his favorite heels, wrapped himself in the terrycloth robe, and took his first steady breath since Adam had left him standing behind Benton's, gun in hand.

He leaned against the bedroom doorjamb, eyeing the weapon on the end of the kitchen counter. It was then he realized the significance he'd missed—or had been too distracted—to comprehend outside the restaurant. Adam had been packing regular bullets, not silver ones. Either Adam didn't know what he was, or more likely, given his pointed assurance that they were not silver bullets, he did and trusted him enough not to carry silver. Trusted Icarus enough to protect him if other paranormals had attacked them in public.

Icarus pushed off the doorjamb and circled the living room rug, lowering himself onto the far end of the couch. He wasn't going anywhere. Not unless a coyote or raven showed up on his doorstep and told him Adam was dead. He tossed his phone onto the cushion beside him, braced his elbows on his knees, and scrubbed his hands over his face. Fuck, he hoped that wasn't how this night ended. He peeked at the time on his phone. He could give Adam a few more hours. He just had to leave himself enough time to get to Portola on foot before the sun came up. It was doable in the dark and would be necessary, as the trains stopped running at midnight.

Hopefully the trek would be unnecessary.

But Icarus's hope waned, his stomach sank, and his steadiness faltered with each passing hour. He forced himself to stay on the couch but only by the grace of his crochet hooks, yarn, and a half-knitted sweater he'd pulled from his go bag.

The bag sat by the balcony door, taunting him. Screaming silently that he needed to run, and that he needed to run now, screaming louder and louder until hope was a whisper on the cusp of dawn. Sunrise the opposite of the widening black hole in Icarus's chest, sorrow and sadness for a man—the Devil—he would've liked to know better. Whatever fate Adam had met, Icarus was almost certain he didn't deserve it; no one should die with that much pain and loneliness on their shoulders. It was not a fate Icarus wanted for Adam, but one he had to assume by now had likely befallen him. A similar fate would befall Icarus a second time if he didn't get the fuck out of there.

Forcing himself to his feet, he retrieved his jeans, a sweater, and his combat boots from his bag, stuffed his knitting inside the outer pocket, and was halfway to the bedroom when a knock sounded against the door.

He dropped the boots in surprise, then had to move at full speed to catch them. Not knowing whether it was friend or foe outside, he didn't want the thump of boots hitting the floor to give his presence away. And why the fuck hadn't he put on clothes before now?

A second knock, and on its heel, a familiar heartbeat.

Icarus took a lurching step toward the door, then froze as a second heartbeat joined Adam's. He traded the clothes and boots for the gun and inched toward the door. If it was Adam out there, why wasn't he saying anything like he had last night? Because he wasn't at liberty to do so? Or because he wasn't sure if Icarus was? Could this fucking night—correction, morning—be over already?

Shoulder to the door, using his speed, Icarus peeked out the peephole. Adam stood outside, Jennifer beside him. He listened once more, just two heartbeats in the immediate vicinity. Icarus opened the door but still didn't lower the gun from where it was half-raised at his side. It wouldn't do any good on the coyote, but thankfully, what Icarus saw with his eyes matched what he'd heard with his ears. Adam and his second were the only two beings in the hallway.

"You alone?" Adam asked.

Icarus opened the door wider. "Not anymore."

Adam passed his gun to Jenn, then took the one out of Icarus's hand and passed that one to her too. "Knock if it's an emergency," he told her, then, without another word or glance, he stepped over the threshold and shut the door behind him.

They reached for each other at the same time, Icarus curling his hands in Adam's sweater, Adam clasping either side of his neck, drawing him in and slamming their mouths together. Like at the club the other night, Adam kissed with a hunger Icarus was powerless to resist, his own instincts racing to keep up. He splayed his hands on Adam's chest, pushed him back against the wall, and Adam's whimper, his satisfied sigh, was the stuff Icarus's fantasies were made of. He plunged his tongue between Adam's parted lips, his thigh between his legs, and pressed their bodies close, diving deeper into the rising heat between them. Adam rocked his hips, undulating between Icarus and the wall, grinding all their hard parts together, and another wave of desire crashed over Icarus. Fuck, when was the last time he'd wanted someone this badly? But could he truly have what he wanted? And for how long?

He broke the kiss, drew in a gasping breath he didn't need, and caught Adam's hands on their way to the knot of his robe.

Lacing their fingers together, he lifted their joined hands to the wall on either side of Adam's head, forcing a cease-fuck he hoped was fucking brief; he wanted a moment to catch his peace of mind. "What happened?"

Eyes closed, Adam leaned his head back against the wall, his chest rising and falling rapidly, gulping in air he did need. "It's done."

"Done?"

"We got Paris out. He's safe. You're safe."

Icarus squeezed the big, callused hands he held pinned to the wall. "And you?"

Righting his head, Adam opened his eyes, and there was a flicker of something in their blue-gray depths, something that caused a prickle at the base of Icarus's spine, but then it was gone with the next blink, burned away by the rising fire, the inferno blast caused by Adam's words. "Safe with you."

Icarus melted, inside and out, consumed by the flames.

FIFTEEN

ICARUS ERASED the distance between them, bringing their lips and bodies back together. Releasing Adam's hands, he slid his own down Adam's sides to the hem of his sweater and shoved the garment up, exposing the lightly furred torso he'd gotten a glimpse of the other night and wanted to taste every inch of now.

Adam pushed off the wall, stripped the sweater off over his head, and used the momentum—and Icarus's admitted distraction with where his lips and hands would land—to walk them deeper into the apartment, untying Icarus's robe as they stumbled toward the couch. Adam turned them so he went down first on the cushions, and Icarus eagerly climbed onto his lap like he'd wanted to at Benton's. He shucked the robe the rest of the way off, then tilted forward, embarking on his quest to taste every inch of Adam's skin. "I'm sorry I didn't get the jeans back on," he said between kisses across Adam's collarbone.

Adam skirted his hands along Icarus's thighs, over the lace

tops of his nylons and under the garters. "No, baby, this is good." He nuzzled Icarus's temple and dropped a kiss there.

The soft gesture made Icarus shiver. He moved on from Adam's collarbone to his neck, alternating nips and licks with gentle brushes of his lips and nose, returning the intimacy Adam craved, even in the heat of lust. "What do you want?"

One of Adam's hands crept higher. "Everything." Skirted Icarus's groin before palming his cock. "Anything." Icarus groaned and rocked into the tempting touch, the lace adding a dizzying degree of friction. Adam's lips brushed his ear, his breath as hot as his plea. "As long as this is inside me."

Fuck yes, Icarus wanted that. But he wanted—needed—to make this good for Adam too. Something inside him demanded it, as did Adam's dry spell leading up to now. Icarus needed to be careful with him, which meant he had to slow this down.

"We'll get there. I promise." He levered upright. "Are you inoculated?"

"I am. Annual vaccine package."

"Same," Icarus said with a nod. "Debatable if I need it, but that whole nurse thing. For the safety of my clients." He reached past Adam for the satchel he'd left on the back of the couch. "All right, then, you're going to help me get this on."

Adam eyed the bag hungrily even as he asked, "Do you need that?"

Icarus climbed off his lap, but only far enough to slide to the plush rug on the floor, tugging Adam along by the hand and the promise of what lay ahead, including himself, splayed out on his back on the rug. "I do if I'm going to make this good for you too." As Adam knelt between his legs, Icarus fished out the cock ring. His fingers brushed the massager and the remote, which gave him another idea. Another way to repay the trust Adam had shown him earlier by giving him his gun and being with him now. "And to give you control." And just that thought was making him harder. He handed the ring and lube to Adam. "You need to get this on me now while we still can."

Adam's grin was devilish, and it only continued to widen, to darken deliciously with heat and lust, as he unhooked the garters and peeled the jockstrap down Icarus's legs at a maddeningly slow speed, kissing the inside of his thigh, his knee, his ankle as he went. Then kissing back up the other leg as he reattached the garters and spread Icarus's thighs with his hands, making room so he could bury his nose in Icarus's groin, breath hot against Icarus's sack and cock, lips so fucking close.

And Icarus was going to be too if Adam didn't get a move on. "Now, Adam."

Smiling, Adam mercifully retreated, rising onto his knees and lubing up the cock ring. He eased the ring around the base of Icarus's dick and balls before clamping it closed.

"Tighter," Icarus directed.

"I'm gonna come in my jeans before you get it in me."

"No you're not."

Adam gulped, eyes flicking up to him, pleading and thankful all at the same time. Yes, this was exactly what Adam wanted. Intimacy on a whole other level.

"Tighter, Adam," Icarus directed again, and Adam did as told, eyes darkening and drinking up the sight of Icarus's rapidly plumping cock and balls. But it eased some of the strain for Icarus, reminded him of his role, except this wasn't the usual performance. It wasn't really a performance at all.

Only insofar as it was needed to give Adam the pleasure, the intimacy he so desperately craved, which Icarus was craving more by the second too.

He removed the massager and remote from the bag. "We're going to lube this up too and get it inside me, then you're going to turn it on with the remote when you're ready for me to come inside you." Groaning, Adam palmed his cock through his jeans. Icarus grinned. "Now, do you want to put it in or watch me do it?"

"Watch," Adam stuttered out.

Icarus figured. "Okay, then you get out of those jeans while I get this inside me."

Adam worked quickly, jeans and boxers gone, getting his dick in his hand, stroking, while Icarus put on a show for him. He lubed up the massager, put a pillow under his ass, hole on full display, then stretched himself, fingers teasing his rim, widening his hole, so he could slide the massager inside and nestle the curved external tip against his taint. Both would vibrate and tease him to the extreme.

"Fuck," Adam grunted. "I want in there too."

"I can take you both," Icarus purred. "But that's not what you need right now, is it?"

Keening, Adam fell forward again and buried his nose under Icarus's balls, his hot breath puffing over Icarus's taint, his lips brushing the sensitive skin as he pleaded. "Fuck, Icarus. I need this. Need you." He licked a stripe up either side of the silicon tip, then around his rim at the base of the massager, and fuck if Icarus didn't worry about his own ability to hold out. Such naked, unembarrassed hunger—for him— from someone so powerful, who'd done fuck only knew what tonight to secure his safety, made Icarus's head spin, his chest ache. He'd seen a lot of clients over his working lifetime, but not a single one had ever made him so dizzy with hunger and desire.

"Let's get you what you need, then." He got his knees under him, then lured Adam upright as well, into a slow measured kiss, smoothing over the rough edges of his own need and Adam's. Letting his hands smooth over warm skin and tight ass cheeks, fingers teasing Adam's crack, getting him used to where this was going.

Their cocks brushed, and the massager turned on. He grinned against Adam's mouth. "Now who's playing dirty?"

Adam nipped at his lips. "That's only an ounce of how badly I want you right now." He nipped his jaw as he ground his cock against Icarus's. "How badly I want to drown in all this."

Icarus chuckled and slapped his ass and got a tick up in vibrations for it.

"Turn around," he told Adam. "Lean against the couch. Arms spread, face down, ass out for me."

He was pleased when the only expression that raced across Adam's face was pure, unadulterated lust. Not a hint of fear. Adam assumed the position, and Icarus rewarded him again for the trust, kneeling behind him, spreading his ass cheeks, and licking around the rim of his puckered hole.

"Fucking hell," Adam cursed.

"Need to get you ready." He speared his tongue and thrust inside, wetting and stretching Adam gently at first before adding lubed fingers and working him open more. Adam was tight, as promised, and Icarus's cock was fattened up by the ring. It was going to be a snug fit, and he didn't want to hurt Adam. Icarus wiped a hand off and tiptoed it up Adam's spine, loving the shiver that followed in its wake. "Are you sure about this?"

Adam shivered again, then ramped up the vibrator. "Icarus, inside me, now."

The gruff order sent a tremor up Icarus's spine and made the plea impossible to resist. Cock in hand, he closed the scant distance between them and lined up at Adam's hole, beginning the slow slide in. Unsurprisingly, he met resistance, and Adam groaned in frustration.

"Easy does it," Icarus coaxed, with gentle hands sweeping over Adam's ass, hips, and back and a line of kisses peppering his spine. His body blanketed Adam's, absorbing the heat and reflecting it right back on the man, reflecting back the closeness Adam—and he—needed. With the intimacy came relaxation, and Icarus stretched his arms along the backs of Adam's, wrapping his fingers around his wrists and nuzzling the nape of Adam's neck, dropping kisses there. Icarus eased the rest of the way inside Adam, cock buried to the hilt.

Adam let out a giant sigh, and Icarus smiled. He stretched enough to kiss Adam's cheek, and Adam turned his face enough so Icarus could capture the taste of satisfaction on his lips. Adam was the first to move the lower halves of their bodies, pushing gently back, rounding into the body spread across and inside his. Icarus rocked, countering Adam's movements, slowly at first, his thrusts measured, aimed at getting Adam used to his length and girth, to having anyone back inside him.

It didn't take long for Adam to adapt, for the heat and hunger to chase away gentle intentions. "More, please," he whispered against Icarus's lips.

Icarus obliged, pumping harder, deeper, faster, and Adam

tore his mouth away, planting his forehead in the cushion and letting out a wanton groan. He ticked the massager's vibrations up again. "That's it," he panted. "Harder."

Icarus bit back his own groan with his fangs, chewing the inside of his lip. He desperately wanted to sink them into Adam's neck, but another part of him rebelled against the notion, rebelled at the thought of causing this man any harm. He focused instead on sinking his cock inside him, making this everything Adam wanted and more. He levered up, hands on Adam's shoulders, pressing gently down, and adjusted the angle of his thrusts. If Adam's groan before had been wanton, the next was pure ecstasy. Prostate found, Icarus continued to pound at it, continued to eat up every grunt and groan Adam belted out, barreling ever closer to his own orgasm. The sounds and sensations, the heated vise around his cock, and the massager stimulating his prostate and taint brought him right to the edge.

But he wouldn't leap without Adam. "Do you—" he started.

Adam dropped the remote and grabbed his hand, lacing their fingers and turning his head, glancing over his shoulder. Tears streaked down his blotchy face onto his swollen lips and into his ruffled scruff. Icarus faltered and lost his breath, worried at first, but looking to the source of those tears, he found no sadness in Adam's bright eyes. Only relief, only desire, only sheer worshipful appreciation. Only fire. Fuck, had anyone ever looked at Icarus like that before? He didn't think so, and he didn't think he was ever going to get the vision out of his head.

He leaned forward, licking up the tear at the corner of

Adam's mouth. "I've got you. I'm right here with you. Come for me."

The mouth against his fell open on a groan, and the muscles around Icarus's dick clenched so hard Icarus closed his eyes and let himself drown. Behind his lids, all he saw was the sun as he dove off the cliff with the Devil.

SIXTEEN

TINGLING FINGERTIPS nudged Icarus toward wakefulness. Searing heat and the acrid stench of smoke shoved him the rest of the way there.

"Fuck!" He yanked his dangling hand out of the sunlight that streaked through the gap in the balcony blinds. Flopping onto his back, he cradled his smoking hand against his chest and made sure none of the rest of him was singed.

Flame-free.

And Adam-free.

The realization struck like lightning, and Icarus nearly burned himself again as he hurtled to his feet, tangled in a quilt and tripping across the sunbeam.

Where the fuck was Adam?

Heart in his throat, he raced around the apartment. No sign of the other man. Last night, he'd said they were safe, but Icarus couldn't kick the sinking feeling he was missing some-thing, that *safe* was a more flexible term in Adam's mind than in his. Why had he left without waking him? Where had he gone?

Forcing his racing mind and jittery limbs to still was a monumental feat, but his eyes weren't doing the trick. He flexed his other senses. No sounds but the usual outside his four walls, and inside, nothing but the lingering scent of sex from earlier this morning. Was it still morning? Not likely, given the brightness of the sun streaming in through his balcony door.

He went to grab his phone to check the time and to text her to see if she could pull traffic cam footage to determine which direction Adam had gone. He'd have to deal with her *I told you so*—she'd not been convinced when he'd messaged that they were safe and he wouldn't be running—but he'd eat crow if he had to for Adam's sake. Time to put the kidnap plan into action, regardless of the outcome. It had to be better than Adam dead. He lifted the phone from the charger—the screen flashing half past noon—and found a folded piece of paper under it. He snatched up the note and read the scribbled words.

You still owe me dessert. Don't go far. —AD

Icarus's panic waned, the sinking feeling muted, as a reel of devilish desserts from earlier flitted through his mind. Easing his cock out of Adam's ass and replacing it with his fingers, keeping him stuffed full, helping him come down gently. Adam likewise gently removing the cock ring and massager from his sensitive parts, light touches and lingering kisses soothing the satisfied ache. The two of them on the floor, Adam between his legs, licking up the come that had dribbled on Icarus's thighs. Moving to the couch, limbs tangled, cuddled together under the quilt, Adam's warm breath and steady snores a calming breeze over Icarus's chest, seducing him to sleep as well. Intimacy overload—the kind Adam had needed, and the kind Icarus hadn't realized he'd needed too. They'd had dessert, but apparently Adam wanted more, and Icarus didn't think he meant only the sweet kind.

Wanting to be ready for him, Icarus gathered the toys, his robe and undergarments, and his bag off the floor, careful not to catch the sun's rays. In the bedroom, he withdrew his laptop out of the bag and put it back in its safe, then dumped the rest of the bag's contents on the bed. After a quick shower, he pulled on lace briefs, jeans, and one of his off-the-shoulder knits, then put everything back where it belonged.

He got as far as the fridge in the kitchen, an express meal in hand, when a bird screeched outside his balcony door.

Panic surged, blinding in its intensity, last night's prickle at the base of his spine now sharp as a knife. He dropped the vial and it shattered, blood splattering the white tile floor.

Adam's words from last night came hurtling back at him.

Safe with you.

He hadn't actually answered Icarus's question. He was only safe last night because he was in the company of an apex predator. But now he wasn't. Adam wasn't safe, not like he'd apparently made Icarus and Paris. By doing what? "Fuck!"

Kraa! Kraa! Kraa!

Icarus didn't think it was possible, but the knife in his back twisted, all the way to his gut, making it churn. He was certain the bird outside the door wasn't like the crow from the other day. Certain it wasn't a crow at all, but a different corvid. A much bigger one.

KRAA!

Fighting the wobble of his knees, Icarus stepped over the

mess in the kitchen, snagged the quilt off the sofa, and made his way to the door. Hand wrapped in the fabric, he didn't bother to hide his speed or strength as he reached through the blinds and shoved open the door, breaking the lock and rattling the glass in the metal frame. The raven outside had to know what he was, same as he knew exactly who the raven was.

The giant black bird tottered through the blinds, its violet eyes tracking every step Icarus took out of his way. "Are you here for me or for him?" Icarus asked, recalling Adam's words to the shifter—the psychopomp—the other night.

The bird jumped from the floor to the couch to the end of the kitchen counter, then spread its massive wings and flew into the bedroom. A crash of a lamp, a whoosh, and then several moments later, the black-haired man from the Canyon Lands the other night reemerged, wrapped in Icarus's robe.

Icarus leaned against the opposite wall, keeping his distance. "Well . . ."

The shifter's eyes flicked to the kitchen floor, then back to Icarus. "To be determined."

"Where's he gone?"

"The Canyon Lands."

"Fuck!" Icarus shoved off the wall. "What are you doing here?" He flung an arm toward the door. "Go help him."

"That's not my role in this."

"Bullshit! You helped him the other night."

"I owed him." Arms folded over his chest, fingers clutching his biceps, the raven—Cormac, Icarus recalled—rested on the arm of the couch. Icarus didn't think he liked that answer any more than Icarus had. The words that came next Icarus liked even less. "And I've been looking for you."

"Me?"

"Michael Rollins."

Icarus rocked back a step and froze. "What did you just say?"

"Your name. From before you went missing. Five days *before* the Rift." He withdrew Icarus's phone out of the pocket of the robe and held it out to him, a secure web page open. "You're a cold case in my stack of many."

The picture of the teen displayed onscreen was barely recognizable to Icarus. Had been then too on his first day at the shelter. "Still am."

"You're a soul I was supposed to deliver."

Icarus pocketed his phone. "Which direction?" He wasn't religious—he'd fled those people eons ago—but certain notions lingered and were reflected across ideologies. Eternal peace or eternal torment? Worth asking.

Cormac didn't answer.

Fuck whatever happened to Icarus. He was always doomed. But Adam . . . Adam had had enough loss. Icarus wouldn't let him lose his own life, and certainly not for a life and soul that was already lost. "Not until I save Adam."

Cormac's eyes flicked again to the kitchen, to the blood and glass splashed across the floor. "Saving lives isn't what your kind usually specializes in."

"I have a way of fucking up, but I think you knew that already, Detective Kelley."

Violet eyes shot to his. "You know who I am?"

"You cops aren't the only ones who can excavate."

"Your file is rather thick."

Icarus spread his arms. "I am what I am."

"So go." The raven tilted his head toward the balcony door. "I'm not ready to take his soul yet either."

"Did you miss the sun part?"

"I didn't." Standing, he crossed to the kitchen, took a long-legged step over the mess on the floor, and opened the freezer, withdrawing the single vial. "I also didn't miss the part in your file about this."

In a flash, Icarus closed the distance between them and snatched the vial of Daylight out of his hand. "Then why'd you even come here? Why didn't you just go help him?"

Cormac didn't budge, didn't back down in the face of Icarus's fury or trembling anxiousness. "I had to be sure I was right. About you." Sadness darkened his glowing eyes, and his tan face drained of color. "I owed them."

Icarus turned the vial over in his hand. How much did he owe Adam already? Could he be safe knowing that his safety was bought with Adam's life? With the lives of countless others—like the kid Adam had rescued—who wouldn't have the Devil to keep them safe anymore? Not a chance in hell. He flicked off the cap of the tube and tipped the vial up to his lips, drinking the magic down. Not the emergency he'd planned for, but the only one that mattered right then. He tossed the empty vial into the trash and cringed at the strange magical sensation coursing through his veins, lifting the hairs on his arms and making him impervious to the big ball of light in the sky. He moved into the living room and tested an arm in the sun.

No smoke.

He yanked back the blinds on the balcony door. Still no smoke. "You know where he's headed?" Icarus asked as he shoved his feet into his combat boots. He didn't figure the detective had gone through all this trouble just to sit on the sidelines.

He figured right.

Magic crackled through the air, and then the raven flew over his head and out the door. Icarus bounded over the balcony rail after him, into the sun, chasing the warmth he'd only just found and wasn't ready to lose.

SEVENTEEN

ICARUS RISKED DRAWING attention in broad daylight as he leapt block by block, roof to roof, street to street. Best-case scenario, anyone he flew past wrote it off as a figment of their imagination or as a bird, like the raven that sailed above him. Worst-case scenario, he drew other paranormals to his trail and his perceived supply of Daylight that he'd completely consumed. All risks he was willing to take to make it across town and to the Canyon Lands before Adam took the ultimate risk.

Thankfully, aside from the raven, no one was on his tail as he neared the eastern edge of the city, the thickening fog blotting out the sun by the time he reached the border fence. Without slowing, he took a flying leap over the barrier and landed in a crouch, hand planted on the ground—

And immediately felt it, the perpetual give and shake these parts were known for since the Rift. Except these weren't the usual shifts that came from unstable ground, not like the shifting silt under his feet last week. No, these vibrations were bigger, rippling under the surface, a futile attempt to relieve the pressure that seemed to be pushing up against the ground.

The instability was likely the reason no other eyes glowed out of the fog at him and why no other birds joined the one that landed on a crumbling set of stone stairs across from him.

And hopped right back into the air, wings flapping.

Kraa!

"Exactly," Icarus said. "We're fucked." They had five, maybe ten minutes if he was judging the vibrations correctly. No time to waste. "Do you know where he is exactly?"

Cormac glided down onto his shoulder and gave a plaintive croak.

No, then. He probably hadn't had time to scout ahead, and with the mounting fog, flying solo would be a risk. Icarus could locate Adam instantly, but it would be another risk added to the mounting stack. If there were any paranormals hiding in the fog, it would be a flashing neon light announcing his presence, assuming they were worried about anything other than scurrying the fuck out of there.

Fuck it. What was one more risk at this point? He stilled, closed his eyes, and opened his ears, searching beyond the heartbeat on his shoulder. For the only one that mattered. Racing and strong, his own heart recognized the thump even as the world raged around them. He moved in time with the beats, rushing alongside it. As soon as he heard voices, as soon as shadowy figures appeared at the edge of the fog ten or so yards ahead, Icarus forced his steps to falter, cutting the connection.

But not before a sizzle of magic zipped toward him. If not for the fog, Icarus was sure moss green eyes would be locked on his position. He was surprised when no other spells were cast in his direction. What the fuck was the warlock playing at? Was the initial flash merely an acknowledgement, or was Atlas drawing him in and setting a trap? The obnoxious warlock didn't need to do the latter. Icarus was approaching regardless. Avoiding traps while doing so would be a bonus.

Cormac took off above him, circling, and Icarus waited. The bird returned several seconds later, banking left, and Icarus followed. As he edged closer, the voices grew louder, as did the crash of waves. They were right at the edge, the thinning fog confirming as much, spray dissipating the heavy mist. He ducked behind a crumbling pillar, then peeked around it, laying his eyes on the stomach-churning scene.

Atlas held two shifters to the ground with orbs of magic— Adam's coyote second and the cat from Paris's place the other night. She'd been a plant? *Fuck!* She'd also been the one who'd helped rescue the kid; that's why she'd seemed familiar. Surrounding them were several other shifters and paranormals, including Paris's other guard, the one like Icarus.

"Biggest mistake I ever made was letting you live that day." Vincent's voice drew Icarus's gaze to the nightmare scene unfolding on the jetty. He muffled his gasp in his elbow. Adam was on his knees, Vincent in front of him, a gun pointed at his head. "You've been a thorn in my side for ten fucking years."

Adam didn't look the least bit frightened. Chin held high, eyes steely, he glared at Vincent like he was invincible. "You thought a human wouldn't come after you."

"I thought a cop would be smart enough to know better."

"You took everything from me. I promised myself I wouldn't meet them again until I took everything from you."

Not invincible. Just had a fucking death wish. Cormac had been right the other night.

"Looks like you're going to fall short of that promise."

Not if Icarus could help it. Adam's words from earlier rang in his ears. *Safe with you.* Icarus would hold up his end of that bargain. Fangs descending, fingers stretching for maximum damage, claws growing out from under his black nails, he mentally calculated how many throats he could slash before Atlas downed him, before one of the other paranormals attacked him, before Vincent got a shot off with that gun.

That gun.

He peered through the fog and thought he recognized the weapon—and if he did, if he was right. He had an advantage only Adam realized. He just needed a fucking distraction, a few seconds to buy time, to get the jump on the enemy and put that advantage to use. He put his hand to the ground and silently begged Nature to win this skirmish, prayed she could sense him like she had since they were foster siblings. Like she had since their transformations thirty years ago. Like she had when he'd rung her on the phone the other morning.

Hearing his plea, she entered the battle, ready for a fucking war. With a kick hard enough to topple the pillar he was hiding behind, the ground buckled, and Icarus rolled with it. He came up snarling behind one shifter and broke his neck. Dashed to the next, broke his neck too. Tore out the heart of the third with his claws while tearing out the jugular of the fourth with his fangs.

Cormac shrieked overhead a second before claws tore across Icarus's back. He howled and turned, ready to return the favor, so sure it was the woman from the other night, but he was saved the hassle by Adam's two shifter guards, who took her out from behind.

"Go get him!" Jenn shouted. "The ground's not stable enough for us."

Icarus spun again, and his heart dropped upon seeing Vincent, gun arm raised, backing Adam up to the tip end of the crumbling jetty. Atlas was running in their direction, but the raven dive-bombed him, halting his progress, the delay enough for Icarus to speed ahead of him, out onto the jetty.

But Vincent fired before he could make it. The gun blast echoed, the bullet streaking out of the barrel and heading straight for Adam's head.

Icarus leapt, taking the risk, praying he was right about the gun. Spinning in the air, he landed between the mobster and the Devil, absorbing the impact of the bullet.

The lead bullet.

Vincent's brown eyes widened impossibly as Icarus snatched the gun out of his hand and turned it around on him—

And then the earth shook, more powerfully, more terrifyingly than it had a moment ago. A globe of moss green magic surrounded Vincent, and he was gone with a snap, wrapped in Atlas's magic.

Cormac screamed overhead, and then so did Adam behind him. "Icarus!"

Icarus spun only to see the jetty fall away, Adam falling with it.

"No!" Diving, he slid on his belly across the crumbling, silty earth, arm outstretched, hand reaching for the scrambling one that was fast disappearing over the edge. The waves below raged on as giant chunks of earth fell into the cold, dark water.

Icarus couldn't let Adam join them. Couldn't lose what he'd only just found.

He clasped Adam's trailing wrist, curled his fingers around bone and skin, and dug his nails in deep, holding on with everything he had. The momentum pulled at him. He spread his legs, the toes of his boots dragging the ground, the claws of his other hand shoved into a crevice of creased and buckled earth. Icarus irrationally thought about those old action movies, how this moment was always in slow motion, how the speed at which his future was falling off a cliff was the polar opposite—too fucking fast.

They caught a break. The earth shook again, pushing up the ground they were hanging from and slowing their momentum. But for how long? Seconds at most, Icarus guessed, before another shake would plunge them into the Bay below.

In such a predicament, the very fucked kind he was known for, Icarus didn't expect to look down and see the Devil grinning up at him, didn't expect the words that came out of his mouth to be just this side of gleeful. "What are you waiting for, vampire?" Adam said, confirming what Icarus had suspected all along. Adam knew exactly what he was. "Get us the fuck out of here."

Pride swelled inside him. This he could do right, after all—kidnap the Devil—and Adam trusted him to do it. He firmed up his grip, detached his claws from the earth, and using his toes for leverage, he dove off the cliff with the Devil.

PART TWO

THE DEVIL

EIGHTEEN

FREE FALL.

Countless seconds where Adam's only tether to reality was Icarus's hand clasped around his wrist, his nails—his vampire's claws—digging into Adam's skin.

Despite his law enforcement training, despite the sun poking through the fog, despite the "death wish" his ex-partner had correctly called, Adam couldn't stop the bile from rushing up his throat as he struggled to catch his breath and take in the crumbling landscape racing past his eyes.

Cliffs splitting in two and exposing pre-Rift foundations, rusted metal piles, and broken wires. A new canyon forming, mystical green sparks emanating from its core, a deep dark crevice the fog and water rushed into.

All of it flashed by too fast for Adam to fully comprehend.

And then he was yanked up and flung into the air. Icarus released his wrist, and the free fall from before was nothing compared to floating on fear, on the certainty that he would hit the water at any moment, break his back, and that would be the end. He'd only felt such fear once before as fiery walls had collapsed around him and his family. Loved ones he'd see again soon. And while yes, he did have a death wish and no, he didn't fear the after, he dreaded the impending moment of death. Been there. Done that. Didn't look forward to the repeat. Not like this. At least this time, death would be quick. At the rate he was falling again, he'd hit the water any—

Pink flashed by him, Icarus diving, and the next thing Adam knew, he landed in Icarus's arms just as the spray of crashing waves soaked his back.

The water never touched him again.

They were flying. There was no other way to describe it. It wasn't exactly like Cormac sailing above in raven form, but the vampire carrying him was practically walking on water, pushing off this or that shoal, leaping miles at a time. Two leaps to the peak of Pelican Island. Four leaps to the Huimen Enclave. A giant leap over the swaying light rail bridge that spanned the Bay. On and on Icarus skipped, banking right as Cormac did overhead, toward the more stable ground across the Bay, but never too far inland. He stayed to the shoreline, heading north into the giant estuary and on farther, the fog breaking over the fields of Talahalusi, the fall colors showing off on the rows of vines and packed late harvest fields.

With the threat of death passed, Adam kicked his brain into tactical mode. They were exposed, unlikely to be perceived by human eyes, but other paranormals would notice them. They would wonder where they were headed in such a hurry and why. And if they realized Icarus was a vampire, traipsing through Talahalusi in broad daylight, they'd either consider him a threat or consider how to steal his supply of Daylight. How large a dose had Icarus ingested? Enough to make it to

Monte Corvo at the north end of the valley? Would the bullet Icarus had taken for him dampen the magic's effect? Until Adam had the answers to those questions, they needed to take cover.

He shifted in Icarus's arms, enough to survey the surrounding area. Familiar with the environs, he knew exactly where they could hide while they assessed maneuverability. He stretched an arm toward the east. "Two vineyards over, at the foot of the ridge, there's a farm. Head for the sunchoke fields. Should be tall enough to hide us."

Nodding, Icarus veered right, and Cormac screeched in protest overhead. It was clear the shifter's primary focus was getting Adam to the mountain. Adam, however, was focused on the man who'd saved his life. "Ignore the angry bird," he added, and Icarus's chuckle rumbled against his side.

Adam remembered the way that laughter had felt against his front last night, right before Icarus had slapped his ass and told him to bend over the couch. His ass still ached from how hard and rough Icarus had fucked him. He'd desperately missed that ache, the good kind.

They reached the edge of the Deere farm, and Icarus shortened his strides, slowing as they neared the plot of eight-foot-tall stalks. His last leap landed them three rows in, and Icarus covered him in a protective crouch. Cormac made two circular passes overhead to scout the area before descending several rows beyond them.

Adam patted Icarus's chest. "You can let me down now. We're safe."

Icarus lowered him to the ground feetfirst. "We're gonna have a conversation about your definition of *safe*."

Cormac came crashing through the stalks, naked as the day

he was born. "Have it once we get to the mountain. Why the fuck did we stop?"

Icarus's gaze shot to Cormac's uncovered bits. Adam laughed at his savior's perfectly arched brow, louder still at his teasing. "Impressive, raven."

Cormac wasn't in the mood. "Shut it, vampire." *Angry bird* was right. Detective Kelley was usually the most levelheaded of their crew, restrained and deliberate to the point of frustrating. Unless someone he cared about was in danger . . . or on his list of souls. Both were currently in play; his patience was shot.

Adam stepped between him and Icarus. "This valley is crawling with paranormals," he said to Cormac. "If we'd kept traveling like we were, we wouldn't have made it to Monte Corvo unnoticed."

Cormac ignored him, attention fixed on Icarus. "How'd you do it?"

"You saw me take the Daylight."

"Not that."

But now that Icarus had mentioned it, Adam's most pressing questions throttled back to the front of his mind. "How long will it hold?" he asked Icarus. "Will the bullet dampen the effect?"

Icarus pulled down the collar of his sweater that was already half off his shoulder. There was a tiny pink scar the size of a quarter—a dime a blink later—where a wound should have been. "Bullet's a nonissue." He righted the collar and pushed up a sleeve, turning his hand over in the shafts of sunlight filtering through the stalks. "And the Daylight will hold at least until nightfall."

"You put that hand"—Cormac pointed at Icarus's flitting hand—"to the ground and made the earth shake."

"I can't make earthquakes happen."

"You're lying."

"Have *this* conversation once we get to the mountain," Adam said, throwing Cormac's words back at him. "We need wheels."

Cormac spread his arms. "I don't exactly have my badge on me."

"Please," Adam scoffed. "Old man Deere knows who you are."

"Not this well."

Icarus stifled a laugh behind a cough. "I hardly know you, and yet . . ."

Cormac's violet glare intensified. Adam needed to get them out of not just other paranormals' paths, but out of each other's. He dug his wallet out of his pocket and withdrew a wad of cash. "I spotted a clothesline on the other side of the bean patch," he told Cormac. "Go get what you need. I'll settle up with Deere"—he flashed the cash—"for that and some wheels."

Cormac held his gaze a long moment, then flicked it over his shoulder to Icarus. "If you hurt him—"

"One, you came to me." Feet planted shoulder-width apart, Icarus folded his arms and lifted his chin. Defensive, a low-key flex of strength. "Two, I didn't carry his ass all the way up here to bite him now." One corner of his sinful mouth ticked up, exposing a fang. "Unless he asks me to."

"Adam, we don't—"

Adam cut off the debate before it continued needlessly longer. "Go." With a huff, Cormac spun on his heel and disappeared into the stalks. Adam waited for them to stop swaying before turning back to the vamp. "You're trouble."

Icarus held his arms out, same as Cormac had. "Not hiding it."

But he had been hiding what he was, up until an hour ago. Adam wondered what Icarus's excuse was. Anything like his own? Icarus wasn't hiding now, though, at least not from Adam, who closed the distance between them and ran his hands up Icarus's torso. "Thank you for getting me out of there." He ached—the good kind—to sneak his fingers under the soft knit sweater, to glide his hands over Icarus's cool skin and firm muscles. To watch the scar disappear for good. But that wouldn't get them out of there any faster. He inched one hand higher, cupping Icarus's neck, and settled the other over his too-slowly beating heart.

Icarus curled his fingers into the hem of Adam's shirt. "You knew?"

"The second you clocked your step to *my* heartbeat at Club Sutro."

"What are you?"

Adam could tell Icarus knew he was hiding parts of himself too; that reckoning was coming for all of them. But not yet. "Add it to the list of conversations." Adam rose the couple of inches needed to press their lips together, teasing the vampire's mouth open with a swipe of his tongue, diving in and stealing a taste. He couldn't let this go on either, but on his long list of regrets was leaving Icarus's apartment earlier without a goodbye kiss. He erased that regret with his tongue, his lips, and the groan he freely surrendered.

Smiling, Icarus clasped Adam's ass and held him close,

rutting through layers of denim. "So many conversations." He sighed dramatically.

Adam smiled wider, unable to contain the laughter that bubbled up and out of him. That was something else he'd missed. Something he could hardly remember doing the past ten years until a certain vampire courtesan had marked him as his own.

NINETEEN

THEY "RENTED" one of Deere's rusty old trucks that miraculously got them the rest of the way to Monte Corvo without incident. Worth the extortionate amount of money they'd paid. Once there, Adam ducked inside Cormac's villa to use the bathroom while Icarus hung back, enjoying the outside it seemed. Adam found him under the pergola, staring at the valley of vines below. Adam leaned against a column and looked his fill, eyes roving over the man he couldn't get out of his head. It had taken everything in him to suppress his reaction to the gorgeous, ballsy courtesan when he'd first approached him at Club Sutro. It had been unexpected on a night mired in grief and regret, in memories of the last anniversary Adam had shared with his husband and wife. He'd flexed his melancholy, an initial line of defense, and Icarus had crashed right through it, the first person to do so in a decade. A gentle word and a gentle hand from an apex predator, whispered promises and heated commands that didn't involve kill or be killed, all of it so different from the friends and foes that Adam usually kept.

Icarus was a tangle of juxtapositions, a mystery Adam wanted to solve. Wanted to do other things with too. Especially when he saw him like this—the sun filtering through his bright hair, reflecting off his pale, muscled shoulder, and highlighting the wide expanse of his back, his trim waist, his firm round ass in threadbare jeans . . . Resistance was futile.

He pushed off the pillar and followed the sandy path along the reflecting pool's edge, scattering the crows there. He approached behind Icarus, wound his arms around his waist, and drew him close, back against his front.

Icarus melted, hands covering Adam's where they rested at his waist. "This is the outparcel?" he asked, bemused.

"They could never get anything to grow up here for all the crows." He pressed his lips to Icarus's sun-warmed shoulder, and Icarus shivered. "Hence the name."

"Hence the name." His shiver lengthened into a roll, aligning their bodies closer but taking it no further, no doubt attuned to Cormac moving around in the house, moving in their direction. "Why does Cormac live up here alone? At least one of his parents is also a shifter."

"Both are, and as are his siblings. But once Cormac was old enough, his parents chose to create life instead of ferrying it elsewhere. The burden fell to the oldest." To the man approaching behind them, steps heavy, scuffing in the dirt, as if they needed the warning. As if his tossing peanuts on the ground for the crows didn't cause a loud enough flurry.

"I get that," Icarus said, voice full of familiar melancholy. Adam held him tighter, not loosening his embrace even as Cormac joined them under the pergola.

"Jennifer and Abigail called," he said. "They got out safely with your Camaro."

Icarus dropped his head back. "Thank fuck for that."

Adam chuckled, a cover for his own relief, not about the car, but about two of his best soldiers surviving today's shit-storm. Abigail had been instrumental in two rescues this week after months of undercover work inside the Cirillo organiza-tion. She was a wealth of information and skill they couldn't afford to lose. And Jennifer . . . well, Jenn was a professional—and family. "Tell them to go by the house and grab what they can. Weapons are the priority. What about Robin?"

"A few hours out. On his way back from a job."

Icarus righted his head and shifted in Adam's arms, enough to split a glance between him and Cormac. "The growly coyote?"

Adam nodded.

"He took a job elsewhere?" Icarus scoffed. "In the middle of all this?"

Adam appreciated the affront on his behalf, but this wasn't even the biggest shitstorm Robin had missed. Robin would carry the guilt of not being there the day his sister had died until he met the same fate. But that particular absence hadn't made him any more attentive to matters at home. If anything, his perceived failure only pushed him further into his ill-advised quest. "Robin does what Robin does."

"What the fuck does that mean?"

"Let it go," Adam gently chided.

There was nothing gentle about the strength Icarus used to shove out of his arms. No longer hiding what he was, Icarus took a giant step forward and spun on his heel. "Also, how is this hiding?" He spread his arms and circled in place. "We're in a villa on top of a bald hill." He gestured between Adam and Cormac. "And you two are ex-work partners and still tight. They've seen you"—he pointed directly at Cormac—"at both incidents. And the name of this fucking hill is *Crow Mountain*. I'm not the sharpest tool in the shed, but even I can figure this shit out. Won't Vincent and company figure out the same?"

Adam eyed the crows that had reassembled along the water's edge, none of them startled by their raised voices or Icarus's erratic movements. "Good luck getting through them to us."

"And I can have more here in an instant," Cormac added.

Icarus snapped shut his lips, but lingering doubts danced across his furrowed brow. Adam stepped forward, only to have Icarus move in the opposite direction. "I need to make a phone call," he said, then asked Cormac, "Can I use your study?"

Cormac nodded, and Icarus trudged toward the house, his combat boots kicking up enough dirt to clear a narrow path among the crows who were busy picking apart peanut shells.

"What is this?" Cormac asked as he pointed at Adam, then at the door where Icarus had disappeared into the house. "What's between you two?"

"I don't know," Adam replied. "I'm just . . ." He tore his gaze from the house. "I'm drawn to him."

"That's not you." Cormac sank sideways onto one of the loungers, elbows braced on his knees. "That's the thing inside you."

Adam had considered that, of course—his heat drawn to Icarus's cold, the promise of rebirth drawn to walking death. The thing inside him was sparked by certain situations, by certain emotions, by certain instincts, all of which Icarus fired. But Adam was practiced with keeping the Devil buried for everyone's sake, that kid the other night an example of what could happen if he ever let the thing inside him loose. But the Devil wasn't the only part of him that Icarus appealed to. There was also the cop who recognized someone in need of protection and the submissive in need of someone to handle him the way Icarus had so expertly done. Adam lowered himself onto the lounger across from Cormac. "It's some of me too. More of me than it's been in a long time."

"You've known him less than a week."

"I slept with Deb and David the night I met them. The two feds I was supposed to be working a case with. I married them a month later."

"For a cop, some of your instincts are shit."

"When you fall in love, then we'll talk." Adam instantly regretted his words, Cormac's immediate flinch as good as any punch. He'd been on the cusp of love once and had had it so cruelly snatched away that he'd sworn to never tempt that fate again. He'd only told Adam about it one night after too much bourbon, after a ferry that had hit too close to his own heartache decades before. "Shit, Mac, I'm sorry."

Cormac wiped away the pain the next second, face blank again. "You're right. I don't know. I can't risk that. But it doesn't mean I don't worry about the risks you take." He closed his eyes and hung his head, hands clasped behind his neck. "Vincent Cirillo sent Icarus after you. How do we know he's not still working for him?"

"When we were partners, what was the one instinct of mine that was always right?"

Cormac eyed him through his dark lashes, conceding. "Who to trust."

"I'm not discounting what you're saying. Vincent knew

who to send to me and knew enough about Icarus to figure he wouldn't take no for an answer. But Vincent miscalculated. The connection between us was immediate, Mac. Same way it was with Deb and David. And just like with them, I knew from the start I could trust Icarus. *Me*." Adam tapped his temple. "Not the thing inside me."

Cormac lifted his face and pinned him with a glare. "You didn't see what I did out there today."

If Cormac relied on Adam's instincts about who to trust, Adam relied on Cormac's powers of observation. The raven saw everything. "Okay, tell me what you saw."

Cormac reached between his own spread knees and flattened his palm on the ground. "He put a hand to the ground like this, closed his eyes, and asked Nature to help him. And it did. I fucking felt it, Adam." He righted himself and mimicked Adam's earlier motion, except he tapped the center of his chest. "The raven felt it."

If Cormac saw it, heard it, felt it, then Adam had no reason to doubt it. But he also needed to understand the why and how of it. "I'll find out."

"Find out what?" Icarus called behind them.

Adam twisted on the lounger and was struck breathless again by the sight of him. Exiting the house, he strutted toward them, his long limbs, blue eyes, and magenta hair all glowing in the sun. Adam wanted to see more of him in the daylight, assuming Icarus had enough of the other sort in his system to last. "You sure that Daylight will hold?"

"I'm sure."

He stood and met Icarus at the edge of the pergola. "How do you feel about some time in the sun?"

"You can't—" Cormac started.

Adam silenced him with a raised hand. "I'm not planning to leave the property. Come find us when the others get here." He didn't wait for Cormac's reply. He grasped Icarus's hand and tugged him toward the steps that cut into the terraced hill and led toward the northwest sector of the property. He ignored Cormac's gasp behind them as they continued on the path he hadn't traversed in a decade.

Icarus stuttered. "Adam, what . . . where . . ."

He smiled over his shoulder at the intriguing man both he and the thing inside him wanted. "That conversation I promised you."

TWENTY

ADAM STOOD at the bottom of the terraced hill's steps, the third time he'd had to stop and wait for Icarus to catch up. Not that he minded. Watching Icarus step to the edge of each terrace, close his eyes, and lift his face to the sun was its own kind of joy. Light filtered through his long, burnished lashes, fell across the sharp lines of his cheekbones, and kissed his full pink lips, as if the sun was as happy to spend an afternoon with him as Icarus was with it.

As Adam was with both of them. Joy had been absent from his life for so long.

Icarus lowered his chin, a smile teasing the corners of his mouth. "You're staring again."

"When's the last time you were out in the daylight?"

"A few months ago." Ignoring the rest of the steps, Icarus leapt off his present terrace and landed next to Adam.

"Around here?" Adam asked as he started them along the gravel path that bisected two of the vineyard's lots.

"Portola."

Where Icarus had lived. In a prior conversation, Icarus had

diverted Adam's follow-up about whether he still had family there. Would he divert again today? "Family visit?"

"Something like that." He held up a hand, fingers spread. "I can count on one hand the number of times I've been out in the sun since I was turned. You don't realize how used to the feel of it you are until you can't bask in it any longer."

Adam let the diversion go—family clearly not a topic Icarus wanted to get into—and tried another. "How long ago were you turned?"

"Detective Kelley didn't tell you?"

"He tried multiple times. I wouldn't let him."

Icarus drew up short, gravel crunching beneath his boots. "Why's that?"

"I didn't need to know then."

"And you do now?"

Adam returned the earlier grin. "Just making conversation."

"Conversation . . ." Icarus rolled his eyes, and Adam laughed out loud. Laughed louder when Icarus put his hands on his waist and cocked a hip. "How do I know you're not going to stake me out here in the vineyards?"

Adam spread his arms and pointedly swept his gaze down his body. "You see a stake on me anywhere?" When he lifted his gaze, it was impossible to miss where Icarus's had gone. Right to his semihard cock. "Actual wood," Adam teased— and acknowledged. He closed the distance between them and took Icarus's hand in his. "Trust me."

"Why do you trust *me*?" Icarus traded his joking tone for one that was earnest and adorably confused. "I'm a vampire. I can kill you before your next breath."

Adam drew him closer, and Icarus twined an arm around

his waist. Pressed together, the last thing Adam felt was threatened. Turned on, yes. Comforted, yes. Life in jeopardy, no. "You had multiple chances to kill me the past week, personally or through Vincent's hand. You didn't."

Icarus lowered his chin, gaze downcast. "I agreed to help them initially."

"How long did that agreement last?"

"Until I saw you at the club the first time."

"Exactly." Adam curled a finger under Icarus's chin and lifted his face. "And I'm guessing extortion was involved."

He tried to duck his chin again, but Adam wasn't having it, wasn't letting this point go. His tenacity was rewarded with another eye roll and a dramatic huff. "They hacked my cock cage and my vibrating plug. Threats of death and destruction. The usual."

When Adam failed to stifle his laugh, Icarus stifled it for him, capturing his lips in a scorching kiss that sorely tempted Adam to drag him off the path and into the rows. He was dying to shove his hands inside Icarus's jeans, cup his ass, and grind against him. Desperate to lower the zipper, sink to his knees, and take Icarus's cock in his mouth. Ready for Icarus to tangle his hands in his hair and use him. But he wanted all that to happen in the place he dearly missed, the place he hadn't wanted to return to until Icarus had walked into his life.

He drew back and rested his forehead against Icarus's jaw. "You didn't have a choice," he said between heavy breaths. "And even if you did, I'm not sorry. I think you're the key."

"The key to what?"

"That's a longer discussion." Fire and destiny, all of it wrapped up in the past and the future. Adam wanted to enjoy the present with Icarus, at least for today. He reluctantly extricated himself from Icarus's arms and, putting a hand in his, tugged Icarus farther along the path. "And there are some other conversations we need to have first."

Surprisingly, Icarus let it go. "Where are we going?"

"My favorite place up here. Plenty of sun for you to bask in."

Neither of them spoke for several minutes, only the rustling leaves, the crunch of gravel, and the errant *caw* disturbing the silence. This part of the property had once been a chorus of animal sounds—birds, squirrels, weasels, rats, the occasional fox or deer—but they'd all fled.

"Still not used to the quiet," Icarus said, as if reading his mind. "Even after thirty years." Adam whipped around his gaze, surprised by the slip. "Trust nugget for a trust nugget," Icarus said with a shrug. An intentional slip, it seemed.

And if Adam's math was right . . . "The Rift?"

"Just before."

At the end of the path, Adam veered right, past the ends of the rows and into the grove of olive trees. He stopped short of the field ahead and drew Icarus close, offering another trust nugget, saying what was on the tip of his tongue the way he used to. "I haven't felt like me in ten years. Not until I met you."

Icarus swooned into him, forehead landing on his shoulder. "Fuck, Adam."

"That . . ." He ran a hand up Icarus's back and into his hair, using it to gently tilt his face, to draw his gaze again. "That's the real me. The one who doesn't hold back. But he's had to stay locked down, be Adam, the Devil, since . . ."

"Since the night they died."

"Everything changed." That man who wore his heart on his

sleeve had burned with his husband and wife, leaving only Adam—and the thing inside him—behind. But pieces of their past remained. "Except this place."

Untangling, he let go of Icarus's hand and stepped the final few feet through the trees and into the field of wild mustard, wanting to get there first so he could witness the expression on Icarus's face, expecting his reaction to be even better than the one at the edge of each terrace.

Icarus didn't disappoint. He cleared the line of trees, and as their shadow receded and the sun greeted his steps, Icarus's eyes grew wider, round saucers of joyous blue, matched only by the smile that stretched across his face, as he took in the field of yellow and green. This late in the season, so much of Talahalusi was brown and dry, but protected as this property was by the mountain and the trees, blanketed with roving fog each morning, wild mustard could grow in the spring and fall, the bright yellow flowers stretching as high as Icarus's knees. Icarus flattened his hands by his sides, brushing the tops of them, laughing at the bees and butterflies that scattered. Without predators, they'd flourished and kept the vineyards, fields, and flowers pollinated. Adam strolled ahead, backward, never taking his eyes off the blissfully happy vampire playing in the sun.

He eventually came down from the high, following Adam to a thinner patch toward the far edge of the field, pulling a sexy pout as he plopped onto the ground next to him. "Do you bring all your lovers here?"

"They brought me here."

TWENTY-ONE

ICARUS'S POUT DISAPPEARED. "ADAM, I—"

He reached out and skated a thumb over Icarus's lower lip, wanting the pout back, wanting more. "I've never brought anyone else here. I haven't been here, haven't been with anyone else, since—"

Cursing, Icarus rose on his knees, and for a heart-stopping moment, Adam was terrified he was going to leave. But then he threw a leg over Adam's lap, grasped his chin, and slammed their mouths together, giving Adam the lip he wanted and more, grinding down onto his cock that had been erect since that pout had first appeared. Adam grasped his hips and rolled, pressing up against him. Icarus gasped, and Adam didn't waste the opportunity, diving inside Icarus's mouth, tongues colliding and twining, parrying until Icarus tore his mouth away long enough to rip off his sweater, giving Adam access to all the skin he hadn't had time to fully enjoy the night before.

Adam leaned forward, swirling a tongue around one pert nipple, toying with it and relishing the answering rock and grind of Icarus's hips. He traveled from one cool pec to the other, administering the same torture and receiving it right back, Icarus's glide over his cock sublime. Hands climbing Icarus's back, he felt the vampire's cool skin heat with the sun and his touch. Heat further as he trailed his fingers back down and inside Icarus's jeans, palming the cheeks he'd craved all day.

Icarus angled his ass up, forcing more separation, creating a path for where he clearly wanted Adam's fingers to go. And in case he wasn't sure, the bossy courtesan told him so. "Touch me. There."

He slid his fingers down the cleft of Icarus's ass, found his rim, and circled. Tapped. And damn near came in his pants from the wanton moan that rumbled up Icarus's throat. The spike was enough to bring his mind back online—a little. "We need to talk," he mouthed against the underside of Icarus's chin.

Icarus tilted back his head, giving him more access while at the same time shoving a hand between them and palming Adam through his jeans. "We need to celebrate the fact we're still alive." He stroked, hard and rough. "And I need to feel this inside me."

Adam was torn. Not about whether to have that talk. Fuck talking. With the gorgeous man in his lap, his hand fondling Adam's cock with maddening, wonderful strokes on the edge of too hard and too slow, there was only fucking on his mind. He was torn over whether to lie back and let Icarus torture him to death or push his finger past Icarus's rim and find out if his insides were as warm as his skin was becoming under the sun. Icarus made the decision for him, thrusting back on his finger, and fuck yes, furnace-hot muscles clenched around his finger.

He groaned, and Icarus smiled against his lips. "You want in there?"

More than anything right then, with one caveat. "Yes, but I need—"

Icarus reached behind his back, grasped Adam's wrists, and pulled them around front. He let them go only long enough to rid Adam of his Henley, then with his grip firm around Adam's far more breakable bones, he laid him out, pinned to the ground. "Don't worry. I'll still be in control while I ride you."

Relief washed through him. "Yes," he groaned. "I need that."

"You keep your hands right there."

Easier said than done, especially when Icarus stood, stripped out of his jeans, and teased a view of his erect cock, straining against his black lace underwear. Adam bit his bottom lip and fought his warring urges—shove his hand down his pants and stroke his cock or shove his hand down his pants and grab his balls to stop from coming. Either case, his hand was halfway to his fly when Icarus lightly kicked his arm back in place, tutting, "Be good now. I'll take care of that, I promise."

Step one, relieving Adam of his pants and underwear, stripping him naked. Step two, straddling his lap once more and dragging his lace-covered taint across Adam's cock in a slow, tortuous glide, making Adam bite his lip and arch his back. Step three, streaking his torso with precome as Icarus knee walked the rest of the way up his body until his knees were on either side of Adam's head, cock so close Adam could feel the heat, smell his and Icarus's precome combining to stain the lace even darker. "You're going to help me ruin these pretty panties." Knees on the insides of Adam's biceps to keep him pinned, Icarus positioned his crotch directly over his face. "Just with that gorgeous mouth of yours."

There was nothing Adam wanted to taste more. He peppered either seam of the briefs with hot breaths and long, slow licks. Twirled his tongue around one ball, then the other. Nipped along the seams until he flattened his tongue and mouthed both balls at once through the lace. Everywhere but Icarus's cock. He wanted to return some of the torture. Icarus keened above him, his broad chest beading with sweat, his head thrown back and mouth hanging open. "Get those lips on my cock. Now. I want you to taste it when I come. Then I want to taste me on you."

Adam followed orders, but not without tasting every inch of Icarus's cock, licking a slow trail up the underside, swirling a tongue around the lace-covered tip, then sealing his lips around the ridge of him. He mouthed a path to his root, then kissed every inch on the way back to his crown, lashing it with his tongue before closing his lips around the tip again, dampening the lace with his spit, wetting it further as he greedily sucked.

Icarus fell forward, stretching over him and riding his face with abandon that Adam relished. He lost himself in the scratch of rough lace, Icarus's musky scent and taste, the aching pressure building in his own balls, the breeze that wafted across his bare, heated flesh, and the pleasure of being so completely used.

Icarus tunneled a hand in his hair and forced his gaze up to meet his. "I'm going to come, but you're not. Do you understand me?"

Adam groaned, not altogether certain he could oblige.

Icarus's fingers curled in his hair. "I'll pull off. Won't give you that come you want so badly. Not if it means I can't have what I want most in the world right now. Your cock in my ass. Do you understand?"

He swirled his tongue around Icarus's crown again, and two thrusts later, Icarus came with a shout, come leaking through the lace and mesh. If Adam was greedy before, he was ravenous now, swallowing and licking up all he could, whining in protest when Icarus lifted off his face.

He slid back down him, smearing come across his chin, his chest, and then once he was straddled across Adam's hips, he smirked, fang teasing the upturned corner of his mouth. "I had to save some for myself." He reached a hand in his briefs, gathered the moisture there, and reached behind himself.

Arms freed, Adam threw one over his eyes, the sight, the pressure in his balls too much. Icarus's laugh was the definition of uninhibited and sexy, fitting here in this place where Adam last remembered being the same. The sound of fabric ripping drew Adam's gaze back to Icarus, who tossed the tattered lace aside, grasped Adam's cock with his slick hand, and guided it inside him. Adam scrabbled for mustard weeds, anything to grab hold of, to keep from reaching for Icarus so he could follow orders.

"Get your hands on me," Icarus said.

Thank fuck. Adam levered up, arms twining around the beast in his arms, holding him tight. He thrust up as their lips met, Adam giving Icarus the moan-inducing taste he wanted while demanding Adam keep up with the frantic roll of his hips, working his cock, building him fast and furious.

"I'm gonna count us down, and you're gonna come on one."

Adam nodded.

"Five."

He grasped one of Icarus's ass cheeks.

"Four."

Clutched his shoulder.

"Three."

Licked a stripe up his neck.

"Two."

Found his lips again.

"One."

Held Icarus close, thrust up inside all that tight, hot heat, and exploded.

TWENTY-TWO

ADAM COULDN'T SAY EXACTLY how long he'd been dozing when the sun-warmed body nestled against his side tensed, Icarus instantly on alert. A second later, growling echoed from the direction of the tree line. The second after that, Icarus was crouched above him, claws digging into the ground on either side of his head, lips pulled back in a snarl around fully extended fangs.

The growls grew louder—and more familiar. Adam tilted back his head to see what Icarus had locked onto. A large honey-blond coyote prowled the edge of the field, hackles up, canines bared. No immediate danger, then, assuming two apex predators posturing didn't kill them all.

Adam reached up and patted the side of Icarus's face. "That's my second, Jenn. You know her."

The coyote snapped and gnashed its teeth. Icarus seethed through his.

"Jenn!" Adam shouted as he rolled onto his side under Icarus. "That's enough."

Abigail, in human form, strolled out from among the trees and ran her fingers through Jennifer's scruff. "Back off, baby." A little more coaxing—a scratch behind the ears, a hand flattened between her shoulder blades—and Jenn finally lowered her hackles. Abigail turned her dark eyes back to them. "You need to get to the mansion," she said, expression grim and foreboding. Granted, Yerba Buena earlier had all gone to shit, but he'd figured Abigail being back with her lover would at least take the edge off, might blunt the reality of the trouble they were in. Apparently not.

He tapped at Icarus's hip, and the vampire must have seen enough to believe the threat had passed. He moved from atop Adam, standing, then offering him a hand up. "What's happened?" Adam asked Abigail as he and Icarus dressed, the latter commando in his jeans. Not thinking about that. Not if he wanted to get his own jeans zipped. Abigail approached, and the waft of smoke that tickled Adam's nose pushed all other thoughts away. "Where's the fire?"

"Your house." Abigail reached into her back pocket, and by the size and shape of the item she withdrew, Adam knew what it was even before she unfolded the photo and held it out to him. "They torched the place. We were able to rescue some weapons from the armory, but upstairs . . . This was all that was left."

Icarus approached behind him, his hand appearing in Adam's periphery, an arm on its way to wrapping around Adam's waist, but Adam put out his own, holding Icarus off. The man in the picture, smiling on his wedding day, his husband and wife kissing his cheeks, had no business in this world, no matter how close to resurfacing he'd been with Icarus.

That man was gone, Adam was here, and the Devil was so close to getting what he'd been after the past ten years. And once vengeance was had, that man in the photo could join his husband and wife like he should have done that day ten years ago. That was the future and fate that awaited him, no matter how much he enjoyed the present escape with Icarus. "Let's get back to the house."

As if sensing Adam's mental shift, Icarus kept his physical distance the entire walk back, but he remained emotionally close, timing his steps to Adam's heartbeats, making his claim clear to Abigail and Jenn. Adam didn't tell him to do otherwise, didn't want to cut that tether completely, and besides, he was certain Abigail and Jenn could smell the come on both of them.

So could the other coyote whose head whipped their direction the second Adam and Icarus stepped through the door. Even in human form, Robin's growl shook the windows.

"Let it go," Adam said as he dropped onto the couch across from him.

"Dog," Icarus sniped from the armrest he claimed beside Adam.

"Bloodsucker," Robin sniped right back.

Cormac, in the chair at the end of the couches, was his usual droll self. "Now that introductions are out of the way."

Jenn reappeared from the bathroom in human form, dressed in jeans and a tee. "Why is he here?" She jutted her chin in Icarus's direction as she sank into the couch next to her cousin. "If you haven't noticed, shit goes sideways whenever he's involved."

"Shit is going sideways, with or without him," Adam

replied. "At least with him, I'm still alive. Without him, I'd be dead."

"Vincent's unhappy you're not." Robin—a slight drawl in his voice, lingering from whatever job he'd returned from—tossed his phone onto the table between them, screen open on an encrypted app. "Raised the bounty to ten million."

"Fuck." Icarus stretched an arm behind Adam across the top of the couch cushions. "This is more than a thorn in his side. Why does he want you dead?"

Adam flicked his gaze to his concerned one. "Because I want him dead."

"That can't be the entire story."

"It's not." Cormac dropped a file onto the table beside Robin's phone. "Only file I have that's thicker than yours," he said to Icarus. "Vincent Cirillo has become a billionaire by enslaving other people's magic."

"What does that mean?" Icarus asked.

"That kid you saw me and Abigail rescue the other night?" Adam waited for Icarus's nod, then continued. "He'd been kidnapped by Vincent's crew and nearly drained dry."

"Okay, but that's not enslaving. That's flat-out stealing."

"He was a runaway," Abigail said. "No one noticed him missing. Since I'd been inside, I knew he was stashed there and about to flame out."

Icarus opened his mouth, no doubt to ask what that meant too, which Adam was not getting into today. He picked up where Abigail left off before Icarus could. "In other cases, Vincent offers 'private security' to paranormals, and before they know it, they're doing his bidding. He takes their money, then uses their power to make more money."

"Say someone wants a soul stolen," Cormac explained,

"and would pay handsomely for it. Vincent finds a soul eater or a psychopomp—like my kind—in need of protection, strikes a deal with them, then uses all that magic he's stolen from nobodies to turn his client into his tool, to convince them to steal that soul for Vincent, who turns around and sells it to the highest bidder."

"And the client can't tell anyone because now they're implicated too." Icarus lowered his chin, features pinched in sympathy. "Just like a fucking dealer."

"Only he's dealing in magic," Adam said.

Icarus jerked his head up, eyes wide. "Is that how he has a warlock in his thrall?"

Twin growls emanated from Robin and Jenn.

"Easy," Adam said, appreciating the response, not appreciating the person it was directed at. Once Abigail moved into position on the armrest next to Jenn, positioned to pounce into referee mode as was often her role, Adam turned his attention back to Icarus, explaining, "Atlas has his own agenda."

"To be even more powerful than his master," Robin said.

"That's not what it looked like to me," Icarus said.

"He's a warlock," Adam said. "You can't believe anything you see." He expected Icarus to argue, but he backed off instead, contemplative and quiet.

Robin gave them more to think about. "He's still not told Vincent what *you* are, assuming he's figured it out. If he had, Vincent would be trying to take you, not kill you."

"I still think we should take this to law enforcement," Cormac said, then when they all looked his way with raised brows, added, "Officially. With Vincent's operations escalating, there's more incentive to do something."

"There wasn't incentive enough ten years ago?" Robin

barked. "He had two cops and two feds on his ass, and he still got away with murder."

Icarus rocketed back to attention beside Adam. "Wait! He's been doing this for ten years?" Then split a glance between him and Cormac. "And you haven't taken it to law enforcement yet officially?"

"We can't trust them," Adam said. "He's got moles all in law enforcement."

"Couldn't trust them then, can't now," Robin said, then with a flick of his hand in Cormac's direction, added, "Present company excluded."

"What if I had a contact?" Icarus said, the last thing Adam expected. "Someone you could trust."

Cormac scooted to the end of the chair. "How can you be sure?"

Icarus shrugged the single shoulder bared by his knit top. "He's thirsty. And I have pics of his dick."

Abigail's hand on Jenn's shoulder was the only thing that kept the coyote from leaping across the table. "Someone get him out of here before I rip his fucking throat out."

Icarus grinned, a fang snagging his lip. "I'd like to see you try."

"We don't have time for this," Cormac interrupted. "Not with a ten-million-dollar bounty on Adam's head."

A ten-million-dollar bounty and two leads. "What if we work both?" Adam said. "We continue to work our angle, Icarus works his. So long as one of them lands Vincent in jail, it'll be a success."

"Do you think jail is going to stop him?" Icarus said, equal parts doubtful and curious.

"No," Adam admitted. "But I think jail is going to put him in a single place for at least a few hours where we can get to him."

Across from them, Robin purred around a grin that was just this side of feral.

TWENTY-THREE

"YES, I KNOW, YOU WERE RIGHT." Icarus sighed, heavy and dramatic. "Do we have to go through this every time?"

Adam leaned against the wall outside the sunny second-floor bedroom Icarus had disappeared into and barely stifled his laugh.

Whoever was on the other end of the line was giving Icarus hell. And he loved it, judging by the affection in his voice. "Thank you for answering the call this time. You saved our lives."

Adam inched closer to the door, recalling what Cormac had described. Had there been someone else on the scene they hadn't seen? Adam didn't think so, but he hadn't been with them. Maybe this person was there? Or helped in another way?

"I'm fine, I swear, safe and sound," Icarus said, then after a pause, added, "Talahalusi." Another pause, then a chuckle. "Yes, I know it's fucking sunny up here."

Adam bit his lip. Icarus wasn't complaining, good-natured

or otherwise, about the sun earlier this afternoon when he'd been naked and riding Adam's cock. He'd basked in the warm rays, same as Adam, enjoying a respite from the characters they had to play.

Which Icarus was shifting back into, same as him. "Do you want to come up here? I think you'd be safe. They're on our side." Protective and assessing. "And if they try to hurt you, I can take them."

So someone more important than what Adam's team was planning. The family Icarus wouldn't talk about? Another vampire, another paranormal, or someone human? Adam would bet the last, given the protective streak, but then how had that person saved their lives? Certainly not the Daylight; that had come from Paris. It must have something to do with what Cormac had seen, but with Icarus's protective streak, how would Adam ever get that information?

"Fine," Icarus said, his tone indicating grudging assent. "But I want check-ins every six, and if you sense anything off, you call me. I'll get down there as fast as I can." Down there as in back to Yerba Buena or somewhere else? Portola? His bags had been packed last night when Adam had arrived at his apartment. Was this who Icarus planned to flee to? Or with?

"Love you too. Keep me posted."

A spike of jealousy kicked Adam in the gut, unwarranted. Like Cormac had said, he'd known Icarus less than a week. He had no claim over the vampire, even if Icarus was broadcasting a claim over him. For protection, because that was his role. But who else did he have to protect? What if by *family*, Icarus meant someone more than a sibling? A partner in Portola? Someone more important than him . . .

"You can come in now," Icarus said from inside the room,

accompanied by the creak of bedsprings. "I can hear your heartbeat."

Adam pushed off the wall and into the bedroom, finding Icarus sprawled on the bed in the sun. He was perfectly still, not bothering to hide what he was anymore. "I thought you didn't keep in touch with your family," Adam said as he moved to sit on the windowsill.

Icarus shifted, staying in the sun. "I never said that."

"Whoever it was, they were giving you hell."

Eyes closed, he smiled, soft and fond, affection with fangs. "She always gives me hell."

"Sister?" Adam guessed, going for the option that would hurt the least and was rewarded with a nod. He crossed his arms to hide the relieved rise and fall of his chest. "Older?"

"Depends how you look at it."

"She's human, then?"

"Not exactly." He eked open one eye, pinning Adam with it. "She's something *else*, like you."

"Like me?"

"Well, I don't know what you are yet, but you're not completely human." He opened the other eye and levered up on his elbows. "There's magic in you, same as with her."

Which meant she was a target, same as him. Icarus's protective streak made even more sense now. "If she needs protection, she can come here."

"I wish she would, but she does things on her own terms." He clenched his fists. "No one else's." Forced his hands open again. He was more of a wreck about her than he was letting on.

"You care about her?"

"I promised to protect her." He lifted all the way up,

crossing his legs on the bed and dropping his hands in his lap, his gaze downcast, his voice as small as Adam had ever heard it. "She's all I have left." Commiserating, Adam pushed off the window and sat on the bed next to him, hand on his knee. Icarus covered it with his and squeezed. "I'm sorry they burned down your house. It was a lovely home."

Home. It had been. A place of so many firsts, of so many hopes and dreams, of so much love. He looked out the window, looked back in time, then shut his eyes and the door on his memories. It was fitting in a way that it was gone now. It was one less thing tying him here.

Icarus removed his hand. "You know, at first, I thought Adam was the real you, and this was the Devil, but they're the same, aren't they?"

Adam returned his gaze to him and nodded. It wasn't exactly how he saw it, but close enough. Adam was both the face the Devil needed and the Devil's keeper.

"I thought so." Disappointment flashed across Icarus's face, but fast on its heels was determination. "All right, what does Adam, aka the Devil, need Icarus to do?"

"Stop picking fights with Robin."

Icarus laughed out loud. "Have you met your friend?"

Adam chuckled. "Fair, but he's set in his ways at this point. He's an asshole, but a loyal one."

"What does he do exactly?"

"He's an assassin."

Icarus startled to full attention. "How's that work with a cop and ex-cop as friends?"

Adam shrugged. "Worked even less with a twin sister and brother-in-law who were feds."

Icarus covered his gaping mouth with a hand. "Deborah

was his sister?" Adam nodded, and Icarus squeezed his knee again. "Deborah and David were the feds on Vincent's trail?"

"He's responsible for their deaths." They'd had a perfect night at Club Sutro, a perfect anniversary celebration, and the next day, his spouses were dead by Vincent's hand. "They were building a case against him. Were close to shutting him down on a federal level. They had juice beyond YB."

"Vincent couldn't have that."

Adam nodded. "The federal case died with them, and the more YB was cut off by the ongoing war, the more Vincent's power grew. He thinks he's invincible. Might be trying to make himself magically so, depending on what he's planning for later this month. Either way, Robin and I can't let him get away with it."

Icarus narrowed his eyes, and his forehead creased, creating the putting-it-together expression Adam caught on his face from time to time. "So you, Robin, and Cormac have been carrying on Deb and David's work? Building a case and disrupting his organization?"

"And rescuing those who need it," Adam said. "Destroying his stores of magic, cutting off his source of funds, interfering with his business."

"So those warehouse fires and gunfights I hear rumblings about?"

Adam pointed at himself. "Not all the time, but some of the bigger ones. Disruption to the point of destruction."

"Because that's what he's done to you." Icarus unfolded his legs, stood, and began to pace the room, hands on his hips below his sweater. "Are you stealing from him too? Is that what pays for the whiskey and meals at Benton's?"

"No. Inheritance, my pension, and the Devil pay for those things."

Icarus paused in his circuit, hip and brow cocked.

"The Devil solves problems for people," Adam clarified.

"Problems that typically involve Vincent Cirillo?"

Adam shrugged.

He rolled his eyes and resumed his pacing. "And the casework?"

"Makes Mac feel better. We've been building it for an opportunity like the one you brought us. We can use it to get Vincent where we need him."

"In jail."

"Like I said, makes him an easier target."

"For the assassin. Makes sense." He stopped in front of Adam, head tilted. "But you had him right in front of you earlier today."

"I tried to make a move without my team." Sometimes, the man Adam used to be whispered in the Devil's ear, and the thing inside him would slip its leash. Would do something impulsive, like the man Adam used to be.

"You were protecting me."

"You made *me* feel invincible. And human again." He reached out and lightly grasped one of Icarus's hands. "I don't know how to turn it off, Icarus." None of it—the lover, the cop, the gatekeeper, the fire. "It's who I am."

"Who you are . . ." Icarus threaded their fingers together and stepped closer. "Why did Vincent tell me your name was Adam Devlin if he knows who you were before?" He glanced over his shoulder toward the door. "Why do they all call you Adam?"

"Why do you call yourself Icarus? Why do you only refer to your sister as *she*?"

He pressed his lips shut.

"That's what I thought." Adam released his hand and pushed to his feet. "We all have our secrets, our reasons for keeping them and for inhabiting the skin and personas we're in."

"Okay, so back to my original question . . ." He laid a hand on Adam's forearm. Still warm, still kind, still more than Adam deserved. "What does Adam need Icarus to do?" He wrinkled his nose. "Besides play nice with the stinky, grumpy dog."

Adam took his hand in his again, not immune to the warmth and comfort, but stopping himself short of everything the old him wanted to drown in. "Get us the details on your police contact. Let us check them out. If we don't spot any immediate red flags, you can proceed."

"I've already done the excavation on him. It's solid."

"Atlas managed to fool you."

"Atlas is a warlock with skills. This is an overworked cop, married with three kids, who jerks off to me fucking myself on a dildo." He spread his arms far apart, taking Adam's arm with him. "Big difference."

Adam chuckled. "Okay, then, set it up."

"What are you going to do?"

"Shore up defenses, work with my team, and consider different angles." He rested his other hand on the strip of skin exposed between the edge of Icarus's sweater and jeans. "Get you a change of clothes."

"That would be appreciated. Little hot up here in knits, even for me. I'm surprised you're not sweating."

He'd learned to live with the heat, here and inside him, long ago. He twined his arm around Icarus, hand settling at his lower back. "We have a contact checking on your place. If it's still standing, I'll have them grab your go bag and computer. I assume you need that for work?"

Icarus nodded. "I'll get you the safe code for the laptop. Would also be nice to get my crochet stuff and my robe." He snuggled closer. "For when it gets cold here at night."

"We'll get you the crochet stuff." Adam dipped his hand below Icarus's waistband, palming his ass and imagining how good Icarus would look in that robe and nothing else. "The robe was already on my list."

Still, it wasn't the time to entertain those fantasies. He had a long list of to-do items, and Icarus wasn't on it. But when he tried to pull away, Icarus slung one arm over his shoulder and grasped his shirt with his other hand, holding him close. "Whenever you need to take a break from Adam and the Devil"—he leaned in and kissed the corner of his mouth—"I'm here."

TWENTY-FOUR

IT WAS near nightfall when Robin's familiar tread echoed down the stairs. Icarus, who'd been relegated to the cellar when his fingers had started to smoke, must have also recognized their approaching visitor. Shoulders tense, he turned from the overstock metal tanks he was pretending to be interested in and let his arms hang loose at his sides, at the ready, fingers spread as if preparing to flex his claws.

"Easy," Adam coaxed. "If he wasn't here in peace, you wouldn't hear him coming."

"I'd hear his heartbeat."

"Maybe." Adam tilted his head. "Maybe not."

Icarus's brows raced north. "Oh, really? How's that?"

"My secret to tell," Robin said as he cleared the bottom step. "Not his." He met them beside the retired tasting table in the middle of the cellar great room and dropped Icarus's jam-packed go bag at their feet. "Your apartment building was still standing. Too big to burn down."

Whereas a fire at Adam's house in the Terrace looked like just another arson in a dying neighborhood. A blaze caused by a squatter or a property owner trying to collect insurance. Barely a blip on the radar. It was what Adam wanted—as erased as he could make it—but memories were harder to scrub clean, the mental door on them impossible to keep shut.

He turned away, chest burning and eyes stinging.

Icarus skirted a hand across his back, a gentle sweep of comfort, enough to steady him on the edge of the abyss, to anchor him while he caught his breath. Icarus, meanwhile, interrogated the messenger. "What about the apartment itself?" he asked Robin. "Atlas broke in before."

"He'd been there, but it didn't look or smell like he stayed long."

"Computer?"

"In the bag."

"Crochet hooks?"

"Plus yarn."

Icarus smiled. "Robe too?"

Robin shook his head. "Wasn't there."

The smile died. "Stinky motherfucking warlock."

"First thing you've said I agree with."

"I get to hit him before you kill him."

"Second thing."

The shared spite forced a stuttered laugh out of Adam. An easier one followed when he caught Icarus's smirk. "Not going for a third?"

The vampire winked and hefted his bag off the floor. "I know better than to press my luck."

That absurdity deserved a full-bellied laugh. "Since when?"

"Since now," Icarus threw over his shoulder as he turned toward the vacant bunk room.

He disappeared into the shadows, and Adam, still chuckling, swung his attention back to the table. Robin eyed him with an expression that was half surprise and half . . . pity? The assassin tossed a dime-sized metal sliver—an embedded lens—onto the table. "Also found that at his place."

"A bug? Someone's been spying on him?"

"Or he's been spying on you."

Adam picked up the sophisticated piece of tech and examined it more closely, considering its other uses. "Or on his clients."

"None of the above," Icarus snapped as he zipped back into the room. He'd left on his jeans but swapped the knit sweater for a strappy tank top that left zero to the imagination, his cut biceps and ripped upper body on full display. For his benefit or Robin's, Adam couldn't say, and he didn't have time to contemplate it further. Icarus snatched the bug from his hand. "That's five grand worth of tech you ruined," he seethed at Robin.

"Who's tech?" Robin asked. "Yours?"

"Hers."

"Hers?"

"My sister's, and it wasn't active." His gaze flicked the direction of the stairs—detecting Cormac's approach, as did Adam—then back to them. "We have a signal. If I gave it, she'd know to turn it on and look around."

Robin planted his hands on the table. "There's only a handful of people with access to that kind of gear."

Icarus pocketed the tech. "My sister is one of them."

"According to your file," Cormac said as he entered the room, "your sister died in the Rift."

"Who do you think taught me how to excavate?"

"That's not an ans—"

"Enough," Adam said, cutting the volley off before it went any further, especially with Cormac-of-all-angles in the debate now. "This is all beside the point." They needed to focus on their common mission—Vincent Cirillo. Adam was done with the asshole who'd destroyed his life, and for the first time in a decade, he had the pieces to return the favor. To destroy Vincent and finish this, for good. "How do we bring this to a close? Because Vincent's clearly ready, and so am I." He gestured at the table, inviting the combatants to sit and strategize. "Help me figure this out."

The stare-off continued another few seconds before Icarus slid into the nearest chair. "I have a call with my client later tonight."

"Why not now?" Robin claimed the seat across from him. "We brought you your shit."

Icarus didn't rise to the bait, his fangs and claws tucked away, his tone carefully indifferent. "While you might prefer brute force, I usually get what I want through more persuasive means." He crossed his legs and shifted his attention to Adam. "What is it we want?"

"A meet." Adam sank into the chair beside him. "We'll try it your way first and hold brute force in our back pocket if needed."

"We'll need to meet on neutral ground," Cormac said as he took a seat beside Robin. "Extracurriculars aside, Icarus's client is still a cop. His defenses will be up. We don't want to be outgunned."

"Portola," Robin suggested.

Icarus fisted a hand beneath the table. Adam covered it with his and offered an alternative. "The Lost Valley."

Robin lurched forward and braced his forearms on the table. "You can't go back into the city."

"It's my fucking home." He tried to keep his voice even, but the unrelenting frustration darkened the already jagged edges of his words. "I'm not going to let Vincent drive me out of it."

Cormac slumped and scrubbed his hands over his face. "Fucking death wish."

Beneath the table, Icarus tangled their fingers. "So we get this meet," he said. "We convince my client to arrest Vincent and bring him in. Then what?"

Cormac dropped his arms. "Yerba Buena Building is a fortress. After the Rift, they rebuilt it to be impenetrable. Not to mention half the cops and guards inside are on Vincent's payroll."

"So we use the in we have," Adam said. "Icarus's client gets us plans and clears us a path."

"How do we separate Vincent from the warlock?"

"We give Atlas what he wants. Me."

Icarus's hand nearly crushed his, and across the table, Robin growled his disagreement. "You can't be serious."

"I don't want this thing inside me. Let him take it and then you kill him too."

"You'll die," Cormac said. "That *thing* is what's keeping you alive."

"They died to give you that *thing*," Robin rumbled.

"I didn't ask for this. I would have rather died with them, but now, all I've got left of my marriage, of my life, is a charred photo and the Devil." He shoved back from the table. Present respite over; it was time to meet fate and the future head-on. "I want it to be over, all of it."

TWENTY-FIVE

IT TOOK Adam thirty minutes and several laps around the reflecting pool to rein himself in. It took another ninety with Cormac, Robin, and the rest of his team on the main level to sort logistics and evaluate potential meet locations. By the time he returned to the cellar, Adam found the bunk room completely transformed.

With most of the winery's business in the main facility down the mountain, the villa's cellar was minimally used as storage for extra equipment and living and sleeping quarters for seasonal workers during harvest, which had ended a month ago this year. But you wouldn't know it for the lived-in coziness Icarus had created in two short hours.

The line of single beds had been pushed together in the center of the room, Cormac's mother's hand-knitted quilts thrown across them in a splash of color. More soft shades painted the walls, cast by the silk and sheer tops Icarus had draped over the room's lamps. Across from the beds, the storage trunks that normally sat at the end of each bed had been stacked and arranged so that Icarus's laptop and webcam on top were aimed directly at the now oversized bed. Everything was perfectly arranged, except for the single bed shoved in the corner nearest the door, Icarus's go bag open and spilling what was left of its contents the length of it.

Adam leaned a shoulder against the door. "Do you have everything you need?"

"Not everything," a silk-robed Icarus said. He dug through the bag once more and produced a bottle of lube. "But enough." His voice was a shade brighter than earlier but still careful, and as Icarus placed the tube of lube on the bedside table and surveyed the room's final setup, he likewise carefully avoided Adam's gaze.

Mentally replaying his earlier outburst, Adam could see how his harsh words might have bruised Icarus. They'd revealed a darkness, an inevitability, that Icarus maybe hadn't fully appreciated—or accepted. He stepped into the room, and as Icarus passed by on his way back to the spare bed, Adam lightly clasped his elbow. "Icarus, please."

He wrenched his elbow free and flicked a dismissive hand in the air. "I can't be in this headspace with you when I need to be Icarus for someone else."

The computer pinged, a guest waiting.

"I want to stay while you do this." It was a wildly inappropriate suggestion that got Adam the reaction he craved.

Stormy blues clashed with his, and Icarus gave a sharp shake of his head. "No way."

"He might say something I need to hear." A plausible enough excuse.

Icarus didn't buy it, his gaze shrewd, but he didn't outright reject it either. "Not without his consent."

"Has he been on a multifeed before?"

"Yes."

"Then it shouldn't be a problem."

Icarus pressed his lips together, and Adam bit his tongue to keep from saying more, to stifle the plea that wanted to escape. He'd become invested in the idea, tangentially for the mission, primarily for the chance to watch Icarus work.

To escape and wind down after hours of planning and debate.

Icarus heaved a sigh. "Fine. You're going to blackmail him with this in the end, anyway. But only if he consents."

Adam nodded. "Fair."

"Where's the meet?"

Adam gave him the address, and when the computer pinged again, he followed Icarus's order to take up residence on the spare bed. He shoved himself into the corner, upright, out of view of the laptop screen and camera but with an unobstructed view.

Icarus clicked the mouse, then sat on the edge of the bed, his legs crossed. "Nate, it's good to see you."

"I'm glad you pinged." There was a slight wobble in his voice, barely contained excitement tangled with I-shouldn't-be-doing-this nerves. "I hadn't heard back from you this week, so I didn't know . . ."

"I've had company in town." His gaze flicked Adam's direction, then back to the screen. "Been more exciting than I anticipated."

Adam stifled a laugh. *Exciting* was one way to put it.

Icarus smirked.

"Company?" Nate said. "Are they still there?" The cop wasn't a fool. He'd picked up on the off-camera byplay.

Icarus must have picked up on something he saw onscreen.

"You dirty minx! Do you want an audience? Because yes, he's still here."

"I like knowing you have one." Nate cleared his throat, tempering the excitement he'd let slip vocally too. "But I don't want to see or hear anyone but you."

"Don't you worry. My friend's going to sit in the corner and be a good boy and just watch." Icarus's eyes pinned him to the spot. "No words and no touching. And he won't come. That's just for you and me, Nate."

Nate half hummed, half gasped his approval, the idea alone clearly turning him on. For his part, Adam nodded. He toed off his shoes and propped his feet on the bed, knees bent and legs spread. He snagged Icarus's crochet hooks, threaded them through his fingers as an extra measure of restraint, then rested his wrists on his bent knees, hands dangling where Icarus could see them and his cock already stiffening behind his zipper.

Icarus smirked and shifted his attention back to the screen. "Are you going to be a good boy too?" He crawled to the center of the bed and untied his robe.

Adam nearly swallowed his tongue.

Turquoise lace hugged Icarus's torso, a form-fitting camisole that dripped from thin silk straps, dipped low in front, and ended at the tops of his thighs. It was an inch or two shorter in the middle, balls peeking out below, owing to the stretch caused by the bulge of his erect cock that was tucked up against his pelvis.

Nate wasn't nearly so quiet, cursing and groaning.

He only got louder as Icarus ditched the robe completely. Unrestrained, Icarus ran his hands through his hair, down his long neck, over the gap in the lace, then under its edges, playing with his nipples, dipping into every ridge of his abs, tracing his V-cut to his groin, spreading his legs wider and subtly thrusting forward. Touching everywhere but his dick that swelled. All while directing Nate—how to tease himself, when to take out his cock, how to lather it up, how to stroke it.

It drove Adam crazy. His dick ached as he imagined his lips tracing a path down Icarus's neck, his hands tangled in lace, his fingers slipping inside to feel the cool heat of Icarus's skin, slipping behind to palm the ass the cami didn't cover all of.

Intentionally.

As Icarus pulled a dildo from under a pillow, his earlier words came back to Adam. *An overworked cop . . .who jerks off to me fucking myself on a dildo.* He suctioned the base of the dildo to one of the wooden headboards, grabbed the bottle of lube, and coated it. Then he hiked the cami up, exposing a plug in matching turquoise.

He'd prepared himself. He eased it out with a mewl that nearly undid Adam. But then he went down on all fours, rammed back on the dildo, and let out a relieved, shuddery sigh, and Adam was fucking gone. He closed his eyes and tilted back his head, white-knuckling the crochet hooks as his hips rocked up, aching for friction, hungry for the man he couldn't touch less than ten feet away.

"Look at me."

He wasn't sure if Icarus's sharp command was for him or Nate, but regardless, Adam whipped up his head, righting his gaze just in time to see Icarus reach down and free his cock from the lace. Stroked once, twice, then bowed like a cat, the hand in the bed fisting the sheets, Icarus coming with a deep groan that was echoed onscreen.

Adam wanted to groan too, wanted his dick in Icarus's ass instead of that dildo, wanted to be under him with his mouth around Icarus's cock, drinking up every drop of his come, wanted Icarus to flip him over and come inside him again.

Adam bit his cheek so hard he tasted blood.

Icarus's head jerked up, nostrils flared and eyes wide, his body practically vibrating. He was every inch the predator.

Adam's heart raced, but he wasn't afraid. He wanted . . . The thing inside him wanted . . . more.

Icarus blinked, and the predator was gone.

Adam closed his eyes, mind swirling, body revolting, heart on a roller coaster he didn't want to get off of.

"Wasn't that good, Nate?" Icarus said, focused again on his client. "Maybe you'd like to do this in person?"

Nate's "I can't" was wholly unconvincing, even to Adam's half-lucid brain.

"You don't have to touch," Icarus cajoled. "You can be like my friend over there watching me fuck myself, smelling the come as it drips from my dick for you, hearing every slide of the dildo into my hole."

"We've never . . ." Nate groaned, and if Adam had to bet, Nate was getting hard again just thinking about it.

"I might not be in town much longer, Nate. Last chance."

"When?" Nate panted. "Where?"

"Tomorrow night." He rattled off the address, confirmed once more, exchanged payment details, and then Icarus signed off.

The bed springs squeaked, and Adam righted his head. Icarus climbed off the show bed, left the camisole in its hiked-up state, his dripping cock and ass bare, and stalked in his direction. The blank face was gone, but the predator remained tucked away too. Adam didn't taste blood any longer, and Icarus apparently didn't smell any either.

"That turned you on," Icarus said once he reached the side of the single bed.

Adam flicked his gaze down to where his cock was at war with his fly. "Obviously."

"You weren't jealous."

"Watching you do what you do best?" He shook his head. "Not at all. Wanted to be that dildo, or between your legs sucking your cock, or getting plowed by you. But jealous? No, baby. That's your job, and you are fucking magnificent at it."

Icarus smirked, gaze drifting to Adam's erection. "Do you need me to do something about that?"

"If you want to," Adam replied, and Icarus's gaze shot back up. "I'm not your job. Only if you want to," he repeated. He didn't want an act. If he was going to be real in these moments when he put Adam and the Devil aside, when Icarus tempted him into hitting pause on the future he usually raced toward, he needed to know Icarus was being real in these moments too.

"I want to," Icarus said as he gently removed the hooks from Adam's grip. He tossed them aside, then gracefully lowered to his knees, spreading them to make the cami ride even higher. "Put your hands in my hair and come when I do." He didn't wait for a reply, Adam's "Again?" dying on the tip of his tongue. In a single blink, Adam was yanked to the end of the bed, his jeans and boxers torn down, and his legs thrown over Icarus's shoulders, his dick inside Icarus's hot mouth.

His hands shot to Icarus's head, tangling in the magenta strands, holding on for dear life as Icarus took him apart. Long licks, teasing flicks, suction that had him idly wondering if what was left of his soul was being sucked right out of him. Stolen by the predator giving him the only moments of intimacy he'd had in a decade. As his world splintered, his orgasm rushing up to meet the one Icarus groaned out around his cock, he thought it a fair deal—peace in exchange for the soul he'd already lost, claimed by the fiery beast inside him that spread its wings and flew.

TWENTY-SIX

"YOU KNOW," Robin said from the passenger seat beside Adam, "he could be in there cutting his own deal with the cop."

Adam drummed his fingers on the Camaro's wheel and kept his gaze focused on the strip of retail units a short way up and across the street. To any brave—foolish—passerby on the street this late, it would look like all the units were either empty or closed, including the one on the end, a tasting room for a distillery that had gone bankrupt. Repo was scheduled for later in the week, the job assigned to one of Robin's contacts who'd been happy to lend them the keys for some extra cash. He and Robin were parked at the curb a half block away, Jenn and Abigail were prowling the nearby alleys and rooftops, and Cormac was perched on the peeling wood sign that hung by the unit's front door. It was as safe and covered as Adam could make Icarus without alerting anyone, including their target. "He could be, but I don't think he is."

Icarus had insisted on meeting Nate alone to start. He liked him well enough, wanted to do something nice for him before they blackmailed him. As he'd rightly pointed out, said black-mail would be more effective if Nate was good and compromised before they sprung their trap. But how long would that take? When would the tasting room's outside lights flicker on, Icarus's signal that he was ready for them behind the heavy curtains that blocked the distillery's windows? How long would Cormac have to play lookout from his perch?

Truthfully, Adam was surprised they'd made it to the waiting portion of events at all. Nate was an overworked cop, but not a bad one. He'd stuttered to a stop short of the unit's steps, balking at the seemingly abandoned spot, but then Icarus had appeared in the doorway, backlit by soft candlelight and decked out in heels, nylons, and a sinfully short, sinfully tight, little black dress. Nate had caved on the spot. So would anyone with a fucking pulse.

"I'm sorry about what I said yesterday."

Robin's uncharacteristic apology drew Adam out of his thoughts. "Which part?"

"I know you never wanted to be like us."

"I'm not like you."

Robin rolled his eyes. "Your body temp isn't ninety-eight point six anymore." He propped an elbow on the open window and rested his chin in his hand, golden eyes anywhere but on Adam. "It's just . . ."

"Just what?"

"If you die, if what Deb and David did to keep you alive is for naught, then it makes what I didn't do even worse."

"Robin, you were halfway around the world—"

His gaze shot back to Adam, hard and angry, the emotions directed one hundred percent at himself. "She called the pack, and I didn't answer."

Adam didn't make an excuse for the truth. That same truth had taken Adam a year to come to terms with before he spoke to Robin again. It had taken Jenn longer.

"I can't imagine what it must feel like," Robin said. "To be torn from your soulmates."

Like someone with claws fiercer than Icarus's had dug into his chest, ripped out his heart, and left a raging inferno in the hollow space. The Devil moniker wasn't only about the trouble he caused Vincent. He rubbed a hand over his chest. "Imagine if someone tore the coyote out of you. The heart of you gone. That was what it felt like. What it still feels like."

Robin gulped, the jagged swallow loud in the quiet car. "I'd want to die too." His gaze drifted back outside, and silence settled in the car, heavy and full of regret. "Tell her I'm sorry."

"She knows."

"Yes, but she'll believe it from you." Another truth, but this one made Adam chuckle. Robin smiled, and the melancholy that had filled the car lightened a measure. "How does he make your soul feel?"

Adam didn't have to ask who Robin was referring to. "I don't have one left to feel anything."

Kraa.

Robin laughed. "Even Mac knows you're lying."

The light outside the tasting room flicked on.

"Or," Adam said, "Mac heard Icarus on the move."

He grabbed the bulging folder off the dash, shoved out of the car, and hustled to the door Icarus had left unlocked, Robin close on his heels. Adam pushed aside the heavy velvet entry curtain just as Nate lurched to his feet from a nearby chaise, blinding Adam with his pale white ass.

"You didn't come," the cop said, voice plaintive. His attention was locked on Icarus, who was pulling down his dress and slipping back into his heels—until Robin forced the curtain the rest of the way back, rings clattering on the rod, a blast of cool night air gusting in around them. Nate spun in their direction. "Fuck! Who are you? What's going on?"

"This is my company," Icarus said. "From yesterday."

"But that was—"

Robin growled. "Pull your fucking pants up."

Nate scurried to comply, fumbling his belt, never taking his wide eyes off Robin. "You're not human."

"Neither is your fuck buddy."

His gaze whipped back to Icarus, who'd gone preternaturally still. "We need you to do us a favor, Nate."

Nate began backing up. Instinct, Adam presumed, as the only thing behind the cop was a corner. But with him and Robin blocking the door, Icarus the other exit, and Nate's service weapon on the floor by the chaise, back was the only option for creating more space between him and the threats to his life. Until Icarus erased that distance in half a breath, zipping across the room. Nate backed the rest of the way into the corner, trembling. "Fuck," he gasped between short, thin breaths. "You're a vampire."

"Who generally doesn't eat people." He planted a hand on the wall over Nate's shoulder, crowding into his space. "I like you, Nate. Please don't be the exception."

Adam crossed the room at a more human pace. He leaned a shoulder against the wall near Nate and waited for the cop to catch his breath. "Icarus says you're a good cop, an honest one, even if you are lying to your husband about where you are tonight." Nate looked as chastened as his fear would allow, eyes downcast before darting back up, jumping between him and Icarus. Adam gave him something else to focus on, holding the folder out to Nate. "This is everything you need to arrest and convict Vincent Cirillo."

What little color Nate had left in his cheeks fled. "He's untouchable. Fuck, that man scares me more than you three."

"He's enslaving other people's magic, not to mention murder, arson, and a dozen other crimes." Adam nodded toward the folder in Nate's hands. "All documented in there."

"Your husband is a shifter, isn't he?" Robin asked from where he'd sprawled on the chaise.

"My wife was a coyote," Adam said. "She was the twin sister of my friend over there. My husband had magic too. Magic that's in me now. They tried to stop Vincent and died for it. I almost died too."

Icarus withdrew his hand and stepped back, giving Nate room to breathe, room to settle into the reality he hadn't chosen but was his now too, regardless. "How many other people are we gonna let die, Nate?"

"Or," Robin said, "we can tell your husband about your fang-banging fantasies."

Icarus hissed over his shoulder.

Nate, however, was oblivious to the back-and-forth. The good cop, as Icarus had promised, was flipping through the file on Vincent, taking in all the evidence assembled. He reached the end, then glanced again at Adam. "You were a cop?"

"Before I was a widower."

"I'm sorry for your loss." He glanced past Adam to Robin. "Both of you."

A good cop in more ways than one. There was a heart beneath his badge and playing to it was the right call. "We don't want Vincent to add anyone else to that list. Will you help us?"

"There's a district attorney I work with. He's good. If all this"—he lifted the file—"checks out, I think I can convince him to issue the arrest warrant. But the charges won't stick. Cirillo has all the judges in his pocket."

"We just need you to get him inside a holding cell." Adam pushed off the wall and stepped to Icarus's side. "We'll take care of the rest."

TWENTY-SEVEN

ADAM FOUND Icarus by the window in Cormac's study, the vampire's attention shifting between the early morning dark outside and the phone in his hand. No one had slept since returning from the city, Icarus included, and that phone had stayed in reach the entire time, through his change of clothes into sweats and a tee, through their debrief and an express meal, through the walk he'd taken around the reflecting pool. He hadn't taken a shower yet, but Adam bet Icarus would find a way to take the phone in there with him too. He was clutching the damn thing like a lifeline. To whom? Adam had two guesses; he started with the less likely. "Are you afraid Nate is going to change his mind?"

"No." Icarus stepped away from the window and sank into Cormac's battered office chair. "I'm afraid we put him in the line of fire."

Adam circled the desk and rested back against its edge. "You may not believe it"—he nudged Icarus's knee with his—"but you're a good person too."

He tossed the phone on the desk, then slumped back in the

chair. Eyes closed, he tilted his face to the ceiling and sighed. "Keep lying to yourself."

It wasn't easy tearing his gaze from the long smooth column of Icarus's throat, the sharp line of his jaw, the weariness beneath the vibrating tension he rarely let anyone see, but the answer to Adam's earlier question—the guess he'd figured more likely—was right beside his hip. An encrypted chat was open on the phone screen: **You're late**, from Icarus, the only message from four hours ago, and **Are you okay?** the only one within the past hour. "Is that your chat with her?"

"Should've been, but she missed check-in."

"Would you expect her to answer at midnight or four in the morning?"

"Yes."

"Do you want me to send someone?"

"If we don't hear from her by daybreak." He righted his head and opened his eyes. "Neither of us are the most reliable."

"You obviously care about her more than anyone."

Icarus shrugged, the nonchalance fake as hell.

Adam pressed, hoping Icarus's weariness would create an opening for another question that had lingered since they'd first discussed his sister. "Why did you leave her?"

Icarus leaned forward, retrieved his phone, and tapped at the screen a few times. He handed it back to Adam, open to an encrypted picture of a blue-haired Icarus in combat boots, jeans, and a leather halter, a young woman with tan skin like Cormac's, long green hair, a nose ring, and hazel eyes lined in kohl, and another young man who looked nothing like the alternakids beside him. He was white with rich chestnut hair, sky blue eyes, and everything about him—from his pressed dress shirt and khakis to his neatly trimmed hair with its perfectly coifed wave—shouted wholesome boy next door.

But the way the three of them had their arms over each other's shoulders, together with the smiles on their faces and the obvious affection in their eyes, led Adam to the obvious conclusion. "Another sibling?"

"We lost him in the Rift." And yet the pain that streaked across Icarus's face looked as fresh as any Adam had ever seen on the face of a victim's loved ones left behind. As fresh as the pain reflected in the mirror each morning.

"That was thirty years ago," Adam said. "What happened nine months ago to make you leave Portola?"

"I never said that was the first time I'd left. Or the last."

"What—"

CAW. CAW.

KRAA!

Adam locked eyes with Icarus—just half a second—before they were both in motion, Adam shoving off the desk and lunging for the window, Icarus spinning the desk chair to do the same. Both of them looked out to survey the chaos erupting below, only to have purple orbs of magic sail in their direction, slicing through the murder of crows that had taken flight, shattering the study's glass window and singeing the hair on the back of Adam's neck as a fanged, hissing Icarus dragged him to the floor. Magic pummeled the study's walls, sending books and files flying, creating divots in the centuries-old wood and stone, replacing the soft light of the shattered desk lamp with an eerie purple glow.

More glass broke a room over, followed by the howls and thundering rumble of the pack in motion. Adam needed to join them; his place was with his family. He reached toward the desk, only to have his arm slammed to the ground, Icarus pinning him in place.

"Stay the fuck down."

"Weapons!" Adam shouted. "Bottom desk drawer!"

"Well, why the fuck didn't you say so?"

Adam would've rolled his eyes if he wasn't busy scoping their surroundings and monitoring the windows and door. Icarus twisted for the weapons, grabbing the drawer handle and yanking, dislodging the entire drawer. Stakes and throwing stars, guns and ammo scattered across the wood floor, a lined box popping open from the force; silver caught Adam's eye, making his heart race as two gleaming bullets rolled toward where Icarus's bent knee was planted. Summoning his own strength, loosening the leash a careful measure, he shoved a blast of heat at Icarus, causing the vampire to teeter off-balance, giving Adam time to snatch the bullets up before they harmed Icarus.

Icarus whipped around, eyes wide. "What the fuck was that?"

Adam opened his fist, a puddle of silver evaporating in the glass-scratched palm of his hand. "Me saving a fighter we can't afford to lose right now."

Me saving the person I can't bear to lose right now.

"How?"

Robin's appearance saved Adam from answering. Still in human form, Robin, arms over his head, ducked into the room and stayed low, scurrying over to join them.

"Sitrep," Adam demanded as he wiped his hands on his jeans, then began loading the lead ammo into pistols. It was dark out; lead would be safer, would slow instead of potentially killing one of their own.

"Two warlocks, two vamps, and half a dozen shifters."

Icarus swept up the stakes and handed those to Adam too. "Atlas?" he asked Robin.

The assassin shook his head. "No sign of him. No sign of Vincent either."

"They're not letting up," Adam said. "They took a loss, but they don't want us to know it."

"They're not going to let up until you're dead."

A howl reverberated down the hall. Jenn was calling for backup.

"We need you out there," Robin said.

Adam shoved the last of the stakes in his waistband and moved to stand, only to be held down again, this time by Robin. "Not you. Him," he said with a nod to Icarus. "He's a weapon we didn't have before."

"I'm not staying here," Adam protested. He needed to be out there too, not hiding inside while everyone else fought to protect him. That was how he'd lost the loves of his life last time.

"He's right," Icarus said.

Adam turned to say thank you, but one look and he knew Icarus was agreeing with Robin, not him. "Fuck you."

"I can't let you die."

"And we can't afford to let Vincent capture you and find out what you are," Robin added. "Go to the roof and provide cover. Be the backstop." He didn't give Adam a chance to argue further, turning and moving out, joints cracking, the shift complete by the time he crossed the threshold.

Icarus's departure was even more abrupt. A rough, hard kiss, the cell phone shoved into his hand, a "Don't fucking die" mumbled against his lips, and then he was gone, disappearing after Robin.

Everything in Adam screamed to follow, a physical pull the likes of which he'd never felt before. An almost painful amplification of the tug he'd felt that night in Club Sutro when Icarus had first approached him, when confusion, desire, and betrayal had converged to spark an awareness inside him that he'd been unable to ignore. At the time, he'd glared over his shoulder, trying and failing to back fate off, but Icarus had sauntered right into his space, right into places Adam had held reserved for others. He wasn't supposed to feel this way about anyone else. He was supposed to take what Deborah and David had given him and use it to end Vincent. Burn in the process so he could join them.

None of that was going to happen if he stayed there, if those fighting for him outside, including Icarus, lost this battle. And fuck, they were too close to ending this to lose now. Adam checked his weapons were secure, then staying low, he dodged more magic on his way out of the study, down the hall, and up the stairs, emerging two flights later onto the roof and slinking across the narrow widow's walk on hands and knees. He reached the edge, hidden in a dark corner out of the moonlight, and lifted his head enough to peek between the rails, raising one pistol enough to be at the ready.

Jenn in coyote form, Abigail in mountain lion, and the rest of the pack were handling the shifters. Cormac and his corvid brethren had one of the warlocks virtually walled off, which left the two vampires and the purple-orb-wielding wizard to Robin and Icarus. Off the field of battle, they were practically enemies, but faced with a common foe, Robin and Icarus were an impressive pair. Two incredibly powerful beings, two creatures with unrivaled attack instincts and training. Adam knew Robin had it and had glimpsed a hint of Icarus's at the Canyon Lands, but seeing both in action now, Icarus held his own beside Robin, the two of them working together to dismantle one vampire, to swiftly stake the second, and to dodge and deflect the warlock's magic as they closed in on him.

Movement to their left caught Adam's eye. A bobcat broke through Jenn and Abigail's line and charged in Icarus and Robin's direction, leaping for Icarus's blind side.

Adam fired and instantly knew the lead bullet wouldn't reach the cat before the cat reached Icarus. He let more of the leash go, fire and heat licking off his fingertips, forming an invisible mire between the cat and Icarus and slowing the former's speed enough for the bullet to catch up.

The bobcat fell and howled at Icarus's feet.

The warlock ceased his spell casting long enough to see where the other had come from, zeroing in on Adam's location. He got as far as raising his arm before Cormac slammed into his face talons first. Robin crashed into his body and took him the rest of the way to the ground, and Icarus finished it, ripping the warlock's head clean off with one twist of his hands.

Victory vibrated through him, through the heated stare he shared with Icarus, until Adam realized something on his person was actually vibrating. It took a second to breach the fog of adrenaline and realize what it was. Icarus's phone in his pocket. He shoved a hand in, withdrew it, and glanced at the screen. At the picture that appeared in the encrypted chat. Vibrations of a different sort took over, and he followed his sinking heart to his knees.

TWENTY-EIGHT

"WELL, this explains why Vincent didn't send Atlas."

Adam barely heard Robin's words over his thundering heart, over the flapping wings of the thing inside him desperate to beat its way out and wrap those wings of warmth around the vampire frantically pacing the length of the cellar he'd had no choice but to retreat to. The rising sun had trapped Icarus, preventing him going from after the one person Adam knew he put above all others.

Including him.

"What does he want?" Jennifer asked. "There's no ransom request, no message, just the picture."

The picture—a smug, grinning Atlas with his arm around the shoulders of a much shorter woman with long green hair and hazel eyes, only the slightest creases at the corners, far fewer than one would expect on a woman who, by Adam's math, should look closer to fifty than thirty.

Adam circled one end of the cellar table. His legs were steadier now, the battle rush of adrenaline faded, the initial shock of that picture internalized, the pain he'd felt for Icarus better tamed though no less intense. He leaned a hip against the side of the table near where Icarus was pacing. "Did they take her to leverage you?"

"I don't know." Icarus stopped in front of him, his eyes wild with fear and with self-recrimination Adam recognized all too well. "Maybe. Fuck!"

"Why else would they take her?" Adam asked, sensing that he'd finally get the whole truth now, that Icarus was either ready to share it or had no choice.

It would be the latter, judging by the frustrated twist of his lips, as if they'd sealed in the truth for so long that his body was fighting to keep it in still. "For her own power. Because I fucking showed it to them."

"You both did," Cormac said, rejoining them from upstairs where he'd been questioning two of the shifters they'd detained. The rest of Vincent's strike force, including the other warlock, had retreated. "You showed them yours tonight," he said to Adam. "And you"—he jutted his chin at Icarus—"showed them hers at the Canyon Lands that day, didn't you?"

Icarus's eyes slipped shut, a powerful cocktail of guilt and fear pinching his features, answering Cormac's question. The raven had been right.

"Which is what?" Adam asked more gently than Icarus was being with himself.

"If they don't know already, and they find out . . ." He covered his face with his hands and roared, loud enough to rattle the metal tanks and light fixtures. Everyone in the room took a step back.

Except Adam. "Icarus, what power?"

He lowered his hands and opened his eyes, locking his

gaze with Adam's and drawing whatever strength he needed, everything Adam had left to give him. A slight nod, a silent thank-you, before Icarus shifted his attention to Cormac. "You weren't wrong about me putting my hand to the ground and asking for help. That's exactly what I did. And she answered."

"Your sister?" Cormac said.

"Nature." His blue gaze returned to Adam's. "Her name is Mary, and she's Mother Nature."

TWENTY-NINE

"MARY AND MICHAEL ROLLINS." Cormac dropped a bulging file folder onto the cellar table and flipped it open. "Crossed paths the first time at the homeless teen shelter in Portola. In 1979." He withdrew two photos and slid them to the center of the table. Teenage versions of the blue-haired man and green-haired woman from the picture on Icarus's phone, except in these older shots his hair was the color of carrots and hers was so dark brown it was almost black. "Michael was fifteen, Mary was fourteen."

Adam looked up at Icarus, who stood behind Abigail, stitching a cut she'd taken to the shoulder in the earlier skirmish. Something to steady him, he'd insisted. "I thought you said she was older."

"In every way that counts, and now technically too." He tied off the stitch and snipped it with a claw. "She's like you. She ages still, but more slowly because of the thing inside her."

"She wasn't always Mother Nature?"

"You weren't always whatever you are." He patted Abigail's shoulder. "You're good. Thank you." He quickly washed and dried his hands, then blinked as he returned to the table, and Adam sensed he was more fully in the room with them again. He slid into the chair beside Adam. "Carry on, raven."

Cormac claimed the chair at the head of the table. "Michael and Mary became inseparable. Fostered together by Brenda Rollins." He withdrew two document copies from the file and passed them to Robin's side of the table first. "Brenda filled a missing persons report for Michael and a death certificate for Mary."

"After the Rift?" Robin asked as Abigail glimpsed the docs, then slid them across the table to Adam. "I thought missing persons reports were all shoved in a corner somewhere."

"We work our way through them slowly."

"But his"—Abigail flicked a glance at Icarus—"was filed five days *before* the Rift."

"What the—" Robin started.

Adam cut him off with a raised hand. He shifted in his chair toward Icarus, toward their best avenue for answers, toward the person Adam sensed needed to give them now that he'd finally started. "Tell me about her."

Icarus smiled as he drew the photo of Mary closer. "Sharp-tongued, sass for days, and smarter than anyone I've ever met. I was at the shelter first, she sauntered in, I sauntered over, and that was that. She's the balance I need, the one who keeps me from flying too high most of the time, and who cleans up after me when I accidentally do."

"And she named you Icarus?"

"No, he did."

"He who?" Cormac asked.

Icarus shifted, withdrew his phone, and slid it in his direction. On it was the picture he'd shown Adam earlier. "Our brother, Canton. He joined us at Brenda's about eight months after we were fostered there. He fit right in and fell head over heels for her."

"Your sister?" Robin said, and at Icarus's nod, followed up with, "You didn't?"

"She's always been just a sister to me."

"I don't have any record of Canton," Cormac said as he rifled through the file again.

"Because she erased him."

"Why?"

"So no one would arrest me for almost murdering him."

Robin growled. "You sure you weren't interested?"

Icarus rolled his eyes. "He was never just a human who fell for my sister. Hell, I'm not sure if he ever really fell for *her* at all." He took the phone back and pocketed it. "Canton was in love with Nature, who was losing the war and needed to take drastic action, then hide afterward."

"Canton identified your sister," Adam said, putting it together, "as a host."

"He was a fucking spy," Icarus spat. Anger and hurt laced his words, thirty years of it that had lingered and stewed. That had kept Icarus at arm's length from everyone but her, who no doubt shared his pain. "A warlock who inserted himself into our lives, buried into our hearts, and stayed there for years. Then, ten days before the Rift, he gave me a choice."

The rest of the awful pieces slotted together, and Adam's heart ached for the selfless man beside him. "You traded your soul for hers. To protect her."

He shrugged, the most helpless gesture Adam had ever seen from the apex predator. "She's my sister. The only person who's ever given a damn about me." He glanced across the table at Robin. "Deborah was your twin?"

A begrudging nod.

"We're not blood related," Icarus carried on, "but how I feel about her is how I imagine it must feel between twins. Like she's the other half of me. I'll do anything to protect her."

Guilt and self-recrimination clouded Robin's expression, a mirror reflection of Icarus earlier. He shoved back from the table and staggered into a shadowed corner, his back to the table, a shaking hand skirting over the back of his neck as his torso heaved up and down.

While his brother-in-law gathered himself, Adam returned to his line of questioning. "Why did you leave her? The first time."

"Do you know what happens when a vampire is turned? What happens to our emotions?"

"You become a bloodsucking asshole?" Jenn chimed in.

Icarus ignored her and focused instead on Cormac. "When you shift, what's it feel like"—Icarus thumped his chest with his fist—"here?"

"Like it wants to explode out of me," the raven answered.

"No different," Icarus said. "And I died with equal parts anger and love"—he flattened his hand over his heart—"right here."

"You went after him," Adam guessed.

"He was smart enough to hide, but I found him. The only reason I didn't kill him was because she already had." He propped his elbows on the table and hung his head in his hands, fingers raking through his magenta strands. "She loved me more than Nature loved Canton, and I'll never forgive myself for putting her in that position. I made sure she survived the Rift and the transformation, and once I was sure she was safe, I left so she'd be safe from me too."

"What about your mother?" Cormac asked.

"She's never forgiven either one of us. Canton was her favorite."

"But she signed the missing persons report and death certificate?"

He lifted his head. "Do you have a pen?"

One came flying out of the shadowed corner Robin had disappeared into. Icarus caught it without missing a beat, flipped over the copy of the missing persons report, and perfectly replicated Brenda's signature. Another talent that Adam added to his mental list. "I forged them, and my sister filed them."

Robin returned to the table. "Why don't you use her name?"

"Because she's supposed to be dead. If someone found out she wasn't, found out what she is . . ."

"Someone like Atlas or Vincent," Abigail said.

"This war is older than time, bubbling up through history. The Rift was the last major eruption and the first time in ages where Chaos gained the upper hand, where it forced Nature to retreat."

Adam covered the frustrated fist Icarus had made while talking. "She hid in your sister."

Icarus flipped over his hand and laced their fingers together, squeezed, and took a deep breath before continuing. "If they find out what she is, if they harness all that power for Chaos and darkness, or worse—if they kill her while trying to manipulate all that magic, that's ball game. Humanity and what's left of this planet dies with her, and we're plunged into a dark age we'll never come out of." He slumped in his chair, as weary as Adam had ever seen him. More than just the past week on his shoulders, he shouldered thirty years of an impossible weight, of a responsibility like no other. "None of us, human or paranormal, can exist without her. She's the only thing keeping this world in balance."

THIRTY

AN ASSASSIN, two detectives, and a vampire with better than average hacking skills could make quick work of excavation. Throw in a coyote and mountain lion working every contact they had between Talahalusi and Portola, and their team had an Atlas and Mary sighting by late morning. They were holed up at a motel on the coast just south of YB, and pressure applied in the right place—a source Abigail had nurtured inside Vincent's organization—yielded news of a broad daylight meet happening at Portola University later that afternoon.

That meant it was impossible for Icarus to join the extraction op they spent the rest of the morning planning. If Adam hadn't personally witnessed Icarus lock down his instincts at least twice, he would have been more worried about approaching the man pacing the cellar bunk room, the long maxi skirt and tunic he'd changed into after a shower swishing around him. Icarus had come a long way from the baby vamp who'd almost killed his brother, with no one by his side, no one to fight for him other than Mary. Well, that was over, and Adam wouldn't let him lose her too. He stepped behind Icarus, clasped his shoulders, and held his ground when Icarus whipped his head around and hissed.

Icarus's face fell the next second. "I'm sorry," he whispered.

"I'm not afraid," Adam replied, likewise speaking softly, the moment a quiet one, too much teetering on the precipice. He coasted his hands down Icarus's arms, rubbing warmth into them, before he circled his arms around the taller man's waist, embracing him from behind. "When did you realize?"

"Realize what?"

"That you could lock down your instincts."

"Senses, technically, which in turn dampens the instincts. And I'd realized too late. She showed me how after Canton. I kept my senses off until it was safe to leave her. It's saved me since a million times over." He tilted his head, back against Adam's. "Saved you a few times too."

"I can make a call," he said. "Offer to trade myself for her."

"And give Vincent exactly what he wants?" Icarus scoffed. "No, and the extraction op is good. Your team is good."

He kissed the back of Icarus's shoulder, bared by the wide neck of his tunic. "We pulled Paris out of the fire. We'll rescue her too."

"Where is Paris?"

"I don't know." He rested his cheek in the valley between Icarus's shoulder blades. "Mac hid him somewhere. The less people who know, the better."

Hands folded over Adam's, Icarus didn't speak for several long minutes. When he finally did, his voice was hoarse, struggling around a lump in his throat Adam could feel him fighting. "I failed her."

"She's still alive." He loosened his arms enough to nudge

Icarus around in them. "You were going to go to her before I returned to your apartment the other night?"

Icarus closed his eyes and nodded.

Adam would have felt more guilt if this right here, Icarus in his arms, didn't feel like a fate none of them, including she, could escape. "Why did you continue to stay away?"

He rested his forehead on Adam's. "She's part of a hacker collective. I didn't want anything to happen to those around her like what happened to Canton. I couldn't put her in that situation again."

"The fact you didn't shut off your senses and still totally ignored my bleeding hands earlier tells me you wouldn't. Also the fact you haven't killed Robin yet."

Icarus's chuckle was a welcome sound. Adam leaned back to see if the smile reached his eyes. Not quite, but he was more firmly on the stable side of the precipice now. Not so close to the abyss.

Taking Icarus by the hand, Adam led him to the bed still shoved in the corner, the coziest spot that Icarus, in the short amount of time he'd been there, had made his own. "She was in trouble the last time you were in Portola?"

"Yeah, several months back," Icarus said as he lowered himself next to Adam. "Hacked the wrong person."

"Vincent?"

"No, a different job. Unrelated."

But was it? "Could that be what this is now?" he speculated aloud. "A hack gone wrong? Maybe he'd been implicated back then?" Or more likely, given the escalation of Vincent's efforts . . . "Or Vincent wants her to hack someone? No connection to us." That would be the best-case scenario. Would be more likely to result in a fast and simple meet and a fast and clean extraction.

"That makes sense, but how does Atlas figure in? We assumed he sent that picture, but what if it was her?" Icarus traced the nearly healed cuts on Adam's hand. "I'm sure it was him who told Vincent to send me to you. What else does he know? Does he know how we're all connected?"

"Did he know when you were in Portola last or why?"

He shook his head. "He'd have no reason to. He wasn't a client then, and like I said, she's good at cleaning up my messes. I'm sure she'd try to clean this up herself if she could do so without drawing undue attention to herself or me."

Utter devotion, the two of them walking a ridiculously high tightrope for three decades with virtually no safety nets.

Safety net. Fuck!

Adam's stomach roiled. "That's why you had the supply of Daylight?"

"Always kept an emergency vial on hand."

"That you wasted on me."

Icarus's reply was swift, the grip on Adam's hand almost painful. "Not a waste. No matter what happens, I do not regret that decision."

"I'll make sure of it." Adam lifted their joined hands and kissed the back of Icarus's. Then brought his lips to Icarus's, kissing those too, making a promise. "I'll bring her back to you."

THIRTY-ONE

ADAM WANTED to know who picked this location. Portola University's main quad was wide open, very public, and very crowded, especially at four in the afternoon. Knowing who picked the when and where would tell them a lot about how this meet would go.

Vincent was a showy motherfucker, but doing his business in this broad of daylight seemed too showy, even for him. He got away with what he did because he did it in foggy, no-rules YB. Portola was a cesspool, but it was a temperate one with a high-gloss veneer, its seedy underbelly more carefully hidden. It was maybe what Vincent aimed to be, but he wasn't there yet. Unless he'd amassed—stolen—more power than they realized. Unless he thought himself invincible already, which was a truly frightening proposition.

If that horror had not yet come to pass, and Vincent hadn't picked this location, then was it Mary? Did she think it would be safer? If Vincent had contacted her about a job, if he wanted her skills badly enough, then it would make sense for her to set the terms of a meet. But if she was being blackmailed into working for him, which was Vincent's usual MO, then Adam doubted she had the leverage to dictate the when and where.

Which left Atlas. They were so far from knowing anything about the warlock's motives that it was . . . suspect. Who was he trying to protect with this location? Vincent or himself? Or Mary? Did he know Mary was connected to Icarus? Had he told Vincent? Had Vincent then made the connection to the people who wanted to kill him? Was Atlas shoving Vincent or Mary into the open for a possible hit? While taking a shot at Vincent was sorely tempting, Adam couldn't make revenge his top priority today. He'd promised to rescue Mary. And despite how desperately he wanted to end Vincent and his operation, Adam couldn't do it here. This was not the Canyon Lands. This was a location full of people, of humans, of potential victims. Which Atlas was counting on too, if he was the one who'd picked this location.

If he was going to show at all. It was ten past four, and there was no sign of any of them.

"Anyone with eyes on?" Adam radioed the teams.

"Negative," Abigail replied from where she and Robin, both recognizable to Atlas, were posted in a parked car near the quad's south entrance.

"Negative," reported another pack pair lounging on a bench at the north end of the artificial lawn.

"Negative," Jenn radioed from where she and another pack member were pretending to be tourists, taking pictures near the west end.

"Negative," Cormac radioed from beside Adam, the two of them crouched on a rooftop at the east entrance.

They returned to silent waiting, except Cormac, whose silence didn't last a minute. His thoughts, unsurprisingly, veered in the same direction as Adam's. "If Atlas sent that picture, why? There's no demand for a ransom, no demand for a meet with Icarus or us. We don't even know if she's still alive."

"I think we'd know if she wasn't."

"If Icarus is telling the truth about what she is."

Adam side-eyed his former partner. "You're the one who kept harping about what you saw him do at the Canyon Lands that day. Now he's told you. How else do you square that?"

"I don't know exactly what I saw, but I do know something isn't squaring. And you're a good enough detective to know that too."

He wasn't wrong; their mental gymnastics just weren't focused on the same person. Adam's gut told him to trust Icarus, but Cormac's observations couldn't be discredited either. He'd been right about that day in the Canyon Lands, even if they still didn't have all the details. "You think Icarus isn't telling us the whole truth?"

"Have *you* told him the whole truth?" Again, Cormac wasn't wrong, nor was he done examining all the angles. "I'm not sure Icarus knows the whole truth about his sister either."

Maybe not the direction Adam thought his suspicions were headed. He kept his eyes on the quad while continuing to hear the detective out. "What makes you say that?"

"I did some more digging. No record before she showed up at that shelter."

"Sealed?"

"Not that I could find." He drummed his fingers against the roof's ledge like he would his talons in raven form. "Couldn't find anything on Canton either."

"She erased all of them." That would be the safest thing to do.

"Including Atlas?"

He glanced again at the raven. "Why would you look into him? We already knew he was erased."

"Something else I saw at the Canyon Lands that day. Atlas cast an orb at me and Icarus and missed."

"It was foggy and chaotic. The earth was falling out from under us."

Cormac wasn't buying it, his lips pressed into a thin line. "He's better than that."

Jenn cut off further debate, her voice whispered over the comms. "We've got eyes on."

Adam whipped his gaze back to the quad, adrenaline spiking then heart sinking as he spotted the couple who emerged through the west entrance.

Cormac narrated the thoughts Adam didn't want but couldn't avoid. "Does that green-haired pixie look like a hostage to you?"

"We don't know what we're seeing," Adam countered to Cormac and himself. Sure, her arm was around Atlas's waist and his was casually draped over her shoulder, neither of them looking the worse for wear, but why would they want to stand out in a crowded location full of people? They looked like any other couple out for an afternoon stroll. But what did they sound like? What words were escaping their moving lips? "B team, move to second position."

"Copy that." The pack pair on the quad stood, frisbee in hand, ready to extend their reach as needed. Jenn's team also wandered closer, picking a spot just inside the lawn's edge well within their hearing distance, but far enough back from where Atlas and Mary had stopped near the center of the oval, arms around each other.

"If she's betrayed him . . ." Adam mumbled, fear and anger slipping out, even as his training coached him otherwise. Coached him to look deeper, beneath what Mary and Atlas wanted everyone to see.

"She's playing along to protect herself," Jenn said. "I can hear her heart racing from here."

"Look at her posture," Cormac added. "She's playing casual, but her back and shoulders are stiff as a board and her fist is clenched behind Atlas's back."

"Vincent entering from the south," Abigail radioed.

If Adam hadn't been so focused on that fist, if he'd shifted his gaze a split second sooner, he would have missed it. Atlas clasped her shoulder, and a shimmer of green sluiced over her, the outward signs of her distress disappearing.

Masked.

Whose side was the fucking warlock on?

"Three plainclothes trailing Vincent," Robin relayed. "The one in a jacket is human and wearing a shoulder harness. The other two are shifters. I can see an outline of a weapon beneath the one's black shirt. I'm guessing the other is armed too."

A strike was definitely out. Too much firepower and too many people. "Extraction only," Adam confirmed to the teams. They would have to wait and rely on Nate to help deliver Vincent.

If Mary didn't kill him first. Scowling, she snatched back the hand Vincent had made a show of kissing the back of.

"C team, can you hear?" Adam asked.

"Pleasantries with a side of snark," Jenn replied. "She's feistier than her brother."

Adam smiled, brief and fleeting because Jenn soon relayed Vincent's true purpose. It was enough to turn Adam's stomach. Vincent had heard from associates about Mary's hacking prowess, and he wanted to hire her to hack the location of one of the most powerful local covens. Ever since the Rift, covens stayed on the move, no one covenstead for this very reason.

Beside Adam, Cormac stiffened, his eyes flashing violet. Over the comm, Abigail growled. "More power he can suck."

"And yet," Jenn said, "he doesn't realize the ultimate power is right in front of him."

But Atlas hadn't told him either. Because Atlas didn't know? Or because Atlas was a double agent?

But that wasn't all Vincent wanted. He wanted her to dig further into Adam, into Deborah and David, because word had gotten back about last night's attack, about the power he'd flexed. Vincent was finally starting to put the pieces together, which meant their timeline had been accelerated, again.

Mary protested, Vincent threatened, Atlas cajoled, and eventually an agreement—if it could be called that—was reached. Adam suspected it was similar to how they'd muscled Icarus into their employ. Regardless, with the deal made, Vincent departed the way he came, and Atlas, arm back over Mary's shoulder, turned her not west but east, toward the entrance where Adam and Cormac hid. The warlock's eyes flicked up as if he knew exactly where they were perched.

"What the fuck is that asshole up to?" Adam muttered.

"It could be a trap," Robin warned. "Lure us out for his own purpose."

"He could call Vincent back," Cormac said. "Turn you over himself."

"He would have done that already," Adam said. "And she

won't let that happen." He was confident of that much. But if Atlas didn't know what she was, other than someone who was important to Icarus, Adam didn't want to expose her more. "Let's spring our trap first," he said. "We've got him outnumbered. Converge behind our location."

Cormac shifted between one breath and took flight the next, and the flock of ravens that had congregated around them the past hour flitted off the roof, falling into formation behind him. Eyes in the sky while the rest of the pack on human feet drew closer. Adam sensed them on either side of the building as he descended the stairs, then stepped out the back door into the small bricked-over courtyard between buildings. They fanned out on either side of him, and the handful of humans in the courtyard scattered, instincts keyed in enough to know better. By the time Atlas and Mary stepped through the opening between the buildings, they were surrounded. And yet neither of them veered off course or missed a step, Atlas leading her to stand directly in front of Adam.

"I believe this"—he nudged Mary forward—"belongs to a mutual acquaintance of ours."

"Why?" Adam asked.

"Because," Mary said, as she sauntered to Adam's side, all her previous nerves gone, her swagger so reminiscent of Icarus's that Adam almost laughed. "I threatened to flood the internet with pictures of him on a leash."

Robin snickered. "I'd like to see those."

And then a seemingly peaceful exchange went up in smoke. Atlas summoned an orb, and Robin shifted and collided with his chest, making the orb fly off course and barely miss the dive-bombing ravens. Cormac screeched as he sailed low enough to ruffle Adam's hair, forcing him to spin. He spied Mary in a crouch, her glowing green hand an inch from the ground. Adam shot out his own hand—power channeled into it, no idea if it would be enough—and wrapped his fingers around her wrist. "No! We can't. Not yet."

She stared up at him, eyes wide, and then a slow, satisfied smile stretched across her face. "He said you were different, but he has no idea you're one of mine, does he?"

One of hers?

"Adam!" Abigail shouted behind him, and he whipped back around. She was the only shifter still in human form, the rest of the pack having shifted to defend Robin and help him pin Atlas to the ground. Robin stood over his chest, snarling in his face.

"You promised Icarus a punch," Adam reminded his brother-in-law. "And you do not get to kill him until I kill Vincent."

Robin gnashed his teeth, and Atlas snarled right back at him. "Now who's on a leash, dog?"

Golden eyes flashed, murder glowing bright, and Adam was sure Icarus wouldn't get his punch, but all Robin's teeth sank into was green mist, Atlas disappearing with a single snap of his fingers.

"Huh," Mary said, hands on her hips. "And I thought I had Atlas's number."

Speaking of numbers. Adam dug his phone out of his pocket and opened the encrypted chat app Icarus had installed. He handed the device to Mary. "Worry about them later. Text your brother now or there won't be a base camp for us to get back to."

THIRTY-TWO

HE SHOULD HAVE KNOWN BETTER. One touch and she'd immediately sensed what he was. Why hadn't David or Deborah ever told him the creature sharing David's soul and now Adam's was a force of nature? Did they know? Deb had always been a shifter, and Adam had assumed the same of David, but thinking back, there were pictures and fleeting moments from before their deployment when David had seemed lighter, when all of his soul shined from his eyes. Before it had been dimmed by the fire inside him.

Inside Adam now.

Magic.

The same magic—the source of it—bound inside the green-haired woman beside him in the passenger seat. She'd been silently working her phone the entire drive from Portola to Talahalusi, fingers flying, switching between chat boxes and transferring files between cloud-based drives. Anyone passing them on the freeway, if they could catch a glimpse of the Camaro through the caravan of other cars surrounding them, would probably assume she was just another person who spent too much time on their phone. Maybe some would wonder if she was a hacker. But how many would guess she was the life force holding their world together? It wouldn't cross Adam's mind if she were a stranger, but she wasn't, and the questions filling his head were too many to count.

"What do you want to know?" she asked, as if reading his mind. Could she?

He chuffed. "I don't even know where to start."

A small smile turned up the corners of her mouth. "I thought I'd lost you."

"You've lost others?

"Too many."

"How did it happen?" Adam asked. "How did the magic inside David come to be inside me?" He'd been in the safe house when David had come stumbling in, his skin rippling orange and red, Deborah in coyote form in his arms. She had been too still, not breathing, a sizzling, gaping wound on her side. He'd told Adam to run, but there'd been nowhere to run, the battle raging outside, the loves of his life dying in the room with him. He wasn't leaving them; he'd promised until death do they part, and he'd planned on keeping that promise. He'd wrapped his arms around David, holding them both, and withstood the searing heat that burst from their husband and brought the walls down around them. That was the last thing he remembered before waking in a hospital bed with no burns on him. But in him . . . "Why am I still here?"

"He loved you. He made a choice to save you. And in doing so, he also saved the magic."

But how? No one had ever been able to answer him that. "It doesn't normally happen this way?"

"Too many can't control the magic. They flame out and die alone."

"They can't use it to bring themselves back again?" He'd sensed that himself; that the magic inside him was a one-shot deal, at least where he was concerned. It was another reason he'd flexed it so rarely—that and the fear a flame out would sear those around him. Contrary to what he'd told Icarus, it was the primary reason why he hadn't flexed his power when facing Vincent at the Canyon Lands. Icarus, Cormac, Jenn, and Abigail had all been in the blast radius.

"The magic can only bring a being back once." She finished on her phone and set it on the seat between them. "It's why Chaos is winning. Every one of you that's extinguished, whose energy isn't properly channeled, is a black hole that feeds the darkness. Without the power of rebirth, of second chances, there's not enough energy to drive the living."

Again, how the hell did Adam unpack all that? But as he turned onto the narrow road that led to Monte Corvo, his thoughts likewise narrowed, catching on something she'd said and considering it more personally, considering it in terms of the man they had in common.

"Is that what I am to Icarus?" Had Icarus figured out what he was? Or even if he hadn't, had the vampire? Was the thing inside Adam a life force—rebirth—the vampire couldn't resist?

"It's what he is to you, isn't it?" she shot back, then cast her gaze out the window at the rising vineyards. "Irony, fate, call it what you will, it twists like a vine around all of us."

Adam frowned. "So it's not really us?" His awareness of Icarus before he'd even laid eyes on him, the attraction that had ridden him hard since he had, the affection that had grown steadily alongside it. Was it merely rebirth reaching for an outlet? For death? Was Icarus the death wish Cormac so often warned of? Adam the man recoiled at the idea, but Adam the detective couldn't discount the possibility. "It's just fate or the monsters inside us?"

"Not monsters," she said, those two words filled with such sorrow, such exhaustion, it stole Adam's breath. But then her voice, her whole being, brightened as they pulled into the villa's circular drive and the front door was flung open, Icarus barely holding himself back from running into the setting sun to reach her. She glanced back over her shoulder at him. "Don't sell yourselves short. I know monsters. They don't have half the love in their hearts as you and Icarus do."

She smiled, then shoved the car door open, leaving a sparkle of green in her wake as she sprinted across the drive, up the steps, and into her brother's arms. Icarus held her tight, lifting her off the ground and twirling her around, radiating relief that Adam felt in every part of his soul, the parts that belonged to him and the parts he shared with the Devil. Felt it settle deeper as he stepped out of the car and met Icarus's gaze over the roof. Read the silent thank-you on his lips.

Was she right? Was it love filling up Adam's heart and carrying him step by step closer to the person he'd been unable to shake from his life since he'd first sauntered into it? Not because of any mission or any blackmail or any forces other than attraction and affection, other than appreciation for what Icarus had brought to his life for the first time in a decade. He'd known love before, real and true, and fuck if the fullness of his heart, the peace in his soul, all of it, didn't feel the same now as it had then.

Adam climbed the steps, never taking his eyes off Icarus, sliding his hand into Icarus's outstretched one while Icarus kept his other arm wrapped around his sister. "I thought I'd lost you," he whispered into her green curls.

"I told you I'd find my way here when I was ready."

Icarus gasped and jerked back. Adam, however, found his words first. "Repeat that."

"I found a way to you," she said to Icarus, then to Adam, "And a way for you to take down Vincent Cirillo, once and for all."

THIRTY-THREE

MARY WAS PETITE, Cormac's description of her as a green-haired pixie spot on, but as she stood at the head of the cellar table, her presence loomed larger than anyone else's in the room. A power, a threat, a responsibility most of them were still trying to wrap their heads around. The only people in the room who seemed relatively comfortable in her presence were Icarus, which was a given, and Abigail, which was a surprise. They were strangers who gravitated around each other like old friends. Even more curious, Jenn hadn't raised her hackles about it, unlike her cousin, who was still seething from being deprived his taste of warlock. Robin stood against the opposite wall beside Cormac, who predictably kicked off the interrogation. "Explain what you meant outside."

"Icarus told you I'm part of a hacker collective?" When everyone around the table nodded, she continued. "A job came over the wire. Someone wanted a hack on the Redwood Coven's location."

Robin growled and Cormac stiffened, neither of them

dealing with the news a second time better than they had the first.

"It's consistent," Adam said, as alarmed as the others but striving to hold it together, Icarus's hand on his thigh under the table helping him do so. "Steal all the power he can."

"I knew it was Vincent," Mary said. "I wasn't going to let anyone else put themselves in the middle of this shitstorm."

Cormac pushed off the wall. "So you put yourself in his path." He rested his forearms on the top of the chair next to Adam's. "The biggest battery Vincent could ever want."

"He doesn't know."

"Does Atlas?"

"Atlas doesn't work for Vincent."

"He works for you?"

"Not exactly."

Robin growled again. "You didn't answer his question."

She flicked her hazel gaze to where Robin remained by the wall. "Atlas isn't your concern."

He didn't stay there long, charging the table. "The fuck he's not!" He would have shouted in her face if not for Icarus and Abigail standing from their chairs to form a wall in front of her that Robin couldn't breach. "He killed my sister," he snarled over their shoulders.

Adam's chest clenched at the mention of Deb and at his friend's naked frustration, his grief boiling over. He hadn't been there that day, not that it would have mattered, and now someone else was keeping him from the retribution he so desperately needed to move on, to maybe forgive himself.

Mary seemed to sense Robin's turmoil, pushing through Icarus and Abigail to stand in front of Robin and clasp one of his balled-up fists. "Everything isn't what it seems, coyote."

"Fucking riddles." He rolled his eyes and tried to snatch his hand away.

Mary held on tight. "You'll get your revenge, I promise, but it's not your turn yet." She held Robin's gaze for several long seconds until Robin deflated and stepped back, slumping into the chair Cormac spun out for him.

Cormac, however, remained standing. "The coven."

"I don't have their location yet. But I do have evidence for you." She tapped at her phone, and the one in Mac's pocket pinged. "Phone records from the collective, along with an audio recording of today's meet. Everything Icarus's cop client needs to hand over to the DA. To get Vincent where you need him."

"Why wait?" Adam said, swinging toward Robin's position. "We can hit him when he goes after the coven."

"That's your choice, but it's a risky play on multiple levels." Her knowing gaze cut to Cormac, and Adam's stomach churned when his former partner sank into a chair and propped his elbows on the table, hands covering his face.

Adam clasped one of Cormac's wrists and pulled it far enough away to see the color leach from his friend's face. "Why are you so concerned about the coven?"

"Because I hid Paris with them."

"Fuck." Icarus spoke for the first time, succinct and what they were all thinking. "Is that why Vincent wants their location?"

Mary shook her head. "No, Vincent is just a human who wants to be a giant in the coming war. Adam's right. He wants the coven for their power, which is rising as we approach Samhain."

Adam leaned forward. "Then we should keep him away from sources of power, including you."

She pinned him with a stern look. "And you."

She wasn't wrong. Him, her, and a coven of powerful magicians, all in one location, was too much juice to ever let Vincent near. He spun toward Icarus. "Call Nate. Tell him we have more evidence. That it's time to move."

Time to get Vincent in a place where they could get the upper hand and get the revenge and retribution—the peace—they all deserved.

THIRTY-FOUR

IF ICARUS'S phone had been a lifeline earlier, it was as good as a grenade now. Arm hitched back, he was ready to chuck it at the nearest wall, and with his full strength behind it, Adam had no doubt it would blow a hole clean through. He rushed into the bunk room and grasped Icarus's elbow. "You may still need that."

"For what?" He wrenched his arm loose and spun, gesturing wildly. "Everyone I love is here, and the best chance I had to keep you and her safe just fucking bailed." He resumed his pacing and continued his ranting, cursing the DA who'd refused to hear Nate's evidence against Vincent.

Adam, however, was stuck a few words back . . . *Everyone I love.*

Love.

Had it been a careless slip? Did Icarus mean love generally, as in care for, like he meant about Mary? Or did he mean something more when it came to Adam? Something closer to what Adam was struggling with himself? Had Icarus fallen as hard and fast too—beyond what the magic inside each of them wanted?

Did Michael want him? Because Adam—no, Gabriel—wanted Michael, Icarus, the entire package. More than he wanted his next breath right then. Maybe even more than he wanted death. That thought fucking terrified him.

But not enough to walk away. He stepped into Icarus's path. "You need to calm down."

Icarus cocked a brow. "Why aren't *you* more upset?"

"The choice is easy now."

"Easy? What planet are you living on?"

Adam closed the distance between them and laid his hands on Icarus's chest. "The one with you."

Icarus's expression was a riot of confused emotions—soft surprise, harsh incredulity, stark worry—that eventually distilled into frustrated exhaustion. He covered Adam's hands with his. "The one where I might lose you and her in one fell swoop." He leaned in, forehead resting against Adam's, eyelids fluttering closed. "And let's not even talk about how I almost got Paris killed once already."

Adam pressed their foreheads together, then shifted. Kissed a path from Icarus's temple to one corner of his mouth. "No one's getting killed except Vincent."

"You want to go in there."

He kissed the other corner and up Icarus's opposite cheek to his other temple. "I want him to pay for what he did to Deb and David. I want this to be over."

Icarus sighed and leaned more of his body into Adam's. "Fucking death wish."

Adam snaked an arm around Icarus's waist and lifted his other hand to cup his cheek. "Icarus, look at me."

He shook his head and kept his eyes screwed closed. "What am I to you?" His voice was thick, a lump in his throat that he audibly swallowed around. "A last hurrah?"

"No, baby." Adam swiped a thumb across his cheek, did it again, and Icarus opened his eyes, the blues wary and bruised. Adam wanted to see them bright again, full of fire and hope and desire. "You're the person making me doubt how much I really want to die."

He swallowed Icarus's gasp, crushing their mouths together and pushing his tongue between Icarus's lips, sweeping inside and stoking the missing fire back to life. Chasing that life himself.

Icarus groaned, a surrender and then more, arms winding around Adam, holding him tight, picking him up and moving him with preternatural speed. Adam's back hit the corner bed, Icarus stretched above him, the space narrow and perfect for the closeness they both craved. Icarus's hands were everywhere, fisting Adam's hair, creeping under his sweater, pushing it up and off, his own shirt close behind. He hitched Adam's leg over his hip and held him closer, rutting their stiff cocks together.

Content to be manhandled, Adam landed his lips anywhere he could reach, brushing them against Icarus's neck, parting them around his Adam's apple, sealing them over a nipple and sucking hard, eliciting a breathy groan and full-body shiver that rippled through both of them. He rucked up the back of Icarus's skirt and found his ass deliciously cool and bare, only a thin slice of fabric parting them. He clutched the smooth globes, and Icarus canted forward, forearms in the mattress on either side of Adam's head, lips where Adam could reach them again. He rolled his hips as he thrust his tongue between Icarus's lips, and Icarus punched back with his own hips, with fangs that descended in the midst of the messy, claiming kiss.

And nicked Adam's lip.

Icarus jerked back, nostrils flaring, eyes zeroing in on the drop of blood Adam could feel welling. He started to blink, to lock down his senses. He hadn't needed to do that last night, and Adam didn't want him to do that now. He trusted him. But more than that, he wanted Icarus with him fully, all of his senses firing, same as Adam's. He grasped Icarus's chin. "Don't. Stay here with me. All of you."

Icarus's gaze remained locked with Adam's, not once straying back to the blood. Not even when their pulses synched like they had that night a week ago in the club. "I need all of you too."

Letting some of the heat flow from his core, trusting himself and the Devil with Icarus, Adam coasted his hands up Icarus's flanks, warming the cool skin. Icarus groaned and sank down onto him, burying his face in the crook of his neck. "Fuck, that feels good."

Adam wrapped his other leg around Icarus, their cocks snug, and they rocked together, Adam touching every part of Icarus he could reach, Icarus nuzzling his neck, the ridges of his forehead, his cool breath, the press of his lips and the tips of his fangs teasing.

But never a bite.

And yet not a single muscle Adam coasted his hands over was rigid. Icarus had melted under his touch, the predator's body fully relaxed. Everything but his stiff cock rutting against Adam's. The care—the trust—in Adam, in himself, fired all of Adam's senses, stoking the fire and his desire higher.

His heart tumbled head over heels.

Icarus kissed a trail along his jaw. "I can't hurt you."

With his fangs, no, Adam believed it, but this had gone past physical, past instincts, since that first night in his Terrace bathroom, when Icarus had run his fingers through his hair and wrapped safety and intimacy around him for the first time in a decade. Had re-awoken Gabriel from where Adam had buried him deep inside. He didn't think he could go without it again. He drew back enough to meet Icarus's gaze, not hiding anything from him, putting it all out there like he used to. "I think maybe you can hurt me more than anyone."

Icarus wiped away a tear Adam hadn't realized he'd shed. "I won't let anyone hurt you. Especially me."

Adam smiled, a forgotten reflex a week ago, same as joking, which he felt compelled to do then to lighten the suddenly heavy mood. "Unless I ask you to," he said with a slow roll of his hips.

Icarus smirked. "Not right now." He canted sidewise, reached into the bag beside the bed, and retrieved a bottle of lube. Righting himself, he tossed it on the bed, then clasped each of Adam's wrists and spread his arms, pinning him to the bed. "Just let me worship you." He coasted his own hands down Adam's torso and rose on his knees. "Let me drown in this heat, in everything I feel for you, before you run off and do something foolish and heroic."

Adam chuckled. "How about you be heroic and give me your dick?"

Icarus was in his face faster than Adam could inhale. "I'll give you my dick when I'm good and ready." He drew back enough to splay his palms on Adam's chest, nails lightly scratching. "And if all this heat is any indication, I'm not gonna last that long once I'm inside you, so I'm going to make sure you're good and ready first."

Adam keened, tried to bow, then shuddered with need as Icarus used his strength to keep his back flat to the bed. Keeping one palm at the center of his chest, Icarus retracted the claws on the other and deftly flipped open Adam's fly. He shifted enough to shove Adam's jeans and boxers down, and Adam kicked them the rest of the way off. Then, in a sight Adam would never forget for the rest of his life, Icarus hitched up his skirt and shoved aside the strappy front of his black thong to free his erection. He clasped it in his hand with Adam's, stroked them together, and that was all Adam saw, his eyes rolling back in his head from sensation overload.

He wanted to writhe, but Icarus wouldn't let him, holding him firmly to the bed with his hand, forcing all of Adam's pleasure, all of his heat into one point. He slapped the bed with his outstretched hand. "Fucking hell, Icarus." He fisted the sheets. "I'm ready, I'm fucking ready."

"I don't know." He rolled his hips, slowed his strokes, and circled a thumb over their heads, smearing precome. "I could edge you like this for hours." Icarus's shadow darkened the light filtering through his lids, his breath floated over Adam's lips, and the palm on his chest trailed out the length of his arm, clawed fingers weaving over Adam's clenched fist. He continued to stroke with the other. "You would lie here for me like this, all day and night, wouldn't you? Let me take you apart piece by piece?"

"Yes," he said without hesitation.

"I'll give that to you, I promise," Icarus murmured against his lips. "But I want you too bad for that tonight. But I promise, Adam."

He forced his eyes open, gaze snaring the blue one less than an inch away. "Gabriel. My name is Gabriel." If he wasn't already in love with the vampire stretched above him, Icarus's smile, bright and fiery and full of desire, would have pushed Gabriel the rest of the way over. He let more of the leash go. And love tasted fucking divine. Icarus brought their lips together in a plundering kiss, and Gabriel lost himself in the heat that freely flowed, everything he felt for this man rushing to the surface, folded together in fire's wings, in life.

Icarus shuddered, losing his rhythm, face buried in the crook of Gabriel's neck again, and Gabriel held him close until Icarus regained his composure and lifted onto his forearms. He stroked Gabriel's temples in time with their heartbeats, and Gabriel laid himself bare, hiding nothing, same as Icarus who looked every bit the predator except for the love swirling in his eyes. He lightly brushed their lips together once more. "I promise, Gabriel."

And fuck if Gabriel didn't want to live long enough for Icarus to fulfill that promise. He smiled again. "I'll hold you to that."

Another big smile from Icarus, free and uninhibited, then fast on joy's heels, a tsunami of desire. And in a flash, Gabriel was on his stomach, his hips hitched, ass in the air, lube trickling down his crack and into his hole. Icarus pushed in a slick finger and worked him open. Fabric ripped behind him, and then all of Icarus's bare flesh covered his backside, dick making a sticky mess of his ass cheek, fingers making a slippery mess of his hole, lips down his spine making a gooey mess of his insides. Gabriel hung his head, panting, so tempted to reach down and clasp his own dick, but not until Icarus was inside him. "Now, baby, please."

He whimpered as Icarus withdrew his fingers, but the emptiness only lasted a second before Icarus slid in, whimpering himself. "Fuck, Gabriel, you feel so good." He slid them both down onto their sides, joined, a knee under Gabriel's to keep it lifted, to keep him open for the slow, long thrusts, while every other part of Icarus wrapped around him. Gabriel returned the hug, letting the leash go completely, letting the fire wrap them up and carry them into oblivion together.

THIRTY-FIVE

GABRIEL WOKE SLOWLY, at peace with the fire inside him for the first time in ten years. Sharing it with someone, basking in it, not fighting it as he gave all of himself to Icarus had made him feel whole. He was left with a comforting warmth inside him instead of the crater that had smoldered for a decade. It had made him consider what he and Mary had talked about yesterday. Maybe the magic inside him wasn't the fiery death sentence he'd always assumed was his fate. At least not yet. Not with Icarus by his side.

"Gabriel."

Gabriel flipped over under the sheets, planted a hand in the mattress, and vaulted his torso up. Mary stood in the doorway, a folded piece of paper dangling from her fingertips.

Wait . . . "Where's Icarus?"

She crossed the bunk room and handed him the folded paper. *Gabriel* was scribbled on the front, and though he'd never seen Icarus's handwriting before, Gabriel knew the note was from him.

His stomach sank and his pulse pounded in his ears as he

shifted on the bed, legs hanging off the side under the sheet. He flipped open the paper. *My name is Icarus for a reason.*

"He flew too close to the sun," Mary said.

But Gabriel's mind had rewound to last night, to Icarus straddling his hips, gliding his hands over him. *Let me drown in this heat, in everything I feel for you, before you run off and do something foolish and heroic.*

Except it hadn't been Gabriel who'd run off to do something foolish and heroic.

I won't let anyone hurt you.

His name was Icarus for a reason.

"He left this for me."

Gabriel looked up and found Mary close with another note she held out to him.

Protect him.

The notes slipped from his fingers, and he curled over his knees, fighting back fear, tears, and the fire that licked across his skin, that raged in his core.

"Stop fighting it." Her voice was close, her presence washing over him as she laid a hand on his knee. "Use it. Use the fire. Help me protect *him.*"

Gabriel lifted his head but continued to keep the core of him buried, the fire scorching his throat as he croaked, "How?"

She crouched in front of him. "Icarus has gone inside. He'll do the job the DA wouldn't. Put Vincent in a place where we—you—can end him. We have to be ready."

"Vincent will see right through him."

"Give my brother more credit." She smirked. "Sure, the plan will go sideways because he's Icarus, but he'll get us ninety percent of the way there."

"I can't let anything happen to him. I just . . ." He gulped, floundering helplessly in this sea of emotions. "I lo—"

"Nope," she cut him off. "Save it for him. Save *Gabriel* for him. I need Adam. I need the Devil. I need the phoenix."

Gabriel closed his eyes once more and rested his head on his knees. One breath, two breaths. He let the memories of Icarus in his arms wash over him and tucked Gabriel into a warm safe space with them. Then he let the phoenix inside him stretch its wings, harnessed the fire, and honed it into an arrow.

The Devil straightened and opened his eyes. "Let's end this. Once and for all."

PART THREE

ICARUS

THIRTY-SIX

ICARUS STOOD beside the same bench where he'd waited for Paris last week, tugging at the sleeves of his too-small suit jacket. The whole damn suit was too small, the Italian threads snug across his biceps, back, and thighs, and good fucking luck buttoning the jacket, even wearing Adam's favorite slinky top underneath. But at two in the morning, Icarus's only option had been Cormac's closet, and he hadn't had time for sartorial debate. He'd zipped in, grabbed a laundry bag, and zipped out before the raven woke.

If he was going to get past the porter of the glitzy high-rise across the street, he needed to look the part. Sure, the pink hair might give him away, but it was all about confidence, right? And he had that.

Confidence that he'd done the right thing, leaving Gabriel sleeping peacefully in his bed.

Confidence that he had the love of a good man he'd do anything to protect and keep in this world with him.

Confidence that this was the only way to do that.

Was he confident this would go as planned? Hell no, but he

was confident it would buy time for her and Adam, because the Devil was who he needed right now. Enough time for them, together with Cormac and Robin, to secure Paris and to be ready for when Icarus delivered them Vincent on a silver platter.

Granted, it was tempting to scale the high-rise's facade, sneak in a window, and rip Vincent's head off himself, but there were three problems with that plan: one, Icarus didn't know which window; two, he doubted he could get past who knew how many guards; and three, it wouldn't give the people he loved the closure they needed. Also, information. Vincent had it; they could always use more of it.

He glanced up and judged the location of the constellations. He had two or so hours left before sunup, before she and Adam would wake, read his notes, and realize he was gone. He didn't have time to waste.

He crossed the street and made it as far as the sidewalk before running into an invisible wall. A magical shield. "Fuck!" He contemplated vamping out and trying to slice through it, but that would stop this party before it even started.

The willowy woman beside the door glared his direction. "May I help you?"

Snotty with a side of static, as if the wall of magic acted like a speaker. Lovely. Icarus barely resisted rolling his eyes. "I have a meeting with Atlas." He doubted saying Vincent would get him anywhere. Vincent would put his guests on the books, and as a human, no matter how criminal, he was less likely to have visitors at four in the morning. But the kinky warlock, Vincent's right hand—that tracked. And if Cormac was correct, if Atlas had missed landing kill strikes at the Canyon Lands, if he'd really turned her over yesterday without caveats and conditions, said kinky warlock was their best bet.

"Your name?"

"Icarus."

Minutes later, the elevator doors inside the lobby opened and Atlas strode out, looking morning fresh in a crisp navy suit that fit him like a glove. He smiled at the receptionist inside, said something, then with a wave of his hand, a shimmering soft spot appeared in the shield. Icarus walked through it, the magic prickling across his skin like it did sometimes in her presence.

The porter, a shifter of some sort Icarus could smell, approached. "I have orders to search you."

Icarus didn't give her any hassle, just spread his legs and held out his arms. He had no phone on him and no weapons other than those magic had bestowed, which he assumed the porter knew, given her watchful approach. "I won't bite, promise."

The porter remained alert as she patted him down then, satisfied with finding nothing, rose and held the physical door open for him. "He's clean," she reported to a waiting Atlas.

"Thank you, gorgeous," Icarus replied, tone sweet as honey, as he stepped over the threshold.

Atlas's tone wasn't nearly as saccharine. "You're late," he snapped.

Icarus smirked and gave a showy little shimmy. "For a very important date."

Atlas rolled his eyes. "Follow me." He nodded at the receptionist, another shifter, then led Icarus to the elevator, murmuring under his breath, "Not a word."

Easy enough as Icarus was too busy holding his breath,

avoiding warlock stench the entire ride to the top floor. He followed a stalking Atlas out of the cab, across the hall, and into a pitifully bland condo. All metal, glass, and black leather, ultramodern with no color, barely lived in with zero personality. The appearance Atlas portrayed ninety-nine percent of the time. The warlock stopped in front of the living room's giant floor-to-ceiling windows and spun to face him, the vivid forest in his eyes giving away the other one percent. "What the fuck are you doing here?"

"My job," Icarus said as he stepped past him to look out the windows, the view of the ocean and coastline to die for, even at this dark hour. If he had to guess, Vincent occupied the end unit next door, the family and guards the other two units on the floor. He drew the map in his head while continuing to speak to Atlas. "I may be a few days late, but I can deliver the Devil. I'm here to tell Vincent where he is."

"We know where he is. Monte Corvo."

"Which we proved your forces can't infiltrate."

"We," Atlas scoffed.

Ignoring the slither of truth, Icarus turned and leaned back against the window casing. "And that was before the entire pack and every fucking corvid in Talahalusi descended on that knobby hill."

Atlas closed the distance between them and grasped Icarus's chin, holding it between his thumb and forefinger. "Fuck me first."

"No."

"That's what I thought."

Icarus wrenched his chin free. "Last time we did that, it ended with you threatening to strangle my cock and tear my ass apart. I wouldn't fuck you again if you were the last person on earth."

"You're lying."

"I most certainly am not."

"About why you're here."

He firmed his jaw and lifted his chin. Confidence. "I will deliver the Devil to your boss. I think he'd want to hear that."

"We have other priorities now." Atlas brushed past him, crossing the cavernous space to the kitchen, his loafers thunking with each step.

Icarus's heels were louder, pinging the marble as he followed. He leaned a hip against the marble island. "*We* who?"

Atlas opened the freezer and withdrew a bottle of vodka and two frosty shot glasses. "*We* as in everyone but you," he said as he filled the glasses to the brim.

Icarus laughed. "I have more at stake than all of you." He held up his glass, and Atlas clicked his against the rim. "Two teams," he said after a sip. "One goes after the coven, the other after Adam Devlin."

"And which one would Vincent and I be on?"

"The latter, of course. I assume Vincent wants to be as done with Adam as Adam wants to be with him, and that after the last time, Vincent wouldn't trust anyone else to do the job."

"Your assumptions are correct." The evil bastard himself stepped out from a shadowed hallway. Vincent wasn't as put together as Atlas, dressed in wrinkled slacks and an under-shirt, but the way he carried himself, and the leather shoulder harness packing two revolvers, put off strong I-do-evil vibes. As did the terrifying thirst for power that still swirled in his lovely brown eyes. Such a fucking waste. "Why should I trust you?" Vincent asked as he joined them at the island. "You fought with Devlin at the Canyon Lands and at Monte Corvo."

"You sent me to him for a reason. To Adam Devlin, knowing I'd be the one who could draw out Gabriel Levin." Vincent's eyes widened, a flash of surprise, then one corner of his mouth ticked up, the hint of a victorious smile. Icarus tossed back the rest of his shot. "Do you care if you lost a few soldiers in the process?"

"You cost me power."

"You stop the Devil, and no one will ever stop you from gaining power again."

Vincent claimed Atlas's empty glass and held it out for Atlas to pour a shot. He eyed Icarus over the rim as he sipped the cold liquid. "I may have misjudged you."

"Most people do, and I wasn't exactly on equal footing last time we met." He cut a glare at Atlas, then snapped his gaze back to Vincent when the boss man slammed his empty glass on the counter.

"Don't mistake this for equal footing now." He jammed a finger in Icarus's chest. "You're bait, plain and simple, and I won't hesitate to throw you to the coyotes."

Confidence waning, Icarus averted his gaze and gulped. Vincent took it as the sign of obedience he wanted. He threw the glass back at Atlas, who deftly caught it, then turned on his heel, heading for what Icarus guessed was an internal door with direct access to Atlas's unit. "Ping the hacker bitch," he tossed over his shoulder to Atlas. The only thing that stopped Icarus from snarling was Atlas's heel digging into his foot. "Get us that coven location. We hit them first, bank the power, then there's no way the Devil escapes. But come fuck me first."

Icarus waited for the door to slam, sniffed to make sure the human was gone, only warlock stench remaining, then shook off Atlas's foot. He shot out a hand for the vodka, then cursed because he was shaking too badly to actually hold the fucking bottle.

Cool as the liquid itself, Atlas refilled both glasses. He handed one to Icarus and held his out for a toast.

Icarus clinked rims, then tossed his back in one go. He needed confidence from somewhere else now because his own was fucking shot, every drop of it spent staring down the real devil. "I don't know what you're playing at, Mr. Magic, but if you hurt her, I will help the coyote rip you limb from limb."

Atlas threw back his shot, then pitched the glass in the porcelain sink, shattering it. "You're not the only one doing what he must to save the ones he loves." On the heels of that truth bomb, Atlas stepped around him, and with the kind of uncharacteristic abandon Icarus was more used to seeing when he was in buckles and kilts, Atlas ripped off his jacket and tie, slung them in the direction of the couch, and snapped his fingers, disappearing to Icarus figured he knew where. He also figured, for the first time, that Atlas wasn't happy about it. That maybe he had the warlock all wrong.

THIRTY-SEVEN

ATLAS RETURNED several hours later through whatever internal passage Icarus hadn't bothered to investigate since Vincent and the warlock had vanished. The shower kicked on, and Icarus kicked into gear, putting into action the plan he'd concocted while watching the sky lighten and the moon descend toward the ocean. The eggs were almost done, the bacon sizzling, the leftover naan resuscitating in the oven, when Atlas emerged from his shower twenty minutes later in a fresh charcoal suit, looking like his usual wound-too-tight self. "I like you better in buckles and kilts," Icarus said as he turned the heat off the eggs.

"So do I," Atlas replied, and Icarus nearly lost his spatula, the truth unexpected. "But that's neither here nor there." The dejection in Atlas's voice was even more startling, but he didn't give Icarus time to dwell, shuffling to a stop beside him. "What're you doing?"

"Well," Icarus said with a flourish of the wily spatula, "once I realized all your windows are tinted and that you may not be as evil as you want everyone to think, I cooked breakfast. Also masks the warlock smell."

"There's an express meal in the fridge."

"Yes, which I already ate. You also have eggs and cheese"—he pointed at the skillet on the stove—"and bacon"—at the sheet pan of greasy goodness—"and naan"—at the toaster oven.

"We don't have time for breakfast."

By the time Atlas had retrieved one of those disgustingly bland protein shakes from the fridge, Icarus had, at full speed, retrieved the naan and filled two folded pieces with eggs and bacon. He knocked the still unopened drink from Atlas's hand and shoved a breakfast wrap into it instead. "Eat it while we go wherever it is we need to go in a hurry."

Atlas warily eyed the food. "Is it poisoned?"

Icarus picked up his own and munched through it.

"You're a vampire. Even if it was, you wouldn't die."

"Oh, for fuck's sake, Atlas, just eat the damn food."

Atlas grudgingly took a bite, then turned for the door and took a few more, his satisfied little hum making Icarus smile. They made their way to the unit at the opposite end of the floor from Vincent's. Atlas knocked twice, then entered. Icarus followed him inside to what could only be described as a command center. Most of the unit's walls had been blown out, the space a true cavern, with only a kitchen and bathroom for dedicated areas. Two cots were shoved in the corner furthest from the windows, while the rest of the open space was occupied by desks, computers, and monitoring equipment.

And paranormals. No other humans. Vampires, shifters, and the warlock from the strike on Monte Corvo. Still pissed off it seemed, magic shimmering in the air when he spied

Icarus. Atlas moved between them, facing Icarus, as he popped the last bite of breakfast sandwich into his mouth. "Tell us where you'll deliver Devlin."

Icarus cocked a brow. "You're licking your fucking fingers, and I don't even get a thank you?"

"Icarus."

Cocked a hip too.

"Fine, thank you, now"—he gestured at the giant map on one wall—"where will you deliver Devlin?"

Icarus stepped around the angry, angry warlocks and studied the map, assuming that was what Atlas-the-not-so-evil wanted. It took a minute for the picture to resolve—to understand that each pin color meant a different source of paranormal power, to realize Vincent was sucking that power from covens, packs, and loners all over the area, creating a vortex at the center right over YB—and less than a second to determine they had to kill Vincent Cirillo.

ASAP.

"Where, Icarus?"

He composed his face, turned, and shrugged, flip as he could seem. "The Canyon Lands, of course."

Atlas raked a hand through his hair, disrupting the blond coif. "Fucking vampire."

Icarus wrinkled his nose. "Not right now, baby." Sparring with him was almost as fun as sparring with Robin. Come to think of it, watching the two of them spar would be epic, assuming they didn't kill each other first. But first, they had to kill Vincent, which maybe Atlas was keen to help them do, which meant maybe Icarus shouldn't piss him off. He dropped the teasing act and channeled a little Adam. "And not there, really. Devlin would suspect something. Club Sutro, where we met."

Atlas stepped closer to one of the other shifters in the room. "Buy the place out for tomorrow night."

While they coordinated, Icarus continued to take everything in before they wised up and threw him out. He drifted toward the vampire who had multiple books open on her desk and a smaller area map with green dots—same as the green pins on the larger map. "Is this what you have on the covens so far?"

"*She* sent us locations this morning," Atlas answered him. Icarus didn't miss the emphasis he'd put on the first word; he knew. But how much? Before Icarus could contemplate further, Atlas held a sheet of paper out to him. "She also sent us this."

It was an email from an alias account he recognized. One that would ping an IP address in Portola, making it seem like she was still there. No subject line. Only one line of text in the message.

tsaEehtnIyL enoloSebotho

"We're working it as a cypher," Atlas said. "To get an exact location."

Icarus laughed. "Stop trying so hard."

The other vampire twisted in her chair. "What's that supposed to mean?"

"I had this client once. Also a hacker." Not really. It was his sister who loved these games, always had. For her protection, he shifted the facts a bit as he explained. "Everything was a fucking riddle. Like the fact he dealt in code all day meant he had to make everyone else work for it too. But with words. He'd give me these rhymes about what he wanted—"

"Icarus!" Atlas snapped, his green eyes practically glowing.

"Reverse it, then read it. 'Oh, to be so lonely in the east.' Then take out the extra space. Ohlone in the East. The Ohlone shellmound in Encinal," Icarus said as he gestured at a location near the concentration of green dots on the other side of the Bay. "Everyone knows it's haunted."

"Recon," Atlas ordered the other warlock. "Go, and take a few shifters with you," he added with a jut of his chin to the dog of some sort that was working the Sutro angle. "Take over for her," he told the vampire.

"Are we sure—" the other magician started.

"No, which is the point of recon, and we're burning daylight, so go." The second of hesitation among the soldiers was enough to blow Atlas's gaskets. "Move!"

Everyone jumped, including Icarus. While the rest of the room scurried into action, Atlas spun back to him and snatched the email from his hand. "We hit the coven tonight, and you're coming with us."

"Wouldn't miss it for the world."

Especially the part where Adam and company intercepted Vincent on the Huchiun Enclave, the Ohlone Island halfway between Yerba Buena and Encinal.

Isle in the Middle.

The message in the message she'd sent. The message meant for him.

THIRTY-EIGHT

ICARUS'S BONES rattled as the gas-guzzling SUV he rode in with Vincent and Atlas and the grumpy warlock whose name he'd learned was Brock rumbled onto the decrepit auto bridge that spanned the Bay between YB and Encinal. Most folks who traveled from one side of the Bay to the other took the light rail. Several miles north, it crossed the Bay at an angle, covering more distance and connecting more stable areas of land. Their caravan, by contrast, was going from one iffy piece of land to another iffy piece of land over the iffiest of iffiest auto bridges left. No other cars dared travel on it, but what choice did they have? Vincent had insisted they roll out with a fleet of gas-powered SUVs, one in front of theirs, two behind them, so there they were, traversing a crumbling metal and cement mass that was one good shake from annihilation.

Icarus was tempted to extend his arm out the window, dig his claws into one of the pylons, and scream through the pain for her to take it all down. Impossible, unfortunately, with his wrists in Atlas's favorite pair of silver cuffs, looped through the passenger door handle to further restrict his movement. At least the asshole had divested him of the too-tight suit coat and wrapped it around his wrists, preventing the cuffs from burning through Icarus's pants where his hands rested in his lap. Trapped, Icarus waited and watched, keeping his ears on Vincent and Atlas behind him, one eye on Brock the Rock beside him, and the rest of his attention on the road ahead.

On the island in the middle of the bridge's span from which Adam and his team would launch their surprise attack.

"You seem tense," Vincent said.

Icarus twisted as much as the cuffs would allow. "I'm in a tank, in a line of tanks, on a bridge that could fall into the Bay at any second. Of course I'm fucking tense."

"But I heard you could fly."

Three days ago. No time at all, and yet it felt like a lifetime had passed since he'd taken the biggest—best—gamble of his life. He'd stared down at a smiling Adam, borrowed some of his confidence, and leapt, skipping across the water with the Devil in his arms, all the way across the Bay and north. He'd used the last of his Daylight and had risked exposure and death because Adam was worth it. Had proven as much every day since. Unlike the power-hungry murderer in the back seat. "You're not worth flying for."

Vincent laughed, and Icarus slumped in his seat, focused instead on appearing calm as they approached the quarter-mile tunnel that cut through the rocky outcrop that had survived the Rift. The neighboring isle had not, but Huchiun's bedrock—its spirit and ghosts—had held firm, prickling as they drove beneath the tunnel's arch and lifting the hairs on Icarus's arms. Atlas stopped speaking midsentence, Brock clutched the wheel so tight it creaked, and Icarus straightened in his seat. Not appearing tense flew out the window.

Vincent noticed. "What's going on?" he asked, a rare quiver to his voice. "What's that smell?"

"Hush," Atlas ordered his master in a rare show of defiance.

"Consecrated ground," Icarus said. "It doesn't like you."

"Wha—"

The tunnel lights flickered.

A flash of green.

The car slowed.

Icarus steeled himself for the pain that would come from yanking against the cuffs.

The van behind them blew its horn, and Brock hit the gas. Icarus slammed back against his seat, and in the back, Vincent cursed. "Dammit, Brock!"

Atlas slapped the back of Brock's headrest. "Go!"

Brock kept his foot on the gas, hurtling them through the short tunnel, so close to the lead van that Icarus couldn't see the other SUV's tires. Adam would have to time the attack just right. As the end of the tunnel neared, Icarus mentally ran through the possibilities.

A road blockade.

An assault from above.

An explosion, man- or magic-made.

Flickering median lamps outside the tunnel reflected off the roof of the lead car, then on the hood of their SUV, climbing the windshield.

They cleared the tunnel.

The cuffs around his wrists disappeared.

And then . . . nothing.

Their SUV continued charging forward, and it took everything in Icarus to not whip around in his seat and glance back, to confirm with his own eyes, what his mind was telling him. That Adam had deserted him. That he'd read her message wrong.

His heart rebelled.

His heart.

He closed his eyes and blocked out the other voices and heartbeats in the car, the rumble of tires over uneven concrete, the waves crashing below, and searched for Adam's heartbeat.

Nothing.

He opened his eyes and shifted enough to see in the rearview mirror, the most he could do without being obvious.

Nothing still.

Just Vincent in the back seat, turned the way Icarus wanted to be, staring back at the now-deserted tunnel. "What the fuck was that?"

Bright green eyes clashed with Icarus's in the mirror. Atlas was as confused as him as to why they were still moving forward without incident. His calm and even voice, however, didn't give his shock away. "Like Icarus said, consecrated ground. Prepare for more of the same at the shellmound."

Would the attack happen there? Icarus didn't think so. He didn't think she would risk the coven or the remains of the Indigenous people buried there either. What the fuck was going on?

Twenty minutes later, Vincent was screaming the same in his face, Icarus shoved against the side of the SUV, all of Vincent's soldiers in a line behind their boss, ready to tear Icarus apart as soon as Vincent gave the order. "I told Atlas you were a spy. That you were still working with Devlin."

"How do you get that?" Icarus shouted back. "Do you see him anywhere?" He would have spread his arms if he could, but the cuffs had rematerialized as soon as they'd reached the end of the bridge.

"I don't see *anyone*!" Vincent roared as he did what Icarus couldn't, spreading his arms and gesturing at the deserted mound of earth behind them. The grass had grown over the layers and layers of shells and bones; this was one of the Ohlone tribe's largest ancient burial sites, seemingly undisturbed by witches or otherwise. "You lied to us about the message, about the coven being here."

Icarus glared over his shoulder at Brock. "You and your recon team detected activity here earlier today, didn't you?"

Vincent wasn't hearing any of it. "You told them to leave."

"When?" Icarus shrieked. He glanced at Brock again, then at Atlas. "When was I alone today?"

Vincent held a hand out behind him. "Stake."

"Vincent," Atlas started.

"Mind your place."

Atlas promptly shut his mouth, back under his master's thrall.

Fuck!

"Someone give me a fucking stake!" Vincent roared again.

The vampire from earlier slapped one into his palm. Fucking traitor. Vincent firmed his grip on the thicker end and drew back his arm.

Icarus closed his eyes and recalled the warmth that had enveloped him last night. Thanked whatever fate had put Adam—Gabriel—in his path and prayed the Devil would keep his sister safe when he was gone.

"Boss," Brock spoke up. "I don't think we're alone."

Icarus popped open his eyes and scanned their dark surroundings. No one in sight.

Caw.

He looked up and gasped. Crows were perched on every roof and eave of the buildings bordering the streets that surrounded the shellmound.

Watching. Waiting.

"Remember what you said this morning," Atlas spoke evenly, as if any inflection would shatter the eerie stillness, would turn whatever was going on here into the battle they'd all anticipated. "He's bait. They're watching him. For the Devil." Vincent's raised arm wavered. Atlas continued to press. "We can regroup and use him like we always intended. We can end this, and then no one will stop you from sucking the coven dry."

Vincent lowered his arm but didn't step back. Didn't give an inch as he seethed in Icarus's face. "Club Sutro, tomorrow night." His brown eyes hardened, and Icarus didn't think he'd ever consider the color lovely again. "You'll die beside him if it's the last thing I do."

THIRTY-NINE

ICARUS FELT MARGINALLY SAFER on the return trip to YB. Yes, his life was more in danger than ever, but with two fewer tanks in their caravan, crossing the auto bridge didn't feel like the same death sentence it had the first time. Vincent had left one van of shifters behind to monitor the shellmound, had ordered one north to monitor Monte Corvo, and had taken the wheel of their van headed back to YB. They were in the middle, Vincent riding the bumper of the lead van driven by Brock. Vincent was paying little attention to the van behind them, unlike Atlas, who had spent extra time securing it before they'd left Encinal and was spending extra energy guarding it still, if the raised hairs on Icarus's arms and the weakened cuffs around his wrists were any indication.

Maybe that was why Atlas missed it.

Or maybe it was Vincent, in all his awful alphaness, cursing the lead car for driving too slow.

Or maybe it was just the shitty, buckled road beneath their wheels.

Whatever it was, the other two beings in the car with Icarus missed the shimmer of green as they entered the tunnel, the water stains on the cement roof that had been dry less than an hour ago, the sway of the island itself. Warning signs that would have cautioned against swerving out from behind the lead car and charging ahead.

Right into a wall of water that crashed over their SUV, that blanketed the windshield and sent them fishtailing across the bridge.

"Fuck!" Vincent cursed as he fought the wheel for control. "Hold on!"

But he was no match for her strength, for the coven she'd spared, for the spirits and ghosts who'd heeded her call and whipped the Bay around them into a frenzy. Walls of water hundreds of feet high splashed onto the already uneven surface, the entire decaying structure swaying. What had been a dark quiet night when they'd entered the tunnel had, a quarter mile later, turned into a maelstrom.

"We can't make it across the span to the other side!" Atlas shouted. "Reverse! Go back!"

"Make this stop!" Vincent countered as he continued to fight the skid. "Do something!"

"Take your foot off the gas and your hands off the wheel!"

"Why would I do that?"

When Vincent didn't comply, Atlas cut a look at Icarus in the back seat, and the next instant, the cuffs around Icarus's wrists were gone. Springing into action, Icarus reached both arms around the driver's seat from behind and clutched Vincent's biceps, yanking his hands off the wheel.

Vincent tried to wrestle free. "Let me go!"

Icarus wrapped his arms fully around Vincent and jerked him higher in the seat, pulling his feet off the pedals too, the car decelerating but still spinning out of control. "I've got him! Stop the car!"

Atlas splayed a hand on the inside of the SUV's roof and cast a spell that created a sparkling green dome over the vehicle. With his other hand, he yanked up the parking brake lever, and finally, fucking finally, the car slowed its skid—until a blast of power pummeled Atlas's shield, shoving their vehicle back toward the tunnel and the two other SUVs who'd wisely stopped before hitting the storm.

"Who's doing that?" Vincent yelled, fear creeping beneath the shock and anger. "I can't see!"

Atlas put a hand to the windshield, and a gap in the wall of water appeared.

So did the Devil.

Icarus had never seen a sexier sight.

Adam stood at the head of the pack, wind-whipped and rain-soaked, his arms extended, his hands flexed. Despite the water, an aura of glowing orange and red swirled around him and over his skin. Like the kid he'd rescued a week ago, but controlled, and at max power. Another blast of that power rocked the SUV, stronger this time without the water filtering it. Strong enough to slam their SUV back into the lead one Vincent had so foolishly passed, all three cars in the caravan piling up inside the tunnel.

"What's he doing?" Vincent said, fighting against Icarus's hold. "How's he doing this?"

"You never wondered how he survived that fire?" Atlas said, voice deathly calm. "The ultimate power was right under your nose for ten fucking years, and you never figured it out." But Atlas had. Same as he'd apparently figured out how to thwart his master's thrall, if he'd ever been under it at all. With one snap, he was gone, only green mist floating where he'd been a blink ago in the passenger seat.

Icarus twisted in his seat, leaving one arm around Vincent. Sure enough, green light appeared in the rear car, and a second later, it was gone again—with someone else, Icarus suspected —but he didn't have long to contemplate. With Atlas and the mysterious person off the scene, the dome over their SUV shattered, and with it, Icarus's temporary view of Adam, water and rain obscuring the tunnel entrance once again. He reached out with his senses, found the heartbeat he'd know anywhere, and latched on.

A guide for Adam, a constant for Icarus, and a silent, shouted warning for any paranormal on the scene who dared lay a hand on his mate.

Vincent fought harder in his arms. "Let me go!"

Icarus did no such thing. He leaned forward and whispered in his ear, "You underestimated him too."

Glass shattered, metal crunched, and the driver's side door was wrenched open. Vincent yelped. "It's me, boss," Brock shouted over the thundering storm. "We gotta go." He summoned a blue orb and flung it in Icarus's direction. Icarus released Vincent and ducked, barely avoiding the sizzling ball of magic, and foolishly turning his back on the door, which was yanked open by someone else. Strong arms banded around Icarus and dragged him out of the car.

Icarus sniffed. One of Vincent's shifters, a horse of some sort. As soon as his feet hit the ground, Icarus bent at the waist, trying to leverage the shifter over him, but the horse had at least fifty pounds on him. Icarus was also fighting at half attention, the other half on Vincent and Brock still arguing beside them.

"We stay!" Vincent wrestled out of Brock's hold and lunged for his shoulder harness tucked in the side door compartment. "We can fight them."

"We don't have the power anymore." Brock pointed toward the third car. "Atlas took him."

What power? Whoever Atlas disappeared with? Was that the juice Vincent was using to keep Atlas and the rest of the paranormals under his thrall? How had Atlas broken through? Had the others? Was it just blind loyalty keeping Brock and the others by his side?

"We don't need him," Vincent countered, the awful lust for power back in his voice. "Not if we can get the Devil. I want his power." He finished readying his pistols and swung his gaze in Icarus's direction. Nope, nothing lovely about those brown eyes anymore. "And we use him as bait."

Icarus kicked and clawed to no avail.

"We need to go back the way we came!" Brock urged. "It's the only way out."

"Cirillo!" The Devil's shout echoed through the tunnel.

Vincent stiffened, and so did Brock and the shifter holding Icarus, all of them turning toward Adam's voice. Toward the army bearing down on them. Adam stood at the center, a gun in one hand, a throwing star in the other, with Robin and Jenn in their massive coyote forms on either side of him and flanked by Abigail and Cormac in human form. Ten more of the pack were behind them, some shifted, some not, the latter heavily armed. Jenn and Abigail had salvaged a lot from Adam's armory—guns, crossbows, knives, and more.

Compared to Vincent and his army of eight, the odds favored Adam. Icarus smiled, and Adam grinned right back before shifting his burning blue-gray gaze to Vincent. "You have someone I belong to. I need him back."

"So trade yourself," Vincent postured. "I'll let him go if you come with us."

"Not a chance, and not a chance you're going anywhere either." He lifted the throwing star and twirled it between his fingers. Icarus counted at least three bone-cracking shifts and as many guns cocking behind him, all aimed at Adam. But Adam only had eyes for him. "Hey, baby, someone's waiting for your SOS." He flicked his gaze to the ground a half second before the throwing star came hurtling the direction of Icarus's captor. In that same half second, Icarus blinked off his senses and prepared for the splatter of blood that coated the side of his face, avoiding the instinctive distraction so that as soon as the shifter's arms fell away, Icarus could drop to a knee, flatten his palm on the ground, and ask his sister for help.

She delivered, shaking the ground so hard the rest of the bridge behind Vincent's caravan collapsed into the Bay, the thunderous booms of cement and metal crashing into the water echoing through the tunnel and driving the waves over the remaining half of the bridge higher. The span behind Adam stretching to YB swayed in an unsteady, disquieting fashion. They didn't have long to end this. Icarus spun, claws and fangs out, and hissed in Vincent's direction. "Fuck being your bait."

Vincent raised one pistol, but before he could pull the trigger, a bullet zipped past his nose. Following the path of his shot, Adam and the pack charged. With no way out, Vincent's soldiers did the same, the two groups colliding just inside the tunnel opening. Icarus rolled and came up slashing beside Adam, engaged in hand-to-hand combat with the other vampire from Vincent's crew. Growls and snarls bounced off the cement walls, joined by grunts and shouts as soldiers fought in human form, and the occasional sizzle and pop of magic as Brock hurled orbs of magic from beside Vincent.

Icarus landed a roundhouse that caught the other vampire by surprise. She fell to her knees, and a ready Abigail swung her sword, slicing the vampire's head off, while Cormac shoved a stake into her chest for good measure. The explosion of dust settled just as Robin and Adam neutralized the horse shifter. With Adam in arm's reach, Icarus blinked his senses back on and grabbed him by the coat collar, dragging him in for a quick, hard kiss, the hit of fire and whiskey intoxicating. "How mad at me are you?"

Adam smirked. "It wasn't your worst plan ever."

Robin butted his head between them, and Icarus could have sworn the massive coyote rolled his eyes. He jutted his muzzle Vincent and Brock's direction. Message received. "How do you want to do this?" Icarus asked as Cormac joined their group.

"You two"—Adam gestured at him and Cormac—"distract the wizard long enough for us to get to Vincent."

"Vincent's thrall over them is broken," Icarus said. "Atlas stole the power source on scene. The warlock with Vincent wants to leave. I don't think it'll be hard to separate them."

"You don't know what else Vincent may have over him," Cormac said.

"I doubt it's Armageddon."

And fuck if the coyote didn't grin. So did Adam as he

dragged Icarus in for another too brief, drugging kiss. "Go be a fucking hero."

Using the van as a shield, Icarus and Cormac crept behind it while Adam and Robin charged back into the melee, making steady progress toward Vincent and Brock.

"I can blind him," Cormac said. "But with the wind whipping through here the way it is, it'll only be for a couple seconds."

Icarus nodded. "That's all I need."

They waited for Adam and Robin to be in striking distance before rounding the back of the car, putting them a few feet from Brock and Vincent while still covered on two sides. Icarus protected Cormac's other two while the raven closed his violet eyes and lifted his arms, murmuring in a mishmash of what sounded to Icarus like Gaelic and Wappo, words he didn't understand but that had their intended effect.

A powerful gust of wind howled down the tunnel and on its heels a chorus of *CAWs* and *KRAAs*. A wave of black undulated through the tunnel and spread like a blanket, unfurling more as the birds neared the intended targets. Focused on taking shots at Adam and Robin, Vincent and Brock were too late in noticing the attack at their back. The corvids swooped in between them and around Brock, disorienting the warlock and giving Icarus time to spring through the narrow opening they'd left him.

He wrapped his arms around the warlock and dragged him away from Vincent. "I will give you one chance to run."

The warlock trembled. "He'll come after me. After my family."

Icarus should have known. Blackmail, thy name is Vincent

Cirillo. But those days would be over soon. "He won't live past tonight. Go!"

One snap—small yet sharp in the booming chaos—and all that was left in Icarus's arms was blue mist.

Followed by two gunshots—louder and more deafening than any other noise—and all that was left of Icarus's future crumpled to the ground.

FORTY

MOVING AT FULL SPEED, Icarus reached Adam before his head hit the ground, cradling the precious weight in his hands. He sank behind him and gathered the rest of Adam's torso into his arms. "No, no, no, no, no," he chanted as his hands moved on autopilot, pushing layers of clothes out of the way, searching and finding the gunshot wound to Adam's chest.

Blood and heat flowed through his fingers. Out of Adam. Too much. Too fast. No sign of healing.

Fuck!

He began snatching back the layers of fabric he'd pushed away, pressing them to the wound. He tore off his shirt sleeves and added those to the compress too, plus all the pressure he could exert without breaking Adam's ribs. "Come on, baby. Stay with me."

A dog whined, and Icarus jerked up his gaze, instinctively hissing, warning back any threats. Robin wasn't one, despite his appearance, his fur matted and muzzle bloodied from ripping out Vincent's throat. Deferring, he lowered to his belly at Adam's feet and stared at Icarus with pleading golden eyes.

"Come," Icarus ordered as gently as the panic coursing through him allowed. "Help keep him stable."

Robin carefully stretched alongside Adam's body, gentle but snug. Jennifer mirrored his position on Adam's other side, bumpering him in blond fur. In his pack. "What do you need me to do?" Abigail asked as she crouched beside Icarus.

"I need to get a better look at the wound." He wasn't optimistic, but keeping his mind engaged, his hands working, was the only thing keeping his heart from breaking and the vampire from rampaging. "Apply pressure on the compress," he told her. "I'm going to lift him, check for an exit wound, and if there isn't one, then I need you to slide into my place." He carefully lifted Adam's neck and head and swiped an arm under him, feeling for a tear in the fabric, or viscous blood, or an output of heat. Finding nothing, he scooted the rest of the way out from behind Adam, and Abigail moved into position, cradling his shoulders and head.

He stepped over Robin, who didn't growl or flinch, a testament to how worried he was for his brother-in-law. Kneeling between Adam's legs, Icarus checked him over for any other injuries. The movement was enough to rouse Adam, his blue-gray eyes fluttering open. Hazy with pain, they bounced around, unfocused, before finally landing on Icarus. "Hey, baby." The gurgling roughness of his voice didn't help Icarus's rising panic.

"Don't—" His voice cracked, forcing him to start over, betraying his attempt to play stern. "Don't fucking 'baby' me right now."

"Michael." So soft yet as sharp as any stake to Icarus's heart. "I love you."

Anger flared, Icarus grasping at any emotion other than the soul-crushing despair nipping at his heels. "No!" he snapped. "You do not get to say that to me as you bleed out on a fucking piece of rock in the middle of the fucking Bay. You do not get to quit on me at all. I belong to you too." He moved with every bit of speed magic had gifted him, peeking under the compress and probing the wound. "Fuck, the bullet's still in there." And there was no way he was getting it out without doing more damage. He grabbed the torn shirt sleeves, packed the wound as best he could, then piled the rest of the compress back on and exerted pressure.

Adam grunted, wincing as he lifted a hand to rest on Robin's head. "You need to go." He ran his fingers through the fur between Robin's perked ears. "Get everyone out of here before I flame out."

Icarus understood those words now and hated the inevitably staring him down, the fire that would steal the man he loved and Icarus along with him because in no scenario was Icarus leaving him alone to die. But did he have to? "Is there a way . . ." He cleared his throat. "Like the kid?"

Adam shook his head. "No time." He petted Robin again. "Go, please."

Robin shuffled closer and laid his chin on Adam's shoulder. His woeful, high-pitched whine was the straw that broke the vampire's back. Leaving one hand on the wound, Icarus turned his face away, giving the brothers a moment and giving himself a moment to choke back the threatening sobs.

"I'll tell her," Adam said to Robin. "I promise."

Robin barked, and Icarus righted his gaze. It was too soon;

the sight was no less painful as Robin rose on all fours, leaned over Adam, and licked his face. A final goodbye. Icarus closed his eyes, fighting the wretched misery tearing apart his insides, the scream of hopelessness rumbling up his throat that escaped on a gasp when the coyote's tongue swiped his cheek, licking away the tears he'd shed for their friend. Icarus opened his eyes, meeting the same grief and despair in glowing gold ones. But he also met a promise. "You'll protect her?" Icarus asked.

Robin nodded his big rusty-gold head.

"Thank you."

He backed away slowly, Jenn and Abigail on his heels. Icarus reclaimed his spot behind Adam, cradling his body as he continued to press the soaked pile of clothes to his chest. Adam turned into him, face buried in his neck, the rising heat of his breath carving open that Adam-sized hole in Icarus's chest again. Adam's words, as usual, tore it wider. "You should go too."

"Not a chance," Icarus managed through his tears. "I've never seen a phoenix before."

"You knew?"

He lifted a hand and cupped Adam's cheek, thumb skating his temple, the corner of his eye. "It burned here when we made love." His voice wobbled. "Like it's burning now."

"We burn together."

Icarus leaned over and brushed his lips against Adam's. "I love you too. Thank you for believing in me."

"Thank you for giving me a second chance."

He pressed his forehead against Adam's and braced for the final, searing burst of heat, expecting it to come from the man in his arms. He didn't expect it to come from their sides. Magic popped and sizzled, green mist coalescing into a dome that formed over them, and inside it with them, Atlas, Mary, and Cormac.

Icarus clasped his sister's outstretched hand. "What are you doing here?" He then cut a glare at Atlas. "Why are you with him?"

She laid her other hand atop Icarus's on Adam's chest. "I need you to give him back to me."

He swung his gaze back at her. "What?"

"He either flames out or you give him back to me."

"What are you saying?"

"You are the balance Nature wants," Atlas interjected, explaining. "Life"—he nodded at Adam's prone form in his arms, then at Icarus—"and death. Phoenix and vampire. *That's* why I sent you to him. *You* have to be the one that kills him."

She squeezed his hand. "You're the one who saves him."

"You want me to bite him? To feed?" They nodded, and Icarus's head spun, but not nearly as fast as his heart tumbled. How did the pieces fit together? Were they a sacrifice or something more? Was this hope or a fucking curse? Did any of it matter beyond the love and life of the man in his arms?

"We can't lose another phoenix," she said. "His is the power we need in the coming war."

"We?" he croaked as he gathered Adam closer, protecting him from all possible threats.

She flattened a hand on the green dome, and the magical shield shone so bright Icarus had to slam shut his eyes, stars sparkling behind his lids. "He'll help me channel the power. Back into the life force, back into Nature."

A gentle hand on Icarus's shoulder urged his eyes back open and drew his gaze to the violet one by his side. Sanity in the swirling storm, an ally like he'd been that day in the Canyon Lands. The man in Icarus's arms was his only concern too. "I'll stay with his soul," Cormac said. "Whichever way he chooses."

Fear gripped Icarus's insides and twisted his gut in a stark reminder of that awful feeling from the day he was turned, that awful, heavy emptiness that had invaded his soul and that had only begun to lighten when Adam Devlin crossed his path. No, not only Adam—the Devil and Gabriel too. Especially Gabriel, who had already lost so much. Icarus would not curse that man or any part of the man he loved to more emptiness. Not when it was the antithesis of what he wanted. "What if I turn him?" He'd never bitten anyone before. He didn't know how this fucking worked. Never wanted to. "This, me, eternal life, it's not what he wants. You know that as well as I do. He wants peace. He fucking deserves it."

"So do you." Cormac squeezed his shoulder. "I'll stay with yours too."

Icarus gulped. "Which direction?" The same question he'd posed just days ago. He hadn't imagined they'd be revisiting it so soon.

"Whichever direction the two of you choose."

He flicked his gaze to Mary. Nature was driving the show, but misery shone from his sister's hazel eyes. "I love you," she whispered.

"I love you too, always." He turned his eyes back to the raven, the too-gentle reaper. "Is back here an option?"

Adam shifted in his arms, his lips moving against the underside of Icarus's jaw. "Icarus, it's okay. I'm not afraid anymore. Not with you. Never with you."

"I can't," he choked out on a sob. "I can't hurt you." He

pressed their foreheads together again. "Your soul has hurt enough already."

"Not hurt. Free." He pressed a kiss to the corner of his mouth. "Wherever you are, that's free."

Icarus drew back enough to meet his eyes, the phoenix there glowing red, only a thin ring of blue-gray left at the edge of his fiery irises. Enough of him left for Icarus to beg and plead with, to confess the only truth that mattered. "I love you. I need you to come back to me."

"You come back to me too." One final kiss, his breath searing hot, the phoenix rising, before he leaned his head back and bared his throat, his Adam's apple bobbing around a last whispered "I love you."

Instincts Icarus had ignored the past however many minutes, the past week, the past thirty years rushed to the surface. And for the first time since he'd been turned, he gave in to them. Gave in to the hope of love. Of peace and a place that was free of emptiness. A place for Michael at Gabriel's side, forever.

Icarus sank his fangs into the Devil's neck and flew into the sun.

FORTY-ONE

MICHAEL LOVED FUCKING in the sun. Loved the heat on his skin, the sweat dripping down his spine, the slick glide of his body against Gabriel's flushed and equally sweaty one beneath him.

Correction: Michael loved fucking Gabriel in the sun.

Loved Gabriel, period.

The handsome man beneath him chuckled. "You're drifting again."

Michael smirked. "As long as I drift while riding your dick, do you care?"

"Not a damn bit." Gabriel grasped his hips and thrust up. "But I'm close."

Michael groaned and tipped back his head, savoring every degree of warmth, every inch of fullness, every racing beat of his pulse, and every second of the second chance he and Gabriel had been given.

They had earned it.

Gabriel bent his knees and bumped him forward, chest to

chest as they picked up the pace, rocking their hips faster, Gabriel thrusting deeper. "I need to come, baby."

Michael pushed back on him harder, driving him deeper, as he flattened his palms on either side of his head, wild mustard under his palms and fresh dirt under his short blunt nails, the smell of earth only adding to the intoxicating moment. He buried his face in his lover's neck, adding sweat and lingering whiskey to the scent cocktail, as he kissed and sucked a path to Gabriel's ear. "We come together."

Gabriel snaked his arms around him, sliding one hand down to palm his ass and plowing the other into his hair, fingers curling in the magenta and ginger strands, holding him close from top and bottom. "We burn together."

Michael exploded, spilling hot, sticky come between them, moaning as he rode back onto Gabriel's cock and watched the body beneath his arch so beautifully. Gabriel came soon after with a shout, filling Michael up. Filling his heart and life with so much warmth and love.

Love that had held their souls connected and guided them back to this world together.

As humans.

Sated, Michael splayed out on top of Gabriel, his limbs like jelly, his entire body happy. And too heavy for his wobbly post-orgasmic arms to hold up. Probably too heavy for Gabriel too. He shifted to his side, taking Gabriel with him, one arm over his waist, a leg still thrown over his hip. Gabriel's spent cock slipped out of his ass, and Michael wasn't the least bit embarrassed by his needy little mewl.

Chuckling, Gabriel combed his fingers through his hair, something they both enjoyed almost as much as sex. "I'll give it to you again, I promise."

Michael snuggled closer, ear pressed to Gabriel's chest, listening to the strong, steady beat of his heart. "If it's not cold and rainy on Solstice, I want to spend all day here, just fucking you in the sun."

"Why Solstice?"

"Shortest day of the year. Human recovery time is a bitch."

Gabriel laughed. "Says the twenty-something-year-old with stamina for days. Me, on the other hand . . ."

"Taking you apart is the best turn-on." He propped himself on an elbow, looking down at the sexy man he was lucky enough to spend his mortal forever with. "So I'll just pin you down and rail you into the ground until you recover."

Gabriel groaned, and his dick gave an interested jerk where it lay pressed against Michael's thigh. "You're incorrigible, and I wouldn't bet on a lazy Solstice. We may not be magical anymore, but the world still is, especially on that day, and you are one of the best medics we have."

"Buzzkill," he pouted. Gabriel laughed out loud, a sound Michael would never tire of, and he laid his head against his chest again to get the full effect, smiling even as he mentally acknowledged the truth of what Gabriel had said. Yes, Vincent was dead, but the war was far from over. As Mary had said, Vincent was just a human trying to be a giant. There were real giants—and worse—and hell, their side was still just trying to sort the good from the bad.

Like a certain warlock. "Any word from Robin?"

"Still hunting."

According to Cormac, as soon as he'd landed back with their souls at the tunnel, the green dome had disappeared, Atlas with it. Robin had waited long enough for everyone to get settled back at Monte Corvo, long enough to question an uncooperative Mary, then left, searching far and wide for the enigmatic warlock. Mary had remained tight-lipped, not bending to Cormac's or Adam's interrogations, insisting that they trust her and that Atlas was not their problem any longer, that Robin would get his revenge when his time came.

In any event, they'd had other more pressing, more present problems to deal with in the past two weeks. Skirmishes had erupted as others sought to fill the void Vincent left behind, and with the anniversary of the Rift four days ago, they'd remained busy. Adam—the Devil—had been needed to fight on the side of Nature, a position staked for the coming war that continued to bubble.

Gabriel gave his ass a gentle squeeze, bringing him back to the here and now. "Do you have a stream today?"

He lifted his chin, glancing up. "Tonight. Multiparty." Business was still good for Icarus—he'd kept the name professionally, same as Adam—though that whole being-human thing meant he had limited repeat performances, making multiparty streams more valuable than ever. His toys were more valuable too, even a few resurrected ones. "I'm thinking about the silver cock cage you bought me and that vibrating plug you love so much."

Gabriel growled and hauled him up his body. "Then I am definitely going to watch."

If they even made it that long, their stiffening cocks aligning. "I don't think we have an issue with recovery time. Yet." Grinning, he grasped them together and stroked.

Gabriel captured his mouth in a searing kiss, their tongues and moans tangling, greedy—always—for each other. Lost in each other. So much so that neither of them heard the intruder until he was nearly on them, branches cracking under hasty, approaching footsteps. They moved on instinct, Adam rolling onto his belly under Icarus, reaching out a hand for his pistol that was never far away, and Icarus springing to a crouch in front of him, his body mass still greater and his reflexes still faster than the average human.

"Adam!" A familiar voice, an unfamiliar alarm. "Icarus!"

"Stand down," Adam said, recognizing it too. They scurried up, grabbing whatever they could for cover, before Cormac shoved through the last of the trees surrounding the meadow.

They hadn't needed to worry about clothes. Cormac was naked too, running to them directly from a shift. He didn't make a quip and didn't even bother to take in their state of undress, as far as Icarus could tell. He was too caught up in whatever tragedy had left his dark hair ragged, his tan skin pale, and his violet eyes bright with fear.

Adam rushed to his side. "Mac, what's wrong?"

Icarus recognized something else besides fear in the raven's eyes. He couldn't believe he hadn't realized it until that moment. Fear—and *love*—cracked Cormac's voice as he sank to his knees and buried his face in his hands. "Paris is gone."

For all the latest updates on new projects, sneak peeks, and more, sign up for Layla's Newsletter and join the Layla's Lushes Reader Group on Facebook.

Reviews are an invaluable tool when it comes to spreading the word about great reads. Please consider leaving an honest review for *Icarus and the Devil* on your favorite review site.

Thank you for reading!

ACKNOWLEDGMENTS

This is one of those books I imagine must feel like birthing a kid. I started noodling Icarus way back in 2020, and several twists and turns (and years) later, *Icarus* is finally here! And so is a whole new series!

This book and series would not have gotten off the ground without a lot of help from my friends:

Beta readers who were invaluable every step of the way—Kim, Rachel, M.A., Kari, Aimee, and Anna.

Editors and proofreaders who helped guide the way and wrangle some of my bad habits into submission—Kristi Yanta, Adam Mongaya, Susie Selva, and Lori Parks.

Awesome PR folks who rolled with my slight swerve in subgenre—Nina Grinstead, Leslie Copeland, and the VPR and GRR teams.

The super talented Kelley York of Sleepy Fox Studios who likewise went through several cover concepts with me. I've loved all of them but the final covers for this series are so on point for the mood of the stories and my brand, with a paranormal flair.

My fantastic PA Kim and my supportive author friends who encouraged me to take this chance—Hailey, Erin, Allison, Annabeth, Aimee, Anna, Connor, the Mermaid crew, and more.

You awesome readers who are likewise taking this chance

with me. I hope you continue to enjoy this new found family I'm creating.

And finally, to the countless fanfic friends, betas, and readers who were cheering me on a decade ago in *The X-Files* and *Vampire Diaries* fanfic communities, I would not be here as an author and certainly not back in this paranormal / urban fantasy romance genre without you. It's good to be home!

ALSO BY LAYLA REYNE

For the most up-to-date list of titles and a helpful reading order, please visit www.laylareyne.com.

Soul to Find:

Icarus and the Devil

Jason and the Storm

Paris and the Reaper

Atlas and the Traitor

Agents Irish and Whiskey:

Single Malt

Cask Strength

Barrel Proof

Tequila Sunrise

Blended Whiskey

Angel's Share

Fog City:

Prince of Killers

King Slayer

A New Empire

Queen's Ransom

Silent Knight

Perfect Play:

ABOUT THE AUTHOR

Layla Reyne is the author of *What We May Be* and the *Agents Irish and Whiskey, Fog City,* and *Perfect Play* series. She writes sexy, intense LGBTQIA+ romance featuring competent adults in kitchens, sports arenas, car chases, and other high-stakes situations. Whether it's adrenaline-fueled suspense, rival athletes, vampires and shifters in alt-realms, or love mixed with mouth-watering foodie goodness, queer folks finding happily-ever-afters is guaranteed.

You can find Layla at laylareyne.com, in her reader group on Facebook—Layla's Lushes, and at the following sites:

BB bookbub.com/authors/layla-reyne

facebook.com/laylareyne

instagram.com/laylareyne

tiktok.com/@laylareyne